The Spy with an Angel's Eyes

An Augustus Benedict Cold War Spy Novel

P.J. Anderson

Nine Lives Original Books

First published 2021

ISBN: 978-1-8383410-4-6

Nine Lives Original Books

The Storey Building,
Meeting House Lane,
Lancaster, United Kingdom,
LA1 1TH.

CONTENTS

A selection of other books by P.J. Anderson available from Nine Lives Original Books (fuller details can be found at the end of this book):

A Man Twice Dead: an almost perfect crime

The Ghost Fabler

ACKNOWLEDGEMENTS

Many, many thanks yet again to Anne and Janet for reading and commenting on the first draft of this book.

In Memoriam

This book is dedicated to the memory of Tony Weymouth, a scholar and a gentleman.

CHAPTER ONE

It was a cold, iced-skin day. The grim, grey sky peppered the air with sleet. The man in the long black raincoat looked like a shadow as he hurried down the mirror-wet path towards the Serpentine. Close behind, another man followed, a bulkier figure with his hands in his pockets and a determined look on his mortician's face. He broke into a run to catch up with the other man and as he drew close his cold, trembling hands pulled a revolver out of his pocket. Three shots cracked through the silence. As the shadow fell to the ground his attacker was already running off across Kensington Gardens, his panic-powered feet sliding and slithering across the sodden grass.

A little crowd hurried over from various far-flung directions and gathered around the corpse. An off-duty soldier attempted to pursue the killer, but was not quite as skilful in navigating the slushy ground and was forced to give up after barrelling face-first into the mud.

The running man in the distance felt more dead than his victim. He was certain he would be betrayed and caught, if not today then tomorrow, or the day after that. He would never know when his journey into the hands of the hangman would begin and his every day henceforth would be spent in terror of it. 1955 had seemed for a while like the year that his life would finally begin. Now it seemed more likely that it would be when it ended.

It had all started with a phone call.

He lived well, well above his means and had been trying to fund the difference through gambling. Things had gone 'swimmingly' at first. He'd paid off everything he owed and moved healthily into profit. Then one big bet too many had turned things round completely the wrong way. He was now in so much debt he'd have to work three life-times to be able to pay it off. Word had got round and he was no longer welcome at gaming tables or even the local bookkeepers. He'd had two firm but polite reminders and two menacing warnings - the second had arrived on a rock thrown through the window of his ground floor apartment. He was on the point of fleeing to France when the voice on the other end of the phone pinned him to the spot so hard it was as if a nail had been driven through his foot.

It was an Irish voice - deep, soft, lyrical, almost as calming as it was menacing. It said,

"Mr. Malone, we haven't met. I'm a contractor who resolves problems for people who can afford my fee and you're the problem I've been given this week. I've been watching you closely, as closely as your beautiful mother used to do, God bless her, and I know you're thinking of joining the owl and the pussycat in their pea green boat and sailing across the sea. So, I need to tell you how terrible, terrible a tragedy such a voyage would be, with you sliding mysteriously overboard half way across the English Channel, never to be seen again. I couldn't bear the thought of those nice young ladies of yours crying their eyes out at your funeral, with not even a body to give a farewell kiss and say goodbye to. Or maybe once they discover that you've been two-timing each of them, they might prefer to give your unfortunate corpse a couple of very black eyes instead, should it ever be hauled from the deep. Whatever their reaction you get my drift - there is no ducking your responsibility to pay your debt, no running away to sea or far-flung lands. Now, I want you to do something for me, something that will begin to solve your little problem. I want you to go to your apartment door, take a look outside and bring into the room whatever you find on the step. But don't open it until I tell you to."

Malone had done as instructed. He found a gift-wrapped package and put it on the small round table on which the telephone sat. He told the mystery voice what he'd done. It said,

"Good. Now, before we deal with that, I want to tell you why

I'm giving it to you. You see I've had a little look into your financial affairs. Getting access to such details is one of my many talents. The long and the short of it is that you haven't a prayer of paying even a tenth of the money you owe. That's very unfortunate, because the people you owe it to don't accept non-payment and they don't extend deadlines. It's very simple, if you don't pay, they get someone to kill you. Their reputation depends on deterrence and they need to show that serious defaulters pay the ultimate price. So, looking at the state of your finances, Mr. Malone, I would appear to be talking to a dead man waiting."

He paused for effect, giving his audience time to sweat blood. He went on,

"The question is, do you want to wait for death to come to you, or are you waiting to find another way to pay your debt, something that will make the Grim Reaper go away?"

There was a pause while Malone tried to calm himself enough to reply. He said, almost in a whisper,

"What do you want me to do?"

The Voice said,

"Well, that depends. Are you a religious man, Mr. Malone? No, let me put that another way. Clearly, you're not anymore, two-timers and liars do not fit easily into the religious frame of mind now do they? But way back, back in your childhood days, you must have had to sit through bible classes and all the riveting lessons on right and wrong that those of us who went to Catholic school had drilled into us. Because you were a Catholic, Mr. Malone, that's one of the things my investigations have unearthed - a little side-show almost hidden and forgotten among the rich fantasies and hypocrisies of your sordid little life, but an interesting one in terms of what I'm going to tell you."

"Who are you?" Malone hissed. "Why are you playing with me?"

"Me? I'm several people and nobody at all. I think the more interesting question is, who are you? Because even if you're not a religious man, all of that belief that was pumped into your brain day after day, the stuff about guilt, mortal sin, heaven and hell is still going to be playing with your mind - and maybe even your soul. Do you have a soul, Mr. Malone?"

"What on earth has that got to do with anything?" Malone

almost wailed.

"Well let's say you have and you've just forgotten the thing, mislaid it a little shall we say. So, when I tell you what I have in mind as a way of paying your formidable debt it won't come as too much of a surprise if that soul of yours comes rushing back from wherever it's hiding and gives you three times four the rounds of the kitchen."

"This is gibberish," Malone said to himself, forgetting that the Voice could hear everything.

"No, gibberish is what you'll be speaking if a man with a very long knife breaks into your apartment and tells you very precisely what he intends doing with it. That's not a fate you'd like to fall upon your head now is it, Mr. Malone? There's few worse messes for a cleaner to deal with than a door that a man's been nailed to."

Malone emitted a strange, incomprehensible noise that sounded more like a squeak than a word. He very much wanted to slam the phone down and end the nightmare conversation, but he had a mortal fear that to do so would be to as good as invite the man with a knife in for a nice cup of tea and a murder.

"Anyway," the Voice continued, "we'll come back to all of that in a little while. I think it's time to open your present and then we can begin to see what all the fuss is about. Will you do that for me now, Mr. Malone?"

Malone looked upon the package with dread written deep into every pore on his sweating face. The man on the other end of the phone was clearly a psychopath and the contents of the parcel might include anything from a human head to a blood-dripping hand. The Voice said,

"I can't hear any rustling - you always get a good rustling when you open a present, Mr. Malone. Are you not going to open yours? It would be a terrible waste of a life if I decided that you were not the man to play ball and had to put the phone down on you. Your only friend then would be the man with a knife and his would be the last face you ever see."

"I'm opening it," Malone said, panicking. He tore off the gift wrapping and ripped open the box. What he saw caused his jaw to drop so far it was in danger of hitting his boots.

"It's a nice gun, isn't it?" the Voice said. "Do you remember when you used to play Cowboys and Indians when you were as small as an ant is tall?"

"What on earth is this for?" Malone asked, simultaneously dumfounded and scared.

"Well, it's not for stirring your tea that's for sure. What do you think it's for?"

"I haven't a clue. The only time I've had anything to do with guns was when I did my National Service. I was a bit of a marksman in training, but even then, I never actually fired my weapon at a real person. It was all targets and that kind of stuff."

"But they taught you how to use a gun didn't they? That's what armies do, train people to shoot things. So, you're just the man for the job."

"What job? Look, this is getting surreal."

"No, surreal is what they have hanging in the picture galleries. This is real, very real. If you look underneath the gun, you'll see there's a photograph of a man. You don't need to know who he is or very much about him, other than what he looks like and where he'll be at nine o'clock tomorrow morning. The details are on the back of the photo. He's been an even naughtier boy than you, would you believe. The people who I work for are prepared to forget about your debt if you'll kindly do them the favour of killing him. There will be no traceable link back to them and if you are stupid enough to get caught, you'll be a sole trader taking one hundred per cent of the blame. So, this little adventure is not without risk from your point of view. But the prize is a very great one if you pull it off and evade arrest. You get to live. There can be no better result than that. What do you say?"

"I'm not a killer."

"I'll bet you the two halves of a horse's tail that you are, Mr. Malone. You'd be surprised how many killers started off by thinking they were nothing of the sort and then discovered, to their great surprise, that they were. Now, left to your own devices you'd spend interminable amounts of time debating the matter in your head and trying to convince yourself that you were not the murdering type. But you don't have even a fraction of that time available to you, so I'm going to cut to the chase and help you see the reality of your position. That gun, you see, has three possible purposes. Pick it up now for me if you would and point it at your head. And before you panic, I'm not going to ask you to fire the

5

thing. I'd just like you to do this for me to help concentrate your mind on your possible fates. Are you holding it now?"

"What? No, this is madness. I don't even want to touch the thing."

"Mr. Malone, pick it up please. If you don't do this one little thing, then I can't help you and I'll have to leave you to your fate. Now I'm going to ask you again, have you done what I asked?"

It occurred to Malone that he could simply lie and say he had done, but he was now in such a state of fear and anxiety that he worried that his anonymous caller would be able to tell simply by the tone of his voice that he hadn't complied. With an unsteady hand he picked up the gun and held it to his head. He said,

"I have."

"Good," the Voice said. "Now, let me explain to you the various things that you might do with it and their likely repercussions. First, you might persist in this wrong belief that you couldn't possibly kill anyone and, in the certain knowledge that an assassin will come for you as a result, decide that it would be better to shoot yourself and die instantly by your own hand. That would cut out all the agony of waiting for what will most likely be a very painful and nasty end. Now, that would be a very Roman death perhaps, some might even see it as noble in a rather classical kind of way. Were you a fan of the classics when you were at that public school of yours, Mr. Malone? Ampleforth wasn't it? I'm sure you swam neck deep in a great sea of the classics there."

"I hated the classics," Malone said desperately, playing for the time to think that he didn't have.

"I'm sorry to hear that. Anyway, the first option is a pointless one because you're simply doing the assassin's job for him and not even getting paid for the privilege. So, we need to look at another option, one that would be instantly recognisable as the path of the hero, to a man who loved classical things that is. You see, you might choose instead to use the gun for self-defence, to try and ward off or even kill the assassin who will be sent after you, should you not shoot the man you have in the photograph there. Now that would be a very brave but very stupid choice, because the assassin is a professional and you are, at best, learning on the job. He would know you have the weapon and would be on his guard and remember, he is an expert in how to kill you before you have the chance to kill him. So, the gun would be about as useful as a one-legged monkey in an ice-skating competition. That means that the second option is simply a variation on the first, with the same outcome - the sad death of Mr. Malone. So, let's pass over that in silence and move straight on to option three, which is where you do precisely what you've been asked and save your skin. Now, when I put things in that way you can see that unless you're a man who wants to jump head first into his own coffin, you have only one choice - and it's that which makes you the killer you didn't think you were. Do you not agree?"

"I can't kill a man," Malone wailed.

"What you mean is that you're afraid of the hangman, Mr. Malone. I think we both know that you're well capable of doing anything at all that will save your godforsaken skin, as long as it doesn't put a noose around your neck at a later date. So, the solution to all your panic, alarm and unmanly fear is a simple one. You will need to be very careful. Be careful and you will not be caught and not being caught will leave you free to enjoy your three score years and ten, should the arithmetic of your later life take on such a neat and symmetrical form. And indeed, as the killing of the man in the photograph is your only passport to such a long and no doubt lustful life, then a careful killing is the sole option available to you. A careful killing will save you from the noose and all your other worries, so shall we get down to discussing the details of how best it might be done?"

That was the point at which Malone had been sucked in. With the news that a failure to kill his man by nine o'clock the following morning would lead to his own death by noon, his resistance collapsed. He agreed to do precisely as he had been told.

That decision takes us back to the beginning, where we find him in terrified flight across the muddy grasslands of Kensington Gardens, in a race with the hangman. Following the instructions that the Voice had given him, he races onto the Bayswater Road and boards the tube at Lancaster Gate. Alighting at Ealing Broadway and emerging once more into daylight, he finds that the sleet has now turned to heavy snow. He marches, as quickly as the treacherous conditions allow, towards the address that he has been given. It turns out to be a somewhat dilapidated looking old terraced house in a silent, depressed looking street. He tries the front door lock with the key that he had found underneath the photograph in the gun box. It fits perfectly and after checking that no-one is watching him, he slips inside.

The interior of the house is dismal - all bare, dusty floorboards, brown, flaking paint and peeling old wallpaper. He enters the back parlour as instructed and finds there that half a floorboard has been removed, ready for him to hide the gun. He wraps it in the dirty old cloth that he has found in the exposed compartment under the floor and then lays it to rest. As instructed, he then replaces the floor board. As soon as he has done so he feels, for no more than a split second, a sickening crack across the back of his head. He slumps forwards, deeply unconscious, a long shadow on the dank, dusty floor.

Outside the snow is rapidly changing the dour street into a cotton wool fantasy of Old London Town. After several hours and the fall of darkness, a car approaches. It stops outside the house and a man emerges from the rear passenger door. His face is almost completely obscured by his high, turned up collar and the hat that slopes low over his eyes. Before he shuts the door, he tells the driver to turn the engine off and to wait for him. The voice is deep, deceptively soft, with the distinctive lilt of County Kerry. It oozes the calm authority of a man who believes he has the power to reprieve and the power to condemn.

CHAPTER TWO

"Eggs! How the devil are you, old man? I've not seen you in ages!"

Augustus Benedict was a man of several names. To all his siblings, cousins and most of his friends he was plain Gus. To his mother, who was primarily responsible for his grand Christian name, he was forever Augustus and that was also the name inscribed in gold on his office door. If anyone called him Eggs it was an instant betrayal of the fact that they were an old school chum. His childhood nickname was something that he always hoped would quietly disappear from the known universe.

"Ollie, good to see you. You haven't changed a bit."

Gus was sitting at a table in his London club, waiting for a one o'clock appointment. His polished good looks might cause him to be mistaken for a Hollywood romantic lead, but he'd been without a leading lady for some time. He stood up to shake hands. At six feet three he dwarfed his diminutive friend, a boyish looking thirty-five-year-old with a winning smile. Ollie said,

"Listen, we must have a drink together and catch up on old times. I've only just joined this club and had no idea you were a member. I've got to dash now, but why don't we meet up some time next week? Here, I'll give you my card - just give me a ring and we'll sort something out."

Gus smiled and said,

"Of course, my treat, I'll buy the drinks."

"That's the kind of music I like to hear! See you next week

then."

As Ollie hurried off Gus went back to perusing his copy of the Times. His brow furrowed as he read about one of his former wartime colleagues having been murdered in Kensington Gardens. The whole thing seemed baffling. No-one had caught a clear sight of the killer and the police were struggling to find a motive. His thoughts were interrupted by a friendly female voice.

"Robin Hood I presume?"

Gus looked vaguely amused by this latest addition to his catalogue of names. The immaculately groomed woman with the mischievous eyes sat down opposite him, her black silk dress hugging her figure in a manner that preoccupied half of the other male diners in the room. He said,

"What makes you call me that?"

"Oh, Henry's told me all about your little racket. You're quite a cause celebre amongst the intelligence community, past and present. 'You wouldn't believe what Gus has turned his hand to,' that's what Henry said. Then he spilled the beans."

"I hope you mopped them up for him," Gus said, with a flicker of a smile. "What exactly did he tell you?"

"That you rob the rich blind to help the poor - that the rates for your unrivalled services are so high as to cause even millionaires to squeak with shock, all for the greater good of those who have little, or no money at all."

"How exotic an imagination Henry has. I don't think a man who lives the kind of pampered life that I do would have much interest in helping the poor."

"Henry thinks that the champagne lifestyle is simply camouflage."

"Well good luck to dear old Henry. That's the type of thinking that comes from spending too much time in the military. It sounds to me like he has camouflage on the brain."

"I think he's spot on. You always were a closet socialist when we were teenagers."

"Well, I'm afraid I don't believe in any 'isms' nowadays - capitalism, socialism, communism, you name it, they are not words that trip lightly off the tongue of Gus Benedict anymore."

"But you do believe in 'esses'."

"What on earth are they when they're at home?"

"Fairness, for example. You can take the 'isms' from a man, but you can't take the 'esses'. I can't think of a fairer man than you my dear Gus. You've just converted your 'ism' into an 'ess' in the hope that people won't notice, that's what's happened, isn't it? Come on, fess up."

Gus smiled enigmatically. He said,

"Alice, you are very welcome to believe whatever you like. Can I get you a drink?"

A waiter had appeared with the lunchtime menu and the wine list. Alice said,

"Oh, yes, thank you. A soothing white wine would be very nice - I'll leave the choice of grape to the man with the champagne taste."

Gus ordered a glass of the best vintage he could think of, together with a whisky for himself. Producing an envelope file from the briefcase that lay on the chair next to him, he said,

"I've set out the salary details and everything I hope you'd be happy to do, should we agree that the job is yours. It's all in here."

Raising her eyebrows, Alice said,

"I didn't think this ultra-traditional gentleman's club allowed the discussion of business during meals. I'm amazed they even let a member of the female sex cast her shadow across their doorway, never mind admit me as a guest."

He said,

"They don't mind people discussing business over lunch, as long as it's done discreetly. Give them another three hundred years and they may even let you become a member."

Alice laughed and opened the file. Her quick eyes speed read everything in less than a minute. She smiled and said,

"How very well organised you are Gus, dear, you seem to have thought of almost everything."

"More camouflage," Gus replied. "I thought I'd impress you now with my efficiency so you'd agree to take the job before you'd seen the chaotic reality of the filing system in the office."

"Well, I'll cross that terrifying bridge when I come to it. Most of what I see here looks fine. The salary's more than generous - as one would expect from a true gentleman. There's just the little leg pull."

"And whatever might that be?" Gus asked innocently.

"The deliberate omission of the key ingredient of the job that got me interested in the first place. You know how much I'd like to help with the research on some of your cases. I'm really rather good at it, as you'll know from my wartime record, and it's something I've always missed since returning to being a civilian. It would be a waste of my talent not to use it. I don't want to be just a glorified personal assistant. You are just pulling my leg by omitting the research stuff, aren't you?"

Gus smiled mischievously. He said,

"Only a little bit. I decided it would make more sense for me to draw up the details of that part of the specs jointly with you. I'd like you to describe how you might most effectively do the research part of your work and then I'll take that into account when deciding the final version of your duties. That will ensure that the job most precisely dovetails with your skills and that will benefit both of us. But I do confess that the thought of seeing the look on your face when you found there was only a blank space amused me."

Alice tut-tutted and said,

"You haven't changed Gussie boots, you're still the sly fox you always were. It's just as well we never got married. Perhaps you could atone for your sins and tell me a little bit more about what goes on behind the plush, oak panelled walls of the Augustus Benedict Detective Agency? I'd like to know precisely what it is that I'm letting myself in for."

Gus said,

"Now that's a very skilful turning of the tables - having thought I would be the interviewer I turn out instead to be the interviewee."

Alice nodded vigorously. She said,

"Well done, got it in one!"

"Well, dear interviewer, as the Mayfair address suggests, most of our business is top drawer stuff. There is the usual depressing divorce related work, but that is extremely remunerative, given the pedigree and desire for absolute discretion of our clients, and is therefore not to be sniffed at. Then things go up a rung or two on the ladder. My allegedly distinguished past in the intelligence services is an open secret amongst those with the right contacts and we get clients who would like us to collect intelligence on rival companies, rival individuals and rival anything really. Powerful people don't much like rivals, full stop. I draw the line ethically on some of the things we're asked to do and that will always be the case. We're not an unprincipled operation. On the other side of the coin there are those who want advice on how best to protect themselves against the intelligence gathering of others. All of that is very remunerative work and we are the primary agency of choice for those who want people who can do that kind of burrowing and counter-burrowing. Then there are the cases which the police haven't been able to solve. Where loved ones are involved, those with sufficiently gilt-edged bank accounts will come to us to find the answers that the boys in blue failed to provide. Most commonly it will be about missing sons, daughters, wives or husbands. Sometimes we will be asked to look into unsolved murders, or to determine the whereabouts of unrecovered stolen money. And then there are the cases that simply grab my fancy, that I might undertake almost as a hobby and at my own expense."

"And that includes helping desperate people with little or no money, without charge, doesn't it? I hear that you maintain a second office in the East End for exactly that purpose, with a pseudonym and a humble location that are designed not to put them off from approaching you. The penniless parents whose child has gone missing and who are at their wits end and all that kind of stuff. You see, I have been looking under your camouflage. And I know also about the money that you've been channelling to East End war veterans down on their luck - a very Gussie thing to do. You are really a very generous man behind this stuffy old clubman image that you maintain to attract your posh clients."

Gus looked slightly taken aback. He said,

"I couldn't possibly comment. Presumably your assumptions are based on more tittle-tattle from Henry?"

Alice laughed,

"I'll take that as confirmation that my suspicions are correct. You forget that I've known you too long not to be able to read you between the lines Gus."

"Well, be that as it may, I rarely confirm or deny anything that people think they can read between my lines."

"You've left something else out I think."

"Have I? I can't think what."

"Porky pies and naughty lies will multiply, take wings and fly. What you mean, dear Gus, is that you're not allowed to tell me. Your past as a very, very *ever* so very secret intelligence man means that, from time to time, a little bit of hush-hush work is outsourced to you for a suitable fee, is it not? Your reputation and skills are far too good for that not to be true."

"Well, once more I'm afraid, I couldn't possibly comment - and if I did have any hush-hush work to do, I would be doubly unable to comment, so a conversation on such matters would be shorter than a full stop that had been halved and quartered with a very sharp knife."

"Ouch, I think I just felt that knife square between my shoulder blades. Forgive me for my annoying inquisitiveness."

Gus said,

"Inquisitiveness is a useful tool to have in my line of business, providing it's combined with an ability to keep things confidential - and you know the drill in that regard. Past experience has shown me that you are, if anything, even more of a nosey parker than I am and that is one of the reasons I thought you would be a good fit for the job."

"Oh, OK, I'll cogitate on whether that's a compliment in disguise, but at least it sounds like you won't get too irritated by having me around."

"Is there anything else you need to know?"

"There is one thing. Tell me, am I the first candidate you've approached for the job or have there been others?"

"There are others on my list, but you are the top of that list and if you accept the post then I will not be offering it to anyone else. I know enough about your talents to judge that you're the best person for the job. How does George feel about the idea of you working for me? My one worry is that there might be some problems in that regard."

"Well, he knows that we went out for a few months before he and I met, if that's what you mean, but he regards you as too much the gentleman to ever try and reignite old flames, as indeed do I. So, George is fine about it, bless him. He knows I've been bored out of my mind simply doing the traditional housewife stuff and he has finally realised that, just like him, I need some kind of career to keep me off the streets."

"Too much the gentleman? You're both right unfortunately, isn't life a bugger?"

Alice laughed. He said,

"I wasn't simply referring to our long-ago fling though, I wondered if George was worried about the risks. This line of business can get a bit hairy from time to time and there is always the chance that somebody who I annoy might try to have a go at you as well as me."

"The risk is part of the attraction of the job Gus, dear," Alice said. "I miss the occasional white-knuckle ride after all the scary stuff I was involved in during the war. George knows that. I think he'd rather have me happy with a degree of risk than bored out of my mind by something that was as safe as houses and deadly dull. I could work in admin for something nice and safe like a shovel making company if you like, but I'd end up burying myself with one of the damn things. And just in case you hadn't noticed, we have a marriage in which it is clearly understood that we are equal partners who make our own decisions."

Gus nodded. He said,

"How very modern of you. I would have asked the same question of George had he been applying for the job - one of the problems with this line of work is that it can cause frictions with significant others, whatever their sex. I'm assuming that you can start on Monday, is that correct?"

She said,

"Sooner is always better than later, so yes, no problem."

"Excellent. Bring me your ideas on how you'd like your research role to develop and if I'm happy with them I'll work them into the specs."

"Will do boss. I'm looking forward to re-entering the real world."

He pushed his copy of the Times over to her and pointed to the story that he'd been reading.

"You could start by using this as a dry run to refresh your research skills. Tony Gregory's been murdered for no apparent reason. The killer got away scot free without anyone getting a look at his face. Perhaps you might like to do a bit of digging to find out why someone might want him dead?"

"He was one of your former colleagues in the very hush-hush

department, wasn't he? Have you been asked to help by an invisible man with no face?"

He smiled enigmatically and said,

"As I said before, there are some matters on which I simply don't comment."

She said,

"I'll take that as a yes then."

CHAPTER THREE

There was the humming of a tune, an Irish sounding tune, gentle and melodic. That was the only sound when Malone regained consciousness. He couldn't see anything. There was a dusty hood over his head that made him cough as he inhaled the cold, dank air through its thick woollen fibres. His hands were tied fiercely behind his back, the rope cutting into his wrists like a blunt, rusty knife. He was on a chair at least, a ramshackle, creaky one that wobbled on uneven legs as he flailed around uselessly, trying to free himself from the thick boatman's rope that bound him firmly to the chair back. His head still ached from where he'd been bludgeoned into unconsciousness. The tune went on and on, a soft, lilting echo from the far Kerry hills. He said,

"Who are you? Why am I trussed like a chicken?"

"Ah, Mr. Malone, you've woken up from your little nap I see. I gather you ignored my instructions and came here during the day instead of after dark. It's very dark now, so at least time has caught up with you. I just happened to be passing and thought I'd drop in to see how you were getting on. Is that chair comfortable enough for you? That and the one I'm sitting on are the only ones on the premises unfortunately, so I'm unable to offer you anything of a grander nature."

"You're him, aren't you? The voice on the phone."

"Well, I may be being a little pedantic about these things, but as there's no phone in the house, I must rather be the voice that's not on the phone. But if you mean that we've spoken before and at some length, then that is indeed correct."

"You said that once I'd done it, I'd be free, that my debt would be paid. That was a lie, wasn't it? I can't be any less free than I am now, bound and hooded like some poor sod about to be hanged. Is that what you intend doing with me, to string me up from one of the rafters in the attic? Or am I going to be left here for the police to find, with the murder weapon at my feet, with my finger prints all over it? I should have known you were lying. I might just as well have shot myself with the gun and have done with it."

"Strong words, Mr. Malone, strong words," the Voice said. "A lie is a very definite thing, a deception that does the teller little credit. What I told you was not so much a lie as a statement of the known facts at the time. The truth of the matter is that the facts have since altered. The gentlemen to whom you owe your debt have changed their minds and decided that your payment is still somewhat short of the mark, given the enormous amount of money involved."

"So, you are going to kill me?"

"Well, if you look at the bigger picture, neither you, nor I, nor anyone is immortal and someone or something at some point is going to kill us all, no matter what we do to try and avoid our fate. So, if you think of matters in that calm and rational light, there's really not much point in getting too worked up about whether your final moments are today, next week or fifty years from now. If you're fond of life, as fond you seem to be, Mr. Malone, then I can nevertheless understand your preference for thinking more of the longer term than the short."

"You haven't answered my question. Just tell me whether you're going to bloody kill me."

The Voice tut-tutted. It said,

"That's a terrible, commanding type of a tone in your voice for a man in no position even to command himself out of the chair he's sitting in. It's just as well I'm such a sweet tempered and forgiving soul is it not? Personally, Mr. Malone, I've no intention of harming a single hair on your head. But when I say personally, you understand, I do so to emphasise the fact that I don't kill anybody at all, you included. To think that I might is to misunderstand my role entirely. You see, I simply give people choices. To the people who may kill you I say that this is what my clients want and if you go ahead and do as they ask, they will pay you an agreed fee for your services. But I simply use my expertise to find suitable contractors and then leave the choice of whether they want to do what my clients ask up to them. I never command anyone to kill anyone, it is entirely down to their own judgment as to whether they go ahead. If they choose not to, then they won't get paid of course, but that is the long and the short of the matter."

"Oh, for God's sake, just tell me if you've given your sodding contractors a nod and a wink and a bullet with my name on it."

"Well, now you put matters in such a precise fashion, I can tell you directly that the answer is no. The person who will most immediately decide whether you should be buried in a cold, damp pit in some godforsaken field, or thrown far into the murky deep, is you, Mr. Malone - yes you, not me. Your creditors, you see, would like you to do another little job for them and if you refuse, then my understanding is that they most surely want you dead. If you agree, you will stay alive."

"For how long?"

"Well, that is a question is it not? You could be flattened by a bus tomorrow and that would be an end of things that neither of us could have foreseen. So 'how long?' is always an impossible question to answer where any man's life is concerned."

"It's going to be job after job after job, isn't it? Until I get caught and the gallows finish me off. What a bloody prospect."

"Only time will tell, Mr. Malone, time will tell. It could be that your creditors grow rather fond of you and feel even a genuine gratitude for all you've done. They might then open the hands in which they clasp you now and let you fly free like a bird, high into the clouds and all the sweet remembered joys of the life that you thought you'd left behind for ever. You must look on the bright side and believe that one day all this will be no more than a bad dream, a terrifying little nightmare that you can push firmly into the darkest corner of your brain and forget forever."

"And pigs might fly," Malone replied. "Why don't you all just end the nightmare now? I can't go on killing people, I can't repeat what I did today. Just put a bullet in my head and get it over with."

The Voice sighed and then said,

"There, there, Mr. Malone, it's always good to get things off your chest when the pressure is on. We all say things we'd very much regret if others acted on them, so here's something to help you reflect upon the wisdom of your request."

Malone yelped as his neck was grasped firmly, his hood pulled up a little below his nose and the icy steel barrel of a revolver forced into his mouth.

"There's nothing that compares to the real experience of being a split second away from death now is there, Mr. Malone, nothing quite like the adrenalin flow you get when a gun is rammed down your throat - that terrifying possibility that the old trigger finger might just slip and blast the back of your head all over the wall. Now, with all the benefit that comes from having the experience for real, do you think you might be a little inclined to modify your views on the desirability of having a bullet in the head? What do you say to that now?"

With his tongue held firmly down by the cold steel of the barrel Malone screamed and wriggled desperately for a full minute before the Voice withdrew the gun and sat down again. It said,

"Now, correct me if I'm mistaken, but I assume that all the screaming and the flailing of legs meant that you hadn't been quite serious when you said what you said a couple of minutes ago: when you swore blind that you'd prefer a bullet in your head to putting a bullet in somebody else's head. I wonder whether that was the old Catholic school upbringing kicking in again? The fear of being catapulted straight into hell through being killed before you had time to seek absolution for the mortal sin of murdering a man. Did that cause the sudden panic that made your knees knock so hard they sounded like a roll on a drum? It's definitely a worry, isn't it? Maybe that's one of the reasons I'm so careful never to be directly responsible for a single death. I certainly had no intention of pulling the trigger on you, you'll be relieved to hear. I carry the gun for purely defensive purposes. I simply meant to concentrate your mind with the aid of a potent bit of the old theatricals. And concentrate your mind it certainly seems to have done. So, are we now ready to start the serious business of discussing the next little job your creditors would like you to do for them? And if you're worried about the old Catholic side of things, you could shoot the target as required and then go straight to the next available confessional. You could unload it all on the priest, in confidence of course. The man would be bound by the Church, the Holy Mother of God and all the saints to keep your sins to himself. So, you could confess without any risk, get your penance and instant forgiveness for the terrible, mortal sin of a thing you'd done. Now you couldn't get a fairer deal than that, Mr. Malone."

Malone emitted a long, desperate groan and said,

"God help me, I'm in hell already. I can't go on killing people, I can't. I'm not a murderer."

"Well on that we must beg to differ, Mr. Malone. If I'm not mistaken, the fact that you put three bullets into the back of a man this morning must make you a murderer in every known sense of the word. Once a man is dead, I'm afraid, you can't wish him back into life, unless he's the Good Lord himself, now isn't that a fact? So, if the poor soul is having his tea with the angels and the reason for that is you, you'll just have to face up to an uncomfortable truth. Once you are a murderer, Mr. Malone, you can't wish away what you've done."

"I've done what you asked, just let me go, please, just let me go."

"Now I would if I could, Mr. Malone. If it was just up to me you could be out in the street throwing snowballs at the moon and having the time of your life. But your creditors have a different view on the matter I'm afraid. If you're to leave this house by the power of your own two legs and not end up being wrapped in a bit of old carpet and carried out to a van, then you really do need to listen to what they want. Would you like me to tell you what it is they'd like you to do?"

"No, I want nothing to do with it. The deal I made should be honoured, just let me go, please!"

"Now then, Mr. Malone, I'm beginning to lose a little bit of patience here. I've got things to do, people to see. If you don't want to play ball with me, I'll just have to leave you to the people who deal with problems like this. It's a cold night to be dropped head first into the Thames with rocks the size of a planet concreted to your feet. You'll catch your death, if you'll pardon my little pun. Do you really want to spend your last remaining minutes on earth with fishes swimming round and round your head, Mr. Malone? Just the thought of that makes me dizzy. Now you might think I'm joking, but I know for a fact that's the method of choice that the boys who'll deal with you will use. So, it's a simple matter. You agree to do what is asked, or you pay with your life for the slice of your debt that your creditors have deemed unpaid. What's it to be?"

"What if I can't do it when I find the victim, what if I make a mess of it and they get away? I'm not a professional killer. It doesn't make sense to use me."

"The fact you're not a professional killer is why using you makes perfect sense to your creditors, Mr. Malone. Your amateur status has advantages that are crucial to the success of the crime. The fact these are not professional hits will be spotted very quickly by competent detectives and that will create exactly the kind of puzzlement as to what is going on that your creditors would prefer. And believe me, you will not make a mess of things, as you put it. You will do what they ask and you will leave the target as dead as Queen Victoria. How do I know this? Because, no matter what you might say to the contrary, you want to live and if you mess it up you won't. Fail and you will be a dead man walking. You will become the target and wherever you go, however cleverly you try and hide, they will have you hunted down and killed. So, let's stop all the whining and the pleas for an easy way out that only the pixies would believe exists. Listen to what I have to tell you, agree to do what your creditors require and you will walk from this house within the hour. Refuse and I will leave you to your fate, the nature of which will be most unpleasant. So, what do you say?"

There was a short silence. Then the Voice said,

"Last orders, Mr. Malone, I either have your agreement in full within the next ten seconds or I'm leaving. You're on your own then, no second chances and your next visitor, I guarantee, will be the last person you ever meet on earth. Now, give me your answer please, yes or no."

There was no reply for a full five seconds, then Malone sighed desperately and said,

"Alright then, there's no alternative, no hope or anything is there?"

The Voice said,

"A wise choice, Mr. Malone, a very wise choice. That's the first chink of light I've seen in this house of overwhelming darkness. I'm now looking at a man who will live another day and that must surely be a cause of celebration for both of us. In fact, that could be the only good thing ever to have come out of this house. Do you know its history now? No, of course you don't, you are not the kind of man to have much familiarity with the poverty that hides behind every window in this blighted street. Well, let me enlighten you a little before we move on to discuss the job our friends have given you. You ate with a silver spoon when you were a child, so you could maybe benefit from learning a little about how the children who lived here fared, little innocents who often went without even the basics of a daily meal. They were all killed you see, killed along with their mother by a madman in a drunken rage, the human wreck that called himself their father. That's why this house has been empty since and is so sad and derelict now. Nobody wants to buy or rent a house with such a history. The strange thing was that nobody ever thought that such a hopeless drunkard would actually kill anyone. He was a shouty man, he'd rage and curse at the sky and the four seasons when the drink was too much in him, but he'd never hurt his family before, never laid a violent hand on anyone. And then, one sorry night, everything inside him exploded and he bludgeoned everyone to death. Had his wife been a wealthy woman, living in a smarter part of town, she could have fled with her little angels long before the drink and madness within him erupted in such a tragic way. She could have been safely accommodated in a flat bought or rented with her own money, or occupied spare rooms in her rich parents' house. But she had no wealth or rich parents and had only this hovel to live in. Her impoverished parents were both dead from TB and had left her only their debts as her inheritance, so she was trapped here, in this house, with the little ones. It must be hard for you to imagine such dire circumstances, Mr. Malone, given your own highly privileged upbringing and all the money you chose to throw away on gambling to try and keep your silk-lined luxury of a life afloat. But you had a choice as to whether or not to put your life in danger and you chose to throw all the dice and fall foul of your creditors. They in turn have given you more choices, which twice now have enabled you to escape otherwise certain death. The woman and her little innocents had no such choices, the harsh inequities of life gave her only a single, tragic outcome. That's why I have little sympathy with all your whining and pleading you see. You have so much more than she had. So, if you want to save your wretched excuse for a life, you need to do exactly as your creditors say. No ifs, no buts, no 'what happens if I mess it up?' If it is indeed your choice to take another life to preserve your own, you need to do the job properly, with no mistakes. Is that understood?"

Malone muttered something of an incoherent nature. The Voice said,

"Oh dear, we seem to be going a little backwards from our firm decision of a minute or two ago, do we not? I need to hear you say very clearly that you understand, Mr. Malone. Now, you have one more chance to do that, so don't get it wrong. If I think you're not up to the job I'll simply walk out of here as I threatened before and inform your creditors that you're not in a position to play ball. Now, do you understand?"

"I do," Malone said weakly.

"Well, that's not the most confident expression of commitment I've ever heard, but I'll give you the benefit of the doubt. So, let me give you the details. I will leave very shortly and somebody will then cut you free. When they've done so, you mustn't remove your hood until after you've counted to one hundred in order to give them time to vacate the premises without you seeing their face. While the room is largely dark, the flea-bitten curtains are letting in just enough light from the street lamps outside for you to make out a detail or two and that could well be fatal for you. It is most important that you never see my face or that of anyone to whom I have contracted your supervision. That being understood, when they have gone you will find at your feet another little box. Inside it there is another gun, an easier fit for your coat pocket I would think. There is a photograph of the man you have to say goodbye to and on the back, you will find the time and precise location of your rendezvous with him. Your creditors have asked that you shoot him twice in the chest and twice in the head. There is presumably some significance attached to this configuration of shots, but I have no idea what it is. You are then to do as you did today and return the gun to this house, from which it will be collected. Only this time, and on the occasion of any further visits to these premises, you must do precisely as you were originally instructed and only come here when it is dark. You have three days to prepare for this next assignment. Do it well and who knows, your creditors may never ask another thing of you, other than to stay well away from their gaming tables. Now, it's time for me to say goodbye. Remember everything I've told you and make sure you get things right on the day. Goodnight, Mr. Malone."

Malone heard the Voice's car leave and then there was silence for a full hour. Then another car drew up outside. He heard the front door bang open, followed by loud echoing footsteps down the hallway and into the room where he waited. He felt a firm grip on his shoulder and then he was cut free. His unseen visitor whispered into his ear,

"Don't mess up now pretty boy, don't miss a single shot or turn up on the wrong day, or at the wrong time. Because if you do, I'll be visiting you again. I'll be your personal Grim Reaper."

The accent was Scottish this time. Had the circumstances been considerably less terrifying it might have occurred to Malone that he was now only missing a warning from a Welshman and he would have been threatened by people from every nation in the British Isles. His creditors, as the Voice called them, were London born and bred, but clearly had a multinational approach to murder.

He heard the military march of the footsteps back down the hall, followed by the sound of the car driving off through the snow shortly afterwards. He was so terrified that he still counted all the way up to one hundred before removing his hood, even though the man of whom he was so afraid had very obviously vanished into the night. Finally, he pulled off the dank and dusty woollen garment and stared at the box that lay in the semi-darkness at his feet. He sat motionless for several minutes, more frozen than the snow outside by the thought of what was inside it. Then he let out a muffled scream, which turned slowly into a long, desperate wail of despair. One or two curtains in windows up and down the street shuffled briefly, but beyond that, nobody thought it wise to take any further interest in the dark house, where no lights ever shone and shadowy people came and went under the cover of the night.

CHAPTER FOUR

"Oak."

"What?"

"You have a solid oak door into your inner office. Very classy, very thick, very expensive - very old. You've acquired that from some stately home that was being demolished, haven't you? And gold-plated door handles, my word. Even my desk looks like a priceless antique."

Gus said,

"That's because it is a priceless antique. It's one of the finest pieces Chippendale ever produced. Cigarettes and lighters are not allowed within five miles of it without a military escort."

Alice said,

"Even your filing cabinets are the finest mahogany. And who on earth has a silver chandelier hanging from the ceiling in the waiting room of a private detective agency?"

"It's all part of the theatre," Gus replied. "It helps prepare the clients psychologically for the enormous bills they'll get for my services."

Alice said,

"You are a card, Gussy boots. Robin Hood would have been very envious of your opulent modus operandi - it's all quite a step up from having to spend cold nights sleeping in Sherwood Forest and hiding in tree branches with one's fellow bandidos, waiting to relieve the Sherriff of Nottingham's heavily armed thugs of their gold."

Gus said,

"Speaking of heavily armed thugs, did you manage to do any research on why somebody might want Tony Gregory dead?"

"I did indeed," Alice replied. "Do you remember Ralph Carter, the Scotland Yard bigwig my section used to liaise with during the war? We always went to him when we needed a bit of extra local knowledge about London-based people who we suspected might be up to no good on Mr. Stalin or Mr. Hitler's behalf. Well, he's still at his desk, believe it or not and was only too happy to be of help – and no I didn't wiggle my eyebrows or any other part of my anatomy at him, he's far too professional to succumb to my charms."

Gus said,

"Well, now that we've established that this was a wiggle-free encounter, what did Chief Inspector Carter have to say?

Alice said,

"Some really interesting things. He ..."

There was a knock at the outer office door, a military tat, tat, tat. The shadowy outline of a tall, thin man in a hat could be seen through the frosted glass. Gus said,

"Ah, that will be the man with no name."

"What, none at all? He must be extremely hush-hush."

Gus said,

"Your predecessor always referred to him as Mr. One. You'll see why as soon as he opens his mouth. I'll be in my office - you can show him straight in."

Alice opened the door and was confronted by a man with ice-hard eyes and a smile that arrived stillborn. He said,

"One has a meeting with Captain Benedict. I assume he's here?"

Alice said,

"Yes, please come in. If you'd like to go straight through, he's waiting for you in his office."

Mr. One nodded in a perfunctory manner and swept past her like a destroyer at full steam ahead. He disappeared into Gus's office, firmly shutting the door behind him. He said,

"Good morning, Augustus. I see you have a new person front of house. It's not your style to have an office assistant who isn't also of considerable use in your investigations, so I assume that behind the innocent warmth of her welcome there's a fierce intellect at work?"

Gus nodded and said,

"As always, Angus, you assume correctly."

"We will need to vet her before she comes anywhere near our dealings with you."

"No need, she's been vetted so many times before there are probably files an inch thick on her. She used to work for Section Two and I've known her longer than I've known you."

"Section Two indeed, right on the inside track. She must be a bright spark. I'll still need to go through the formalities. Six are taking an interest in this matter as well, for obvious reasons. They're checking to see if they can pick up any overseas leads on what's going on and they're taking a keen interest in what we're up to. We have the extremely rare and dubious shared distinction of having worked for both Five and Six during our careers, so you know what they're like - to them Five is little more than an upstairs branch of the police, plodding and a little wooden in comparison to their high-flying intellects and egos. I like to think the reality is the other way around and I certainly don't want them to be able to accuse us of not doing something so simple as running proper checks on people who are involved with our activities."

"If you must, but I've already put her to work on your little matter, with no information beyond that in the newspapers I might add, and no idea of precisely who you are."

"I see. You might have checked with me first before doing that. I hope you're not going to go maverick on me again, Augustus."

"I wouldn't dream of it, old man. As I said, I've given her the minimum of information. I think we'll find that she's turned the minimum into the maximum - if you're prepared to let her into the room and tell you about it that is."

"Can't you just summarise it for me?"

"She hasn't actually told me what it is yet - your early arrival cut her off in mid-sentence. I can give it you later, if you'd prefer not to hear from her now."

"Well, if she's been in Section Two, I suppose I can make an exception on this single occasion, but I will still need to order the full menu of formal checks on her record when I get back. What's her name?"

"She'll tell you herself."

Gus opened the door and asked Alice to join them and introduce herself. He said,

"Our client would like to hear what you have discovered, courtesy of Ralph Carter. He has made the request on the understanding that he was never here and there is to be no paper record made of our conversation."

Alice said,

"Absolutely, understood. I'm Alice Harding and I suspect that Mr. Benedict has already explained my background. Chief Inspector Carter is aware of the case and has spoken with the team investigating it. Their only clue so far has been a tip-off that Gregory had been having an affair with the wife of a mid-ranking official at the Soviet embassy and had been killed because of it. The informant wasn't sure whether this was the unauthorised revenge of a jealous husband, or a Moscow approved hit in the belief that Gregory had used the affair to get hold of sensitive information."

Gus said,

"Did he give you any idea as to who the source might be?"

"No, if the team are to be believed, the information was given to them anonymously. I was told that it was a phone call and that certain aspects of the conversation convinced them that the source was genuine."

Gus said,

"And why did Carter give us so much detail without any apparent quid pro quo, do you think?"

"Because he doesn't buy the story," Alice replied. "Ralph is a very bright chap. He will know very well that through me he is dealing with the invisible people. He's already had people from another intelligence section breathing down his neck and they seem to have taken the tip-off seriously and ignored his reservations. I would imagine he presumes that through me he is dealing with the grown-ups rather than the little boys in short trousers, the people who watch things from the top of the mountain and make their own independent judgments. He wants them to know that the little boys are on the wrong track."

Gus said,

"Did he say why he doesn't buy the story?"

"Yes, it's very simple and I think he's right. The killing looks more like the work of an amateur than a professional. The three shots were from relatively close range, but showed little understanding of the human anatomy. The fact that one wound was fatal appeared to be more by accident than design, given that it almost missed its mark. A Russian assassin would have been precise, of course, and from that range each bullet would have been lethal in its own right. Only a professional assassin would have been involved if it had been an official Russian job. The idea that a jealous husband from the embassy might have been responsible is simply preposterous. Stalin may be dead, but no Russian official would dare act off his own bat for personal reasons. These people still live within a wall of fear."

Gus nodded and said,

"OK. Fine, very useful, thanks Alice. I'll give you a shout if we need to ask you anything more."

As she closed the door behind her Angus said,

"Excellent work, you've chosen wisely, Augustus. I've got rather a lot on my plate with various other antics of our Russian friends at the moment, which is why I've needed to sub-contract the initial investigation of Mr. Gregory's demise to you. I don't want to be wasting time chasing red herrings, so your young woman has been very helpful. We knew all about the supposed tip-off about the embassy link, but I wasn't aware of Carter's thoughts on the matter. From what I've heard today, he's absolutely right in his judgment. Now we know who wasn't responsible I look forward to hearing from you as to who was."

He was on his feet and half way out of the door before Gus had had time to blink. He paused briefly and said,

"I've heard a whisper that Mr. Gregory had a bit of a gambling habit and that his murder might be simply the result of an unpaid and very large debt. Perhaps you could look into that among your various lines of enquiry?"

With that he was gone.

He was followed shortly afterwards by Gus who, to Alice's surprise, was wearing a distinctly battered looking hat and an overcoat that looked like it had seen more winters than Jack Frost and all of his withering relatives. Amused by the look of puzzlement on her face he said,

"Horses for courses. I always dress to suit the occasion. I'll be back around mid-afternoon. See if you can rescue my filing system while I'm out."

The mysterious occasion was his twice a week journey into his parallel life in East London. He arrived at his rather down-at-heel looking second office an hour later, having stopped off at a bacon and egg café for a mid-morning coffee and snack and the opportunity to pick up on the local gossip from the proprietor. He'd no sooner opened the shutters and deposited his hat and coat on his battered old desk, when the door opened and a bull-built man with eyes of thunder marched in. He said,

"Mr. Bendink I presume?"

Gus nodded and said,

"Have a seat. What can I do for you?"

"You've already done it old son," the man with the arms of a wrestler said. He had a voice that echoed off the walls, a constant deep, husky bass. Wedging his considerable bulk into the wobbly chair facing the desk, he looked around the room with curiosity. He said,

"I don't get it. The Flash Harry office in Mayfair, with all the posh clients - and then this shithouse, servicing the poor bloody infantry with hardly a few coppers to rub together between the lot of 'em. And the two names - Bendink and Benedict, so nobody would connect your two lives."

"Well, not exactly nobody," Gus said, "you've clearly managed it."

"Yeah, well, that's part of my job you see, keeping tabs on people, finding out what's what. Mind if I take my hat off?"

Gus said,

"Be my guest. You said I've already done something for you."

The wrestler wiped the dust off the end of the desk and then placed his hat on it. He said,

"That's right, I did. You helped my sister find her daughter after she'd run off with some penniless clown who then hid her away and made her into his bloody slave, knocking her about until she was black and blue. Thanks to you, I was able to find his gaff, punch his lights out and bring her back to her mum, all safe and snug. He wasn't on the list of bad boys round 'ere, nobody knew him from Adam - so we wouldn't have found him without you. I

31

help her mum out a bit with money and things, to the extent she lets me, but she's not a rich gal and you didn't charge her a penny for all your trouble. Nobody does something for nothing round 'ere, so that left me puzzled. I had you followed and that's when I discovered the double life. I don't get it, you didn't charge her, you didn't expect her to pay with any favours either - and when I ask around, I find there's other people who say you've done similar things for them, all with no charge. So, what's the game? Who are you, bleedin' Robin Hood, making the toffs that use your Mayfair office pay through the nose so you can afford to give your services for free round 'ere? And it doesn't stop there old son, does it? I hear there's more than a few families right on the breadline and knee deep in debt who've been helped out by an anonymous geezer who, my sources tell me, is most likely you."

Gus laughed. He said,

"I spotted the tail, now I know who sent him. You must be Marjie Hepworth's brother."

"Yeah, that's the one. Tasty Harry they call me. I could buy her a really nice gaff with the money I earn, but she won't let me. She takes as little as possible because she says my money's contaminated. She reckons it comes from working for the naughty boys round here. What do you think?"

"I think she's probably spot on," Gus said. "She's more honest than the Bishop of London and you've got the fingers of a man who uses a knuckle duster."

The wrestler smiled. He said,

"I think I like you Mr. Bendink-Benedict. Which is just as well really, for the sake of your good health. You still haven't told me what your game is."

"You seem to know already," Gus replied. "My bright spark of a new assistant has reached the same conclusions, so great minds would seem to think alike. I always liked the legend of Robin Hood. But I stay within the law. Nobody delves into their riches to hire me with my enormous fees unless they want to. Their unwitting 'donations' to fund my parallel life are entirely their own free choice."

The wrestler laughed. He said,

"It's a bit different in my line of business, as you'll appreciate. If people who owe don't delve into their pockets, they tend to need an urgent visit to the dentists and a neck brace. But I'm grateful for what you've done for Marjie. I owe you one and I'm going to make you an offer, which you can take or leave as you please."

Gus offered him a cigarette. Tasty said,

"No ta, my nan always said it was a filthy habit and used to box my ears so hard I gave 'em up in the end. The cigs, I mean, not the ears."

His booming laughter filled the room. When it had subsided, he said,

"Listen, this is the deal. A toff like you isn't going to get much change from the underworld round here when you need to get a bit of information about dodgy dealings. You've obviously been getting round that by paying your own sources to ask the questions for you, but you don't have one like me. I can find out things for you that nobody else can and I won't charge you a fortune. All you'll pay will be my expenses. But I'm not a grass, so there's rules and limits to what I'm prepared to do. I'll never tell you who has done things, but I will tell you who hasn't from the list of likely bad boys. That will save you time in narrowing things down. If you were an ex-copper, I wouldn't give you even that, but you're not, are you? You don't smell like a copper and you don't talk like one. You've been something else, some kind of other job where you've been solving puzzles. In fact, I'd go so far as to guess you've been some kind of clever dick in the military, finding out what old Adolf's plans were during the war perhaps? Am I getting warm?"

Gus smiled through the haze of his cigarette smoke. He said,

"I couldn't possibly comment."

Tasty laughed.

"No, I bet you couldn't. I can live with that. Anyone who helped us knock that bastard into touch has my vote. I mean, there's some villains round 'ere, you might even think I'm one of 'em, but every one of us looks like a saint compared to 'im."

"I shall call you Saint Tasty," Gus said, daringly.

The wrestler looked startled and then laughed again. He said,

"Anyone else who'd said that would be seeing a starry, starry night by now, with ten teeth short of a full set. You've got balls Mr. Bendink-Benedict, I'll say that for you. So, what do you say, are you going to take me up on my offer? I won't be offended if it's not good enough for you."

Gus frowned, nearly biting through his cigarette as he did so. Taking it out of his mouth and squashing it in his overfilled ash tray, he said,

"Yes, I am going to take it up Tasty. It's very generous of you and it's much appreciated. In fact, I'd like to take it up straight away, if that's ok?"

Tasty nodded. He said,

"Fire away. Tell me what you want to know and I'll tell you if I can help."

Gus said,

"I'm trying to find out why an old colleague was killed in Kensington Gardens a few days ago. There's a theory that he was a secret gambler and had unpaid debts that were so large and so far beyond the deadline that his creditors pulled the plug and had him shot. I don't buy the theory, but I need to check it out. If I told you his name, could you find out if there's any truth in the rumour? If there is, I don't need to know who did it, because I know you won't tell me and I can check that out on my own. But it would save me a hell of a lot of time if I could find out whether that was a line worth pursuing."

"This was a toff called Tony Gregory, wasn't it? I read it in the paper and nobody I know had any idea who might have done it or why. The geezers who'll know if he was on the gambling circuits - the legals and the illegals - are Geoff the Dice and Jack the Tipper. Geoff bluffs his way round all the posh gambling circuits and when he's not selling tips on bent races, Jack knows who's who on all the rest. If they can't answer your question directly, they'll know someone who can. They'd never speak to you, so I'll have a word on your behalf. It'll cost you a meal though. That's why I got the name Tasty, by the way, in case you were wondering."

He smiled and licked his lips in a slightly disturbing manner. Gus said,

"Done. Where and when do you want to eat?"

"Nothing posh, so don't panic, your wallet's not going to be stretched. I like egg and chips, fish and chips, steak pie and chips, not your caviars and your foreign delights. I'll let you know where to meet when I've got an answer to your question."

He raised his substantial bulk from the chair and said,

"So, that's that then. A pleasure doing business with you Mr. Bendink-Benedict - can I call you Gus?"

Gus nodded and smiled. Tasty stuck out a large paw and they shook hands.

"Nice to meet you Gus. Ta-ta for now old son."

And with that he was gone. Gus watched through the grimy window of his office door as people nervously edged out of Tasty's way, or doffed their hats to him, as he ploughed onwards down the street. The crowds seemed to part before him, as if he were a giant Moses, leading invisible Israelites through the Red Sea.

CHAPTER FIVE

The great tenor bell rang in Malone's head like an omen, shaking his brain and rattling his senses, until it seemed as if the entire contents of his skull would spew onto the ground in front of him. And yet it was a mere memory, a ghost, the giant amongst all the bells of St. Mary-le-Bow, lost in wartime bombing and awaiting replacement, pounding out the judgment of the Almighty on the dark act that he was about to commit. He couldn't get the ethereal echo of its chimes out of his mind as he padded ever onwards towards his latest lethal rendezvous. The bell seemed to be tolling for the soon-to-be dead and for the loss of his own immortal soul.

He arrived at his destination, St. Boniface and all the Angels, an hour after darkness had fallen. The West Door was still open and he slipped in like a shadow, hardly daring even to have full human form. The church was largely in darkness, lit only by the candles on the altar. The saints and angels who towered down from the Great Window behind it seemed to be glaring at him in condemnatory fashion, ready to send him plunging down into hell for the deadly sin he was about to commit.

Checking that he was alone, he crept quietly over to the pulpit on the far left-hand side and slipped behind it, as per his instructions. He shivered violently for a few seconds. He felt even colder than the building, which seemed to be completely unheated. His hands were clammy and gripped in nervous fists inside his overcoat pockets. He could feel the dead weight of the gun in his inner jacket pocket, like a small, malign animal waiting to be unleashed on his intended victim. He checked his watch in the dim, flickering light cast by the altar candles. If all went to plan, he had only ten minutes to wait. The past few days had dragged their crushed and broken feet along the ground as if they'd been ten years. He'd felt increasingly dead to the world, a man who was buying an unknown quantity of further life by killing another man in a church. While his own religious beliefs had long been diluted to the point where he rarely remembered them, they still occasionally surfaced from within his subconscious mind. This was one such occasion and he couldn't escape the deep, guilty feeling that he was about to commit an act of sacrilege. And it was now less than ten minutes away, the point at which he crossed another thick line on his road to damnation, the killing of a man in the Almighty's personal space.

Terrified by the very thought of what he was about to do, he put his head in his hands and uttered a low, soft moan, desperately hoping for some miraculous way out, an escape from his downward spiral into a deep personal hell of fear, guilt and the darkest of depressions. Impulsively checking his watch again, he gasped as he saw that he had only two minutes left. If he was going to do it, this act from which there was no way back and which could easily see him swinging from the gallows, he had to do what he had been most dreading and remove the gun from its hiding place in his pocket, ready to fire. It had been hard enough to do the first time, in Kensington Gardens, but, on this occasion, murder seemed a ten times more difficult act to perform. His procrastination was brought to a sudden and dramatic end as he heard the West Door creak open and then fiercely shut, its echoes bouncing around the church like a drum roll. Feverishly, he reached inside his jacket and pulled the gun out so quickly he nearly dropped it. Peering through the candlelit gloom he could see his intended victim standing, looking around him. Then he started to walk towards the altar, the leather soles of his shoes seeming to count down the moments to his death as they cracked against the ice-cold floor. He stopped and looked around again. He said in Russian,

"Igor, if you are here, show yourself. Don't be shy."

His words made an already nervous Malone jump. He didn't know what they meant, but he recognised the language. He'd heard it often enough during his posting to Germany at the end of the war. The Voice had said nothing about his target being Russian. Why would his paymasters want someone from Russia killed? But he could see enough of the man's features now to know that his was the face in the photograph and he was here at exactly the time he'd been told he would be.

What Malone hadn't realised was that, in his amateur way, he had leaned out a little too far from behind the pulpit in trying to identify his target. The Russian's practised eye spotted him and recognised in a second that he wasn't the man he'd been expecting to meet. He whipped a gun out of his pocket and it was at that moment that Malone snapped and instinctively fired all six bullets in rapid succession. He had no time to put them in the particular parts of the anatomy that his instructions had dictated, simply using his old national service training to aim as well as he could at his enemy in a classic kill or be killed situation. To his surprise, two shots found their mark and one, purely by chance, caught the Russian straight between the eyes. He dropped like a puppet whose strings had been severed. Malone stood momentarily in shock, deafened by the sound of the gun and its echoes that had repeatedly boxed his ears, leaving them ringing. Then the church door banged open and a second man with a gun burst in. Clearly, the victim had come with a minder to stand outside and keep watch. Malone crouched low and observed while the second man cursorily examined the body of his partner, all the while keeping his gun raised, ready to fire at the killer, should he spot him. Terrified to the extent that he wet himself, Malone looked round desperately for some means of defence, having no more bullets for the gun. His luck was in, in so far as there was a large, heavy brass candlestick that had been slid behind the pulpit while not in use. With some effort, he lifted it above his head and waited while the minder checked out all the shadows and places of possible concealment. With a thorough inevitability, he eventually advanced on the pulpit. Malone held his breath. The man's shoes didn't make much noise, but they made just enough for him to tell when he was nearly upon him. He waited until the last possible second and then, at the precise moment his pursuer's gun appeared round the back of the pulpit, he brought the candlestick crashing down upon his skull. There was a low moan and Malone's second victim of the night collapsed onto the floor in front of him. He stood in horror as a pool of blood trickled towards his shoes. Then, shaking so much he could hardly stand, with a fierce, shock-induced pain in his back that made it difficult to breathe for a few seconds, he followed his very precise instructions and staggered towards the side door. That, he had been assured, led to a quiet, poorly lit lane where he was unlikely to be spotted as he made good his escape. When he tried to open the door, however, he found that it had either jammed or been locked. Pull and push, kick and curse, there was no way he could get it to open. His grip on reality now was only tenuous and he felt as if he was in the middle of a nightmare from which he might never wake up. Driven purely by his survival instincts, he turned round and started to run back the way he had originally come in, bursting through the West Door and out into the street. He was startled to find a small crowd of people outside. His shots had clearly been heard by someone and word had got round. He stood like a proverbial frozen rabbit for a few seconds and then, realising that they were far more terrified of him and what he might do than he of them, he ran off as fast as he could. He disappeared down the escalator of the first tube station he came to. He fled away into the night on a train that might just as well have being going to nowhere, for all the idea he had of what he might do after he had returned the gun to the dark and deserted house of the tragically murdered family, as instructed. He was frozen to his seat by the realisation that his face had been seen by enough people to facilitate the creation of a near perfect likeness by a police artist. At that moment, the rocking of the carriage as it hurtled through the tunnels seemed to be a grim precursor to the swinging of his own corpse from the gallows, the fate he had so dreaded since the first moment the Voice had dragged him into the deathly mire that was now suffocating him.

When he alighted at Ealing Broadway tube station, he was in two minds as to what to do next. He could take the gun to the house to which he'd returned the previous weapon, as he'd been originally instructed, and pretend that nothing had gone wrong. But if word had reached the Voice about him having been seen by a bevy of witnesses, that could be hazardous. It might be safer to acknowledge that things had not all gone to plan and that his face was imprinted on the memories of those who witnessed his flight from the church. He would then need to follow the instructions on the back of his latest victim's photograph telling him what to do if anything went seriously wrong. He was to go instead to the Rat and Ferret Inn in Whitechapel and tell the landlord that he needed to speak to the oddly named 'Mr. Shadow'. He was to give him a code word. Given that it was Gibbet, it had been clearly chosen to indicate the nature of what potentially was at stake. Neither the name of the pub nor the pseudonym of his potential helper sounded promising. After some thought on the matter, he decided that all of his possible options carried risks and unknowns. His previous visit to the gun-return house had not gone well when he'd failed to follow his instructions to the letter and he didn't want a similar experience on this occasion. In light of that, it seemed going to the pub would be the simplest and wisest thing to do. He would explain to whoever it was hiding behind the name of Mr. Shadow that he had only been spotted because his specified escape route had been blocked and then see what happened. If the worst came to the worst, the Voice and his paymasters might abandon him and leave him to his fate, waiting for the Russians' associates to find him. He was certain that people like the two dead gunmen would be working for other, far more powerful people who would now be on his trail. Or, should an excellent police artist's likeness of his face be published in all the newspapers, his creditors might simply kill him themselves as a liability that needed to be disposed of. Whichever way he would end up in a coffin. Alternatively, if his luck was in, the Voice might have some further use for him and spirit him away to a safe hiding place. If the police likeness was considerably less than a perfect match for his face, he assumed that his appearance could be disguised enough for him to be unrecognisable from it. His usefulness to the Voice and his general chances of survival would then be considerably higher. That was the best he could hope for. If the picture was spot on then his chances of survival would be small.

The Rat and Ferret turned out to be as unpromising as its name had suggested. Dimly lit and dirty, it was a maze of rooms half-full of hard faces and threatening looks. Malone made his way to the bar, where a man with a scar that ran the full length of one cheek stood watching him from behind the counter. Malone told him of his need to speak to 'Mr. Shadow' and gave him the code word. He trembled quietly while the landlord's boxer's eyes weighed him up in silence. Then, the man with a face as fierce as a knife gave him a key and told him to go to the meeting room at the far end of the pub, to unlock the door and to sit and wait until he was contacted. He did so with a look that would have withered a lion. He seemed to have no interest in who Malone was or the nature of his business with the mysterious Shadow.

The meeting room turned out to be something of a surprise. In complete contrast to the rest of the pub it had been recently decorated. In the centre of the long, polished table that ran its full length was a telephone. Malone seated himself opposite it and waited expectantly. The venerable old carriage clock on the mantelpiece had chimed the passing of two hours before the call came. Trembling, he picked the receiver up and asked who the caller was. The Voice said,

"It is your usual friend, Mr. Malone. Sorry about the subterfuge. It amuses me to have Mr. Shadow as the version of myself that deals with matters of an ominous nature. My sources tell me that tonight's job did not go smoothly. That sounds extremely ominous."

"But it wasn't my fault. The door through which I was supposed to escape had been locked and I had no alternative but to flee out of the main exit. I couldn't help it, there was no other way out. There was a group of people standing there who'd heard the shots and they all saw my face."

"So I believe. How serious a matter this is depends on what they make of your face, Mr. Malone. If their recollections are so good as to give the police a clear likeness and a picture that's nearly as precise as a photograph goes out in all the newspapers, then you're of no further use to your creditors so far as this country is concerned. However, the good news for you is that they have significant interests in Paris as well. You have at least delivered two souls to the Almighty's mercy, as they have required, and even added a third as an unexpected bonus. Those successes have given you a degree of credit and a usefulness that previously you were lacking. I've spoken to one of them tonight and he is prepared to facilitate your escape to France if the need arises. If, on the other hand, the police likeness is so poor as to make you unrecognisable from it, then you will have no cause for panic and can continue as before."

Malone gasped with relief. The Voice continued,

"However, your failure to provide for a safer means of escape has caused both me and your creditors unnecessary and unanticipated inconvenience. You should have checked the side door before your target arrived and if it was locked you should simply have saved a bullet to blow the lock. You should always plan ahead, Mr. Malone, always allow for the unexpected. Because you didn't, I have had to waste valuable time making rapid arrangements for your temporary accommodation in a safe location until we can see what the police picture looks like. If your escape to France is necessary, then that will cause yet more inconvenience and a degree of unanticipated expenditure. So, there is a price for tonight's little moment of incompetence, Mr. Malone and that price is that your creditors will require your services for further jobs. As always, you have a choice, but equally, as always, the consequence of any refusal to take up their offer will be of a terminal nature for you personally, if you get my drift. Do you get my drift, Mr. Malone, or have you developed a death wish of a truly heroic nature?"

"But I can't kill again," Malone wailed, "every time I kill someone a bit of me dies as well. When I send a man to his grave a small part of me follows him into the soil."

"Well, that's as may be, Mr. Malone, but I'm afraid beggars can't be choosers. You're almost as tall as me, so if only a small part of you dies with every killing there should be some time to go before the whole of you ends up six feet under. And that's surely better than the only other alternative, which is to refuse your creditors' kind offer and end up with the whole of you tumbling into the grave at one go."

"That's not a choice at all, that's the Devil's alternative."

"For a man who, before all this began, had lost his religious beliefs, this seems to be a remarkable conversion on the road to Damascus, Mr. Malone. Perhaps it was the location of tonight's job - d'you think the angels and saints in the church windows got into your head perhaps? Or is your old Catholic school conscience coming back to haunt you - the notion of mortal sin and you buying a one-way ticket to hell as a result of your murderous actions?

42

"I'm all kinds of things - a serial fornicator, liar, wastrel and hopeless gambler, call me what you like, but I'm not a killer. I just can't go on doing this - I've paid my debt twice over."

"Not a killer? Now haven't we been over this same ground before, Mr. Malone? How can a man who has made a deliberate choice to kill on two separate occasions not be a killer? I would say that that is now most certainly your profession and one that you might even be proud of. You've been useless in so many aspects of your life, Mr. Malone and yet here is something that you seem able to perform reasonably well. If we dismiss tonight's little hiccup as a beginner's mistake, this may well be the one profession on this earth that you can succeed in. Who knows, your creditors may yet decide to cancel your debt and start paying for your services. So, cheer up, chin up, look to the future. Your three for the price of two deadly acts have bought an extension of your life. All you need do is to keep delivering what your creditors want and you could yet live your full three score years and ten."

Malone groaned and put his head in his one free hand. The Voice said,

"Now then, Mr. Malone, that's not the attitude for a grown man to take. Your continual moans and complaints are beginning to grate and it's time you faced the facts. As I have said so many times that I'm beginning to tire of the words, I am not forcing you to do anything. You have a choice. If you want to take the virtuous path then all you have to do is say so and you will not have to kill another living man. It is a martyr's journey that you will then be on, but, with the apparent resurrection of your old religious beliefs, it is a journey that may well save you from the hell that Catholics fear so much. If you want to live, then your own past foolish behaviour, your reckless gambling and your accumulated debts, have left you with only one choice. You must become the servant of your creditors until they decide to set you free. That means if they say you must kill another man, or even several men, then that is what you must do. The choice is yours. Do you understand? I can't go on repeating all of this forever and a day."

Malone mumbled something incomprehensible. The Voice said,

"For all the sense that made you could be talking in a foreign language. Now, here's the deal. If you choose to live then you must leave the pub at the end of our conversation and go to the following address. Have you got a pen and paper now?"

Malone furtled about in his jacket pocket and retrieved both of the required items, confirming his possession of them as he did so. The Voice said,

"Right. Go to Vittler's Lane, which is about six streets down from your current location, where you'll find a disused hotel, the Van Ginneken. It was bomb damaged during the war and looks deserted. You'll find that the side door is unlocked. When you go in, you'll find that, of the three lifts, the middle one is still working. Go up to the ninth floor and look for room 912. That's yours until we find out whether the constabulary's portrait of your cherubic face is a spitting image or not. Stay inside the room and do not leave it even for one minute until you are told that you can. You'll find enough food in there for a week. When we have decided what best to do with you, you will be contacted by a young woman who will use the name Laura May. She will tell you what to do next. When you leave the pub tonight, lock the meeting room and return the key to Mr. Barnaby, the landlord. The establishment may look unsavoury, but everyone who drinks there understands the house rule that nobody must grass on anyone else. It's a rule that can only be broken on pain of death, so you will not be betrayed. If the police enquire, they will find that no-one in the pub has seen you. That's the end of our conversation for tonight, I'm afraid. If you choose to live, you'll follow my instructions. If you choose otherwise, I'll be sending flowers to your funeral, but they will be the very best, Mr. Malone. I know how expensive your tastes are. Good night and good luck."

Reluctantly and with a feeling of deep dread, Malone did as instructed. Room 912 was surprisingly large and clean, with fresh bedding and a small supply of bread and tinned food laid out on the dressing table. It was clearly in regular use as a hideaway. Even soap and towels were provided, as if the hotel was open for business. The ageing blackout curtains from the Second World War were still in place and when Malone pulled them back a little, he found they concealed French windows, leading out onto a small balcony. The people who had stayed in this hotel in its heyday were clearly worlds away from those who populated the Rat and Ferret, only six streets distant. Looking out at the tapestry of lights of the vast city below, Malone was in the paradoxical position of seeming literally to have the world at his feet, while feeling simultaneously that he was completely powerless, a puppet whose strings were being pulled by people he'd never seen and would never meet - and who could snuff out his life in an instant. He was the man who'd dreamed of winning big time and of having everything he wanted, but who'd ended up with nothing of value at all. He closed the curtains, turned off the light and went to bed.

Unbeknown to him, in another room, five doors down, with its door very slightly ajar, a second man sat. His job was very simple. It was to make sure Malone didn't leave the building during his stay. Now that he was in, there was no way out, unless or until the Voice allowed it.

CHAPTER SIX

"He's sleeping with that nun I tell you!"

Alice had been delayed by five minutes in her arrival at the office and was startled by the accusation that she heard as she opened the outer door. Gus was looking equally taken aback. He was standing in the middle of the front office in conversation with a small but very fierce looking woman in her mid-seventies. Her expensive tweed skirt, along with her cut-glass accent, marked her out immediately in Alice's eyes as a probable member of the aristocracy. As she hung up her coat, she remembered the name of the first appointment of the day - Lady Arabella Witchfield. So, she was correct in her assumption and this was the fearsome Lady A in the flesh. She remembered also the note that her predecessor had put in the relevant client file - 'Frequently Exploding Bomb - handle with extreme care!'

"It's Sister Agnes. She's in and out of that presbytery as if she were his wife. We Roman Catholics do not expect our prelates to have wives Mr. Benedict. I want you to prove that I'm right so that I can have the man defrocked!"

Gus caught Alice's eye and noted the enormous difficulty she was now having keeping a straight face. He said,

"Lady Arabella, may I present my new assistant, Mrs. Alice Harding."

Alice's near collapse into giggles of a few seconds ago was frozen off her face by the laser-like gaze of Lady A as she turned to scrutinise the new member of staff. She said,

"She looks a sensible girl - will you be putting her on the case?"

Before Gus could reply she said,

"And there's another thing I want investigated. I'm convinced the man's a communist and communism, as you well know, is an atheist dogma. He ought to be defrocked for that as well."

Gus was now looking more baffled than startled. He said,

"What makes you think that, Lady Arabella? Canon O'Leary has always seemed a very traditional priest in his beliefs when you've asked us to check on him before."

"His every second sermon is devoted to a tirade about how we rich of the parish should be doing more to help those idle or unwise enough to find themselves in poverty. He's forever showering charity on the most undeserving poor in the parish. The money's not coming from us because we believe the best way to help the poor is to make them work for a living and learn to support themselves. There are some very substantial sums involved and if we're not providing it, it must be coming from the Communist Party. It's a means of persuading the recipients to join the revolution I tell you. I want you to prove that I'm right about that as well."

Gus said,

"Well, you're paying the fees, Lady Arabella and if you want us to look into these accusations we will do. But I can't guarantee that we'll be able to prove what you want. If the man turns out to be completely innocent on one or both counts then that is all we will be able to tell you."

"Oh, I think you'll find I'm right this time," she replied. "What is it they say in these popular cinema films? 'I've got you bang to rights!' That's what I'll say to that abominable excuse for a priest when I've finally caught him."

With that slight misremembering of words from a hoary old film, the formidable tweed-armoured battlecruiser slipped on the coat that she had draped over a chair, picked up her thousand-pound handbag and exited in grand style, saying, as her parting shot,

"The man's in league with the Russians. He must be stopped!"

Her exit overlapped with the arrival of the invisible man, Mr. One, who burst into the office with a perplexed look on his face. He said,

"How does that woman know about the Russians? Who is she?"

Gus laughed and said,

"That was Lady Arabella Witchfield, leading light in the congregation of St. Bartholomew the Miraculous. She and her wealthy chums within the parish have been in high fury since the arrival of a new priest. He's been reminding them that the New Testament says it's harder for a rich man to enter heaven than it is for a camel to pass through the eye of a needle. She wants him sacked by any means she can devise and has been paying me to investigate a host of spurious allegations, the latest of which implies that he's a communist in the pay of the Russians. It's all quite entertaining, none of it appears to be true, but she seems determined to pay us large amounts of money to provide answers that for her, are always a great disappointment."

Mr. One looked completely baffled. He said,

"Oh, I see. Well, I think I would rather side with Lady Arabella on the wealth question."

Gus raised his eyebrows and said,

"Yes, I rather thought you might. Shall we go into my office?"

He had hardly shut the door behind them before Mr. One had thrown two different newspapers onto his desk.

"I presume you've seen this story, Augustus?"

Mr. One pointed to headlines about a double murder the night before in St. Barnabas and all the Saints.

Gus shook his head and started reading the account of the killings on the fourth page of the Times. Mr. One said,

"We've managed to persuade the police to keep it from the press so far, but both of the victims are Russian intelligence officers. First one of ours is killed, then two of theirs. We're being set up by someone, it's being made to look like we've retaliated for a killing we're assumed to believe was done by the Russians. I've spoken to Carter at Scotland Yard on the basis of your assistant's information and he is indeed absolutely certain that the Kensington Gardens murder was the work of an amateur. There is no evidence whatsoever to suggest that professional Russian hitmen were involved. I've checked with every section in the British intelligence services this morning and everyone is clear that last night's church murders were nothing to do with us. But I've seen the bodies and this time it does look like a professional job. One of them was shot right between the eyes from some distance and the other had his skull caved in. The mood music coming out of the Russian embassy is not good. They haven't drawn any definite conclusions yet, but they're definitely moving towards a position of thinking that our fingerprints are all over the killings."

Gus said,

"Have you any idea who's really behind last night's murders?"

"If I had I wouldn't be here," Mr. One said irritably. "If we don't find out what's going on pretty damn quickly everything could get completely out of hand, with the Soviets taking out two or more of our intelligence officers in retaliation and who knows where it would all end. To stop that from happening we need to give them some heads on a platter. I'm mobilising all available resources to that end - and that includes you as our main external contractor in London. Did you get anywhere with your enquiries about the first killing?"

"I've had a well-placed source working on it and should have something for you by early afternoon. I'm meeting him for lunch and he expects to have what we need by then."

"OK, as long as it's no later than then. Last night's killer was spotted coming out of the church by several people. The police have put together an artist's impression of his face, using their descriptions, and it's going out in the late editions this morning. Unfortunately, there were significant discrepancies in the various accounts of the hitman's appearance, so the usefulness of the likeness they've produced is highly dubious. I've brought you an advance copy of the Telegraph's late edition. The portrait is on the fourth page."

He threw it onto the desk. He continued,

"Make what use of it you can. The police don't recognise anybody from it and the only good thing about it is that it doesn't resemble any of our people who the Soviets might expect to be involved in such an operation. That might buy us a bit of time if they take it at face value. I'd like you to get to work with your sources to see if you can pick up any whispers as to what might have been going on. Will this character you're meeting at lunchtime have any useful insights on last night's killings as well as the Kensington Gardens murder d'you think?"

"He has contacts right across the London underworld, so if there are criminal interests involved, he will most likely hear something."

"Good. Right, that's it for now, I'll rely on you to get cracking. I've got two more visits to make before eleven. As soon as you hear something, express it through to me via the usual secure channels."

Gus nodded and Mr. One exited in his customary turbo-charged fashion, his leather soles hitting the highly polished oak floorboards of the outer office so hard and so quickly that the pencils on Alice's desk vibrated as he sailed past.

After he'd made some phone calls, Gus put on his 'East End' hat and coat. As he headed for the door Alice said,

"Horses for courses again?"

He smiled and nodded. She said,

"Before you go, what do you want me to do about Lady Arabella?"

"Ah, Lady A. Well, regarding the communism allegation, I already have all the information we need. You see a sizeable chunk of the money that the good Canon O'Leary has been putting towards helping the poor comes from me. I'm confessing this now because I know you'll discover it anyway if you begin what I am certain will be a very thorough investigation of the matter."

"I didn't think you were a Catholic."

"I'm not. I simply help fund people who I know to be doing a good job helping the poor and whatever his faults or merits, the good canon is one of those people."

"Why didn't you tell Lady A that and stop her wasting her money?"

"She's not wasting her money - it's going to a very good cause. It amuses me to regularly give the canon fifty percent of what she pays us. Lovely irony, don't you think - Lady A is helping provide the funds she thinks are coming from the Communist Party. I'm sure it's good for her soul."

Alice laughed and said,

"You are outrageous Mr. Robin Hood. But what about the rest of the money the canon's being given?"

"He did actually tell me believe it or not. It's from his dodgy brother apparently and he's had all kinds of qualms of conscience about whether he should accept it. He's always suspected that his brother earns his money from illegal pursuits and that he makes charitable donations to hedge his bets with the Almighty. Ultimately, he decided that in this case at least, the ends justify the means and took the lolly. That's up to him, but it's very clear that the money's not coming from the Communist Party. I'll not be telling Lady A that I'm one of the funders by the way, I'll just say that I've discovered that it's a wealthy private donor of impeccable standards who wishes to remain anonymous."

"Hm, I'm not sure about the impeccable standards bit, Robin. And what about Sister Agnes and her secret love nest in the presbytery?"

"Get John Harris to do the necessary surveillance. He's in the freelance contractors' file. I normally use him in divorce cases and anything to do with the underpants department, so he's the best man for the job. If he finds anything incriminating on Sister Agnes, I'll buy you a pink silk hat. As for my own hat, I'll probably eat it."

"Whatever would George say if you bought me a hat?"

"I'll buy him a pink hat as well so he won't feel jealous. I'll be back around mid-afternoon."

Gus arrived at the exotically named 'Nellie Nolan's Pie and Chips Restaurant' at precisely midday. Tasty was living up to his name, being already half-way through a large plate of steak pie and chips. He motioned to Gus to sit down and snapped his fingers at the young waitress who had just finished taking the order of the table next to them. He said,

"My friend here will have the same as me - and a large cup of tea. Make sure you give him the best because he's paying."

The girl nodded and smiled, then scuttled off to the kitchen. He said,

"You can't go wrong with their pie and chips special. Try it and you'll be in heaven. I hope you don't mind me starting without you, I've had a busy day and I'm a growing boy."

He flashed a smile full of interestingly damaged teeth. Gus drank in the lovingly preserved 1930s décor of the establishment and the rich aroma of perfectly fried chips that permeated the air. He was fascinated by the range of customers, who were an eclectic mix of young and old, working class and middle class, the gentle looking, the hard boiled and a few likely lads who would probably cut someone's finger off to settle a debt. Tasty watched the way his eyes scrutinised the room with interest. He said,

"I thought you'd like it here. You get a mix of people that you don't get anywhere else. Just the kind of place that you can meet up without standing out."

It occurred to Gus that Tasty would stand out wherever he went, given his mountainous build and face like a thunderstorm waiting to happen. Tasty said,

"I've asked around as you said. It's absolutely certain that your boy had nothing to do with gambling. Nobody on any of the circuits had ever heard of him prior to his sudden departure from this earth. It seems like somebody's been feeding you red herrings."

Gus said,

"Did you hear any hints as to which alternative direction I might best proceed in with my enquiries?"

Tasty frowned and was obviously in deep thought as he made light of his enormous steak and kidney pie. He said,

"I promised I'd tell you who's not involved and not who is when you want me to find out who's been up to what. I'll narrow the field down for you, but I'm not a grass. But in this case, I can give you a name because it isn't a name."

"I'm intrigued."

"So you should be. This guy's a ghost. Nobody alive knows who he is and nobody who's ever seen him has lived to tell the tale. He's only ever been heard, not seen, by the people I know - over the dog and bone, or in the shadows of darkened rooms. So, I couldn't grass on him even if I wanted to, because I know sweet Fanny Adams about him. But there's now a strong rumour that the Kensington Gardens thing was something he set up. The armourer who supplied the gun apparently let something slip when he shouldn't have done - it suggested who'd organised the hit and the rumour is that it was this invisible man. The gun supplier can't be questioned any further because his loose lips cost him dearly from what I've heard. He's started a new job as part of the foundations of an office block. All I can tell you is that this faceless ghost is Irish, he's big time and he doesn't make mistakes. If you've got him on your tail you've as good as fallen into the hands of the Grim Reaper or Mephis-what's-his-name."

52

"Mephistopheles?" Gus ventured.

"That's the one. I don't know why he'd be after your boy, but the rumour has always been that he's a contractor, so the whys and wherefores would be best known by the people who hired him. There's something else as well. The rumours say that he never does a job himself, that he always sub-contracts it, so you'll never find a smoking gun in his hand."

Gus said,

"You said you can give me a name because it isn't a name."

"That's because it's the nickname, not the real name, of a man nobody knows, if you get my drift. This ghost, shadow, call him what you like, is known as the Kerryman on account of his accent. The Belani mob refer to him as the Voice, because they only ever got to hear from him over the dog and bone when he was on their backs about something, but everyone else calls him the Kerryman."

Gus said,

"This is all extremely helpful. Tasty, you're a man of your word, thank you."

"The missus says I'm a man of too many words," Tasty replied. "She's the only one who'd dare."

Gus said, speculatively,

"You heard about the church killings last night?"

"Who's not heard about them? That story's going round all the houses. There's a rumour they were Ruskies, the dead and soon to be buried that is, not the boys with the shooters. If you're interested in them then there must be a connection to your boy. Am I right or am I right?"

Gus smiled and was about to reply when Tasty pre-empted him and said mirthfully,

"I couldn't possibly comment! I've got your sauce in all the right bottles, haven't I?"

Gus said,

"Have you heard any theories as to who might or might not have been responsible for the killings?"

"Well, sticking by my non-grassing rule, I can tell you that nobody thinks any of the London mobs was involved. They've all got their hallmarks where killings are concerned and they weren't visible on either of the stiffs."

"Did somebody you know see them?"

"An old acquaintance from the local mob checked them out before the bluebottles arrived. He was totally certain that it wasn't a London type of job. It looked more like a military operation, with a precision shot right between the eyes of one of the stiffs. If the targets were Ruskies, then perhaps you ought to be looking more at your old mates in intelligence Gus me old china."

"They weren't involved - like you, I hear rumours shall we say. And nobody that you know recognised the suspect's picture in the papers this morning?"

"That comedy cartoon the bluebottles are putting about you mean? It looks more like a face that was made in a plasticine factory. Naw, Gus, me old china, if it ain't one of the London mobs and it ain't your old muckers, then you should maybe look for the invisible man for that job as well. You wouldn't have asked me about last night's circus if you didn't think there might be a connection to your boy in Kensington Gardens, would you?"

Before Gus could reply his extra-large plate of steak pie and chips arrived. Tasty said,

"Find the people who hired the Kerryman for the two jobs and you'll find out what's going on - but to find them you've first got to find him. I wouldn't try it alone if I were you, anyone who gets too close to him tends to meet their maker. Anyway, enjoy your dinner, Gus, I've got to go - arms to twist, legs to break, you know the kind of thing. Don't look so alarmed, I'm only pulling your leg. It's really my ballet lesson this afternoon. I'm practising the Nutcracker Suite and then I'm going to prune the roses at the vicarage - after my flower arranging class in the church hall."

He let out a huge, ear rattling laugh and as he was getting up said,

"Your face. You are a one, Gus. Let me know when you need my help again. You can usually find me in here on Thursdays, at about this time."

Then, after squeezing his hat onto his substantial forehead, he patted Gus on the shoulder and left, the sea of passers-by in the street outside parting all the way down the middle as he ploughed forwards into the early afternoon sunlight.

As Gus walked back to the tube twenty minutes later, he wrestled a little with his conscience. After all of the excesses and horrors of the war he'd vowed that he'd remain uncontaminated by what he'd seen and heard. He'd had a privileged life that he could walk straight back into, a cushion against the horrors of everything he'd learnt about the Nazis during his time in intelligence. But many of the poorer men and women who'd survived the grim, murderous battle against an enemy from hell itself were not so lucky. He had little faith that the new deal they were offered after the war would last much beyond the grand principle of a health service free to all. He knew that many people in the East End were still struggling desperately, particularly those who had lost everything in the blitz. He wanted to do his bit to help and that was where his 'Robin Hood' scheme had come from - something that would put a smile on his face and those of the people who benefited from it. It was a drop in the ocean when the scale of the problem was considered, but every drop was valuable to those who needed it. He enjoyed investigative work, something for which he'd developed an outstanding reputation during the war, and he could use a significant part of his Mayfair earnings to give some relief and enjoyment in life to those who previously had been in near despair. It was in that spirit also that he'd set out to help people like Tasty's sister. Without his freely provided skills, she might never have found her daughter before the thug who'd imprisoned her had taken her life in some drunken rage. Yet the professional focus of the former intelligence officer never left him. He knew that some among those he helped might in return give him something of great value - information and new routes into the gossip that circulated within the criminal underworld. Their precarious existence, family connections, a whole range of factors, made them much closer to these things than he was. If his Mayfair operation was to be able to justify its huge fees to its wealthy clients, he had to have access to all the best information sources needed to deal successfully with their cases, and that included cases that could only be resolved through help from the London underworld. His acquisition of a source as well connected as Tasty was one of the fruits of his dual-purpose beneficence, a major coup. Yet he worried that the intelligence gathering dimension to his kindness had somehow contaminated and degraded the humanitarian side of what he was about. He did, after all, keep half of the profits of the Mayfair business, an operation that part-

depended on such intelligence, purely for himself. It was a nagging doubt about his own motives that he knew he wouldn't be able to get rid of. For now, however, it would have to be put to one side. There were urgent matters to deal with. What Tasty had given him was real gold, even if, as yet, he had no face to stick on the wall above those two magic words, his first real clue, 'the Kerryman'. But it just might be enough to persuade the KGB to hold off for a little longer before planning retaliation. He didn't want any more of his former colleagues to join Tony Gregory in the grave in a tit for tat killing war that was being provoked by a party as yet unknown and for reasons that needed to be discovered, fast.

As he walked on, his mind deeply focussed on his thoughts, a black Bentley passed by. In one of the random ironies of fate, it was a brief moment when the hunter and the hunted came within three feet of each other, without either realising it. The moment passed almost as soon as it had arrived. The Bentley drove sedately on down the road, the Kerryman reading a copy of the Irish Times in the back. Oblivious to the significance of the occasion, Gus hurried into the nearest Tube station to catch a train that would hurtle into the darkness, in the opposite direction to his elusive prey ...

CHAPTER SEVEN

Claire Riley swept into the oak panelled room with the outer style and serenity of a queen. Her mind, however, was consumed by an inner turmoil. It was visible only in the almost imperceptible shaking of her slim, silk-gloved hands. She was twenty-six years old and deeply afraid she mightn't make it to twenty-seven.

The Maître D was expecting her arrival and led her immediately to the table that usually she shared with one of her two extremely wealthy beaus. One would have been a safe number, two was dangerous. She had become a little over-confident that one wouldn't find out about the other and now her proverbial chickens were coming home to roost.

"Will Lord Learswick be joining you later?" he asked, as he pulled back a chair for her.

She shook her head and half-smiled, a nervous gesture that might most usually be shared with her dentist. It was a particularly busy night and the ultra-expensive restaurant was full of the various London cliques that made it their own on a Thursday. They were familiar faces and several people smiled emptily at her as she passed. The room reeked of tradition, order and wealth. It was the place where several overlapping elites came to dinner and everyone was on their best behaviour. She asked for a few minutes to consider her order. The head waiter nodded with his usual impeccable courtesy and headed back to the grand entrance, where a minor celebrity and his date for the evening had just arrived. She waited until he'd greeted them and then stood up, now visibly shaking, her face a pallid white. She unzipped her dress and let it drop to the floor, then kicked off her shoes. The room was filled with sudden gasps and excited, disbelieving cries. She was completely naked. She joined her hands above her head and turned slowly in a complete circle, first one way, then the other. Then, unsteadily, she climbed onto the table top, bowed and stood motionless for a full minute. She was unable to look into the eyes of a single one of the startled faces in the room. Looking as terrified as someone about to be guillotined, she sat down, drew her knees up almost to her chin and placed her arms round her shins. Her gaze was fixed firmly on a hatchet-faced woman in a black dress, who was standing just inside the polished oak doors at the far end of the room, watching her performance. The observer nodded, made a mocking display of vigorous handclapping and then left. Claire let out a gasp of relief and her head dropped onto her knees.

The Maître D had acted swiftly and by now was at her side, with a large white table cloth that he immediately wrapped around her. He instructed a junior waiter to pick up her dress and shoes and then, with his hands placed gently but firmly on her arms, impressed upon her the importance of getting down from the table and accompanying him to his office, where a female member of staff would help her to get dressed. A taxi was called and sent round to the rear of the premises, where she was escorted out via the service entrance. As the vehicle disappeared off into the distance the name of Claire Riley was being rapidly typed into the restaurant's black list, a once highly valued customer, never to be admitted again.

Sexual exhibitionism of any kind was the number one crime at this end of the 'posh nosh' market.

The taxi headed out of the city and into the countryside. After a tortuous ride through winding, hedge-lined lanes, it finally arrived at the gates of a large country estate. She was following the second stage of the instructions that had been given to her. "After your performance in the restaurant make your own way back to the house. Quickly." The discreetly armed flunkey on duty checked who the passenger was and then waved them past, up the long drive, through the deer park, to the imposing front entrance of the palatial Georgian mansion that dominated everything around it.

58

Claire paid the driver and then walked uncertainly up the steep, stone steps and rang the bell. She was left waiting a good three minutes before the door was opened by the house manager, Mrs. Grant, who ushered her into the marble hallway. She was the same fierce-faced woman in the black dress who had observed her performance. In the centre of the ornately patterned floor two suitcases, one large and one small, sat waiting. Mrs. Grant gestured towards them. She said,

"He said you're to leave immediately. You need to take those with you."

"Oh. Will the rest of my things be sent on, or will I need to arrange that myself?" Claire asked plaintively.

"Everything you arrived with has been packed into those cases," Mrs. Grant replied. "He said that if you want the rest, you'll find it in the walled garden. You'll need to follow me."

She marched off at a pace that said, "Let's get this over with as quickly as possible, I've got better things to do." Claire followed dispiritedly. Quite why her best coats and dresses and everything else had to be in the walled garden was a mystery she hardly dared contemplate. As they exited via the service entrance at the rear of the house, she could see a pall of smoke rising above the garden walls and making lace-like patterns in the moonlight. Mrs. Grant opened the heavy iron gate and led her over to where two of the staff were tending a bonfire. Claire was filled with an increasing dread as it became obvious what was being burned. Her two favourite silk-lined coats were all that remained. Mrs. Grant said,

"He said these were to be kept until last. They can be thrown on the fire now that you're here."

One of the men picked them up and did as instructed. Claire let out a desperate yelp and tried to lunge forwards to stop him, but Mrs. Grant grabbed hold of her arm and held it firmly until both garments were fully alight and unsalvageable. She said,

"He said that we're to give you one bagful to take with you."

She nodded to the second man, the head gardener, who pulled a crumpled brown paper bag out of his pocket. He used a trowel to fill it with the now cooled ashes from the clothes that had been incinerated earlier.

He handed it to Claire, who stared at it in disbelief and then threw it onto the ground. She turned back towards the house and began to run, her entire body trembling. She was afraid that the deal wasn't going to be kept, that the next thing she would feel would be a bullet in her back and that she would be the final item on the bonfire. In her blind panic and the weak light of the moon she failed to notice an ornamental rock that had slipped sideways from one of the flowerbeds onto the path and tripped over it. She went flying onto the stone flags. Momentarily stunned and bleeding from her left cheek and her badly scraped left knee, she was helpless to resist as Mrs. Grant grabbed hold of her arms roughly and pulled her up.

"He won't be pleased that you were so ungrateful for his kind gift," the harridan said. "Come on, it's time for you to go. It wouldn't be wise to be still here when he gets back."

She frogmarched her crushed charge back into the house and handed her the suitcases. Claire said,

"I need to go upstairs to get my car keys."

Mrs. Grant laughed.

"Car? You are a one, aren't you? That's already been sold. That Jaguar raised a very handy little sum. I believe he intends using it to pay for repairs to the ornamental fountain. You can ask the lodge to call a taxi when you get outside the gates. You might need to ask the security guard for some cash to cover the fare. Jerzy has closed all your bank accounts."

"But everything I had was in those accounts."

"Everything indeed. You'll be able to remember it fondly, then, won't you? Think of it as a friend who's suddenly died. You'll never see them again, but the memories of the good times will always cheer you up."

"You're a bitch!"

"That I may be, but the tables have been turned, Lady Jane and I'm now the bitch that's in charge of you, not the other way round. You might think your little ritual humiliation in the restaurant, and being slung out on your ear with nothing, will pay off your debt in full, by the way, but that's a little short of the mark. He's got a nasty job for you to do as the final part of your penance."

"I've done enough, just let me go."

"If you go without agreeing to do it, he said he will get someone to do a little job on you instead. They're laying the foundations for his new club in Hammersmith next week and you'll be part of them unless you do what you're told. He's not joking little miss nobody, so you'd better listen."

"I'm all ears."

"They are rather big, aren't they? Now you're not going to like this, but you're going to do it or die, so listen carefully. Jerzy was very much impressed by how you'd learned how to aim a gun on that stinking farm you were brought up on. You handled a rifle as well as any of the gentlemen when he had shoots on the estate, so he'd like you to use your talent to clean up a little problem for him."

The harridan handed her a slip of paper. She continued,

"You're to go to that address. It's a disused hotel. There's a gent in there who's become a liability and it's your job to get rid of him. We know he's expecting someone to call on him when it's safe for him to leave, a girl who he hasn't seen before, someone the Kerryman will be sending."

"Who's the Kerryman?"

"Believe me, he's someone you should express no curiosity about whatsoever. Forget I mentioned him. Just you remember that you need to get there before the girl he's sending does. You go to the gent's room and tell him that you're her, that you've come with the news that it's safe to leave. Tell him you need to be let into his room so that you can explain the details of where he's to go without the risk of anyone hearing. Once you're in, think of some reason to get him to turn round with his back to you. Say you're parched and need a drink or something. Then shoot him dead. Empty four of the bullets into him, then get out as quick as you can. Wear gloves so you don't leave any prints on the gun or anywhere else and then sling it as far as you can into Old Father Thames."

"Bloody Norah, I can't do all that. If I get caught, it's the gallows and no mistake. There's already been one woman hanged for shooting a bloke this year."

"And if you don't do it, Jerzy will do far worse than hang you. If he's in a really bad mood he'll arrange to have all your finger nails pulled and your tongue cut out before you're topped. You know how quickly he flips from nice to really bloody nasty. This isn't something you've got a choice in girl. It's do or die."

Claire was trembling and was whiter than she'd been during her performance in the restaurant. She said,

"I can't do it anyway; I haven't got a gun."

"Yes, you have. You'll find one's been slipped into your bags - that big grey one with the stickers on it from all the posh holidays you won't be going on again. It's a nice little Luger, already loaded. It'll fit those skinny little fingers of yours perfectly."

"I'm too bloody terrified to do this. I'll make a mess of it; the bloke will survive and probably kill me in revenge. Jerzy's got professional gunmen here, why doesn't he use them?"

"Because they're too busy protecting him and there's a big job on at the moment that needs all of their attention. If you do make a mess of things, then that will be it for you girly. If the target doesn't kill you, somebody else will be sent to do it instead. It's as I said, do or die. If you wanted to avoid all of this then you shouldn't have been so stupid as to play away from home with Lord Earwig and his cute little arse."

"His name's Learswick, as you very well know," Claire said. Mrs. Grant continued,

"You knew what would happen if the master found out that you were two-timing him, so you've only got yourself to blame. You thought you could be a clever dick and juggle two fierce rich geezers at once. You need brains to do that and brains are something that are in short supply between your ears. You can just thank your lucky stars I persuaded him that having you 'disappeared' would waste too much of his time in terms of the cover-up. The fact he agreed with me that ritual humiliation and instant poverty would do the job instead saved your worthless little life. It not only puts a permanent end to any social ambitions you may still have, but the sordid nature of your performance tonight makes you such an embarrassment that Lord cute little arse won't go anywhere near you when he hears about it. I really did you a favour you don't deserve in so far as all of that gave you a big enough kick up the arse for Jerzy to drop the idea of topping you. So, don't start moaning and whingeing when I tell you he's decided to add a nasty job to complete your penance - you just don't appreciate how very lucky you are. Just be grateful it's you doing the shooting and that you're not the one being shot. If you refuse to do it, then make no mistake, he'll go back to his first option of giving you a bath in quick setting concrete. And frankly, given all the times you played Lady High and Mighty with me, if you won't play ball, I couldn't give a shit what happens to you. I've been more than generous in saving your undeserving hide already. Now, I've told you what's what, so get out and enjoy your nice little walk to the gatehouse. Bye-bye."

She opened the door and none too gently propelled her charge through it. Claire stumbled out into the darkness, her knee hurting with every step.

Before throwing her bags after her, the harridan said,

"My, my, how great is the fall from grace - once the lady of the house, now poorer than a mouse."

Her mocking words echoed more loudly in Claire's consciousness than the fierce slamming of the door that followed them. She limped slowly down the drive, trying to avoid stepping in the deer excrement.

While she was waiting for the taxi to arrive at the gatehouse, she checked inside the grey suitcase. Sure enough, there at the bottom was a Luger pistol. The thought crossed her mind that it would be as useful for bumping off her lethal former 'master' and Mrs. Grant as for executing the unknown man in the hotel room. That would solve all her problems and worries at one go. Reality cut in swiftly when she thought of the two hitmen who went everywhere with their demanding boss and how they would probably have shot her straight between the eyes before she was even able to think about pulling the trigger on the Luger. She hoped she might have a better chance of survival in the hotel killing. She tried not to think of the consequences of being caught if the murder was successful. The thought of death by hanging was so terrifying that the only way she could deal with it was to blank it out of her mind. She had to think positively - she wouldn't mess anything up, she wouldn't be caught - just like her childhood fairy stories, everything would turn out fine. She shuddered uncontrollably for a minute, which was her body's way of telling her she was kidding herself. Pulling herself together as far as she could, she realised she didn't even know the name of the intended victim. Retrieving the slip of paper that Mrs. Grant had given her from her pocket, she found that the lucky individual was a Mr. Malone. She'd no idea what he'd done, other than that he was considered some kind of liability. She didn't want to kill him. He'd done no harm to her and she'd much prefer to bed him rather than top him if he was reasonably good looking with enough money to give them both a bit of fun. But fun was no longer on the agenda and it had been made perfectly clear to her that it was simply a case of kill or be killed. Like Mr. Malone, she didn't consider the option of sacrificing her own life rather than taking someone else's. If a coin was tossed it would come down only one way and that was in her favour.

Mrs. Grant's note gave her step-by-step instructions as to what to do. She was to leave her luggage in lockers at Euston so that it wasn't an encumbrance and then catch a bus to within two streets of the hotel. From there she was to walk. The side door would be open and the middle lift working. She was to go to room 912. If anybody was watching the floor, she should tell them that she'd come to inform Malone that it was safe to leave and give him his instructions. Most likely, they would then let her through. She would have to work out how to deal with them after the shooting and might want to save a couple of bullets for that purpose. Her escape was entirely down to her, but if she was caught, she was to say nothing about those who had given her the job. Should she ignore this advice in order to try and avoid the hangman, she would meet a very unpleasant end in jail, courtesy of her former lover's connections inside the prison world. It would be so unpleasant that a hanging would seem like a dance in the sun by comparison. Jerzy and his henchmen would deny all knowledge of her operation anyway and the gun would not have any of their prints on it, or be in any way traceable. She was to get the job done without delay and to destroy her instructions before going to the hotel. No problem there then she thought, all she had to do was do everything absolutely perfectly and then escape through the window on a magic carpet. She started shuddering uncontrollably again, just as the taxi pulled up. Seeing her, the driver said,

"You haven't got the flu, have you? I'm not picking up any rides if they've got the flu. If I end up off sick, I lose money."

Reassuring him that she hadn't and was just feeling the cold, she pushed her luggage onto the back seat and got in. As the car rattled down the country lane, back towards London, she told herself that the only way she could get through this nightmare was to try and act like an automaton - to do everything as quickly as possible and avoid any detailed thinking about what might happen and just get on with it. Hopefully, she would come out of it all alive and well on the other side of the rainbow. Deep down, in the back of her skull, a dull, throbbing voice murmured that she was more likely to end up dead. Much as she might like to, there was no point in trying to run away or go into hiding. The people who would be sent after her would track her down wherever she went.

When she got to London, she did everything as instructed and arrived at the hotel before the pubs in the nearby streets had shut, allowing her to blend in with the throngs of people going in and out of the more popular establishments. She took the lift to the ninth floor and then crept silently down the corridor. Luckily for her, the man on watch several doors down from Malone's room had fallen asleep and she was unchallenged. When she got to room 912, she could see that Malone's light was on through the gaps between the frame and the damp-warped door. She knocked and went through her routine as instructed, trying to hold herself together while she did so. She managed to convince him that she was genuine and he let her into the room. She asked if she could have a drink of something and as soon as he turned his back, she pulled the gun out of her coat pocket. Fortunately for Malone, he'd opened the blackout curtains earlier in the day while it was still light and hadn't closed them since. Observing her reflection in the French windows as he walked across to get her a glass of water, he saw the gun and instantly dived out of the way as her first shot was unleashed. Moving more quickly than he'd ever done before in his life, he sprang upright and seeing that she was momentarily frozen with shock, dived at her ankles, bringing her face first onto the floor. Temporarily dazed, she fired off a second shot almost by accident, missing his head by a hair's breadth. He tried to wrestle the gun out of her hand, but, somehow, she managed to hold on as he worked it this way and that, attempting to prise her fingers from the trigger. Unfortunately for Claire, the gun went off again in the middle of the struggle, at the precise moment it was pointing towards her neck as Malone wrestled it backwards and forwards. The struggle ceased and she went limp. Shaking with shock, Malone pulled the gun out of her hand as she struggled to breathe. She lay on the floor helpless, clawing at her lacerated throat in desperation.

He'd hardly had time to register what was happening when the minder who had been asleep burst into the room, gun in hand. Instinctively, almost without any conscious thought at all, Malone launched himself at the new arrival, wrongly presuming him to be an accomplice of the woman on the floor. He cracked him across the head with the pistol butt, sending him flying and then raced down the corridor and into the lift. Tearing out into the street he tried to make sense of what had happened as he ran. He could only presume that the Voice had turned against him, that the accuracy of the police artist's likeness had been too close for comfort perhaps and that he had arranged for him to be killed. There was now no place of safety. As he ran along, dodging in and out of alleyways to try and ensure that he wasn't followed, he decided that he would just have to take a risk and hope that the police hadn't yet discovered the address of his flat. If he could get there before the Voice found out that he'd survived, he could collect the cash that he kept in a hidden safe in the wall as a small emergency fund, together with as many changes of clothing as he could fit into a suitcase and then make a bolt for it, heavens knows where.

Pulling his hat as far down over his eyes as he could, in the only way that he could think of to reduce the chances of anyone recognising him, he shot down the escalator at the first tube station he came to. In less than half an hour he was back at his apartment. After checking carefully for any sign of it being watched, he hurried over to the front door and let himself in. All seemed to be well. There was no sound other than his own breathing. Rather than risk alerting anyone to his presence inside, he fumbled in the top drawer of the mahogany cabinet in the hallway and pulled out a torch. Switching it on, he made for the hidden wall safe in the dining room. Working the combination in such a desperate hurry that he got it wrong twice, he opened the safe and reached inside for the money. As he did so he was aware suddenly of a sound behind him. He reached into his pocket for the gun and was about to turn round when he felt a sharp crack on the head and for the second time since his nightmare journey into hell had begun, everything went dark and he slumped to the floor, unconscious.

Incongruously, the cuckoo clock on the wall chirped the hour brightly and his unseen assailant hummed along to the tune.

CHAPTER EIGHT

"One sent Two."

"What?"

"Well I assume that's what he's called. One of Mr. One's underlings called in to see you while you were out," Alice said.

"Very funny. Did he leave a message?"

"Mr. One would like you to meet him at his club at lunchtime, presumably to discuss very, very secret things. You'll need to look out for big ears in nearby armchairs and speak in hushed whispers."

Gus was leafing through the mail. He said,

"Okay. How are things moving along with Lady A's suspected love nest at the presbytery by the way?"

"Very efficiently, if I may say so. The required surveillance is in place and I can report that last night Sister Agnes was back at her convent at five-thirty pm and the entire congregation of nuns appear to have been in the land of nod by ten pm. She was not observed slithering down a drainpipe in a negligee and hotfooting it to the presbytery, nor was the canon spotted climbing in through a downstairs window of the convent, wearing only his underpants and shoes. Things are not looking good for Lady A's plan to defrock him at this moment in time."

"Not that that will put her off from trying. Keep up the hard work, ludicrous though it might be. She pays good money and it can go to much more useful causes than would be the case if it stayed in her grasping little hands."

Alice said,

"Be careful what you say, if Lady A hears you uttering such heresies she'll be accusing you of being a member of the Communist Party as well."

"As long as she doesn't try to defrock me, she can think what she likes. How are we doing for other new work?"

"We had a visit from Sir Arnold Bentley shortly after Mr. Two left a couple of hours ago. He wants us to locate the whereabouts of his estranged son so that he can try and effect a reconciliation. I said I'd check with you and if you're happy to take the case on I'd give him a ring by teatime. I've left the file on your desk."

"Okay. He's aware that our fee will be eyewatering, given our one hundred per cent success rate in similar cases?"

"I did float the likely cost in front of his eyes and he said he was well aware of our premium rates. He also said that he expected rapid results for that kind of outlay."

"That we can give him. If I like the look of the file, we'll get started on it first thing tomorrow - or rather my highly efficient assistant will. We have a top-notch freelance subcontractor that you can use for most of the legwork. We've still got three other cases ticking over nicely at the moment. I might need to ask you to take over the running of two of them as well, if that's ok? The surveillance can be subcontracted in both cases. This business with Mr. One looks as though it could eat up a considerable amount of my time."

"No problem. How are things going in the hush, hush department, or am I not allowed to ask?"

"Well, I've got a name, or rather a nickname for one of the men at the top of the operation we're hunting, but as yet no face or address to go with it. I was able to give Mr. One enough information for him to prevent a tit-for-tat shooting war breaking out, so that at least is something. There's a long way to go though."

"If you need any help just say the word."

"I might even say several words."

"All of them complimentary I hope."

"Indeed."

"I hope Mr. One pays well for the use of your services and that he doesn't plead government enforced poverty and try and get you to work for a bag of toffees and the occasional ice cream soda."

"Mr. One doesn't pay as much as everyone else, but in exchange he feeds me regular work and that is a valuable safety net to keep in place for those very occasional periods when business is a little slack. He knows very well that if he doesn't pay a reasonably generous rate, he will lose his access to my services."

"Well I hope he really is paying you properly. The reason he uses you is because you were one of the best people in intelligence and he doesn't have anyone else as good on his staff."

"I presume you've heard that from Henry?"

"I couldn't possibly comment," Alice replied. "You know how much I prize my reputation for protecting my sources."

"I'm the same myself," Gus replied, "I always take particular care of my tomato ketchup."

Alice grimaced and said,

"Some jokes really don't mature with age, Gussie dear."

Gus said,

"No, but they're satisfyingly annoying. I'm just going to have a look at the file on Bentley's son and then I'll be off to see Mr. One."

"Don't forget to choose the right horse for the course - you're to meet him at his very exclusive gentlemen's club, so don't go accidentally putting your East End hat and coat on."

Gus smiled beatifically and disappeared into his office.

At twelve o'clock precisely he arrived at Mr. One's club. He found him in the process of ordering lunch in the dining room.

"Ah, Gus. Lunch is on me. Please take a seat."

He asked the waiter to bring a second menu. With a faintly impish smile on his face his guest ordered the most expensive items he could see, together with a glass of the very best wine. Mr. One gulped, and said, sotto voce, "Ouch." Gus said,

"A dose of bad indigestion, Angus?"

Mr. One ignored his mischievous question and replied with one of his own.

"Have you managed to find out anything more about the Kerryman since we last spoke?"

"No, not as yet. I'm working on it."

"Well, I have some information that might help. The details you provided last time are still enabling us to keep the Russians at bay, but they expect us to come up with something quickly if they're to be convinced that the church hit was down to someone other than us. As it so happens, fortune has smiled on our labours and revealed a little gold nugget of information, one that should help both you and us in our investigations."

Mr. One paused while the waiter arrived with the drinks. As soon as he'd gone, he continued,

"Three nights ago, the police received a report of a young woman crawling along the pavement outside a disused hotel, the old Van Ginneken. She'd been shot in the neck and had somehow managed to drag herself outside to get help. Somewhat miraculously, the bullet missed anything crucial and her powers of speech appear to be intact. As she was coming to after surgery, the nurses told the police she kept repeating the phrase, 'the Kerryman sent me.' She was in a bit of a trance with the delayed shock, the after-effects of the anaesthetic and all the usual stuff one gets with traumatic injuries. Since she has recovered full consciousness and been questioned by the police, she has denied all knowledge of ever having said such a thing and claims that she has no idea who the Kerryman is. She says she has no idea who shot her. She'd gone into the hotel to find a disused room to sleep in for the night, given that she hardly had any money and couldn't afford to pay for a room in anywhere that was actually open. Somebody had surprised her while she was looking round and shot her for no apparent reason. The police searched the place and found that the ninth floor appeared to have been used until recently by persons unknown. Several rooms had fresh bedding and two clearly had been used during the last few days. Room 912 was interesting, in so far as forensics found another bullet embedded in one of the walls, together with evidence of a struggle and her blood on the floor. The bullet was from the same gun that shot her. There were also several bits and pieces of evidence that suggested strongly that a man had been living in the room. They've taken prints, but so far there's nothing that's showing up as relating to any known criminals. Now she's got her act together, she's sticking to her story and there's nothing our Scotland Yard friends have been able to do so far to persuade her to give them the real account of what happened."

Gus said,

"Do they have a name for this woman?"

"Now that's where things start getting really interesting. She's Claire Riley, who made a bit of a name for herself a few days ago by performing an impromptu striptease in my favourite restaurant. Up until then, she'd been known to police undercover officers as the live-in lover of Jerzy Stokowski, as he calls himself."

Gus said,

"And who exactly is Jerzy Stokowski when he's at home?"

"That is a more pertinent question than you perhaps realise, because Mr. Stokowski is not in fact the gentleman of Polish descent that his name might suggest, but the son of a dissident Russian émigré, one of the 'White Russians' who escaped following the upheavals that came with the Russian Revolution. His real name is Sergei Kozmonofski. He's been a subject of interest to both us and the police for some time in his role as one of the fictional Stokowski Brothers, a couple of big-time crooks whose interests occasionally spill over into politics. The other brother is not only not a Stokowski, but not even his brother. He is another individual of Russian descent by the name of Vladimir Polmonovski. The two gentlemen are in fact cousins, but for business purposes, apparently decided it would be more useful to be thought to be brothers."

Gus said,

"Although not Russian brothers, I wonder why? What exactly is their business?"

"Now that is a very good question. We suspect that they're involved in all kinds of illegal gambling operations, prostitution, drug dealing, you name it, but their connections to these activities are so labyrinthine, complex and legally invisible that it has been impossible to produce any usable evidence against them. They also have a fearsome reputation as brutal enforcers of both debt repayments and of a code of silence about them and anything they're involved in, which makes it even more difficult to get anyone to talk about them."

"They sound like a couple of incorrigible charmers."

"Indeed. And we believe there is an additional dimension to their violence. We're pretty sure they're in the contract killing business as well. The police have long been of the opinion that they largely subcontract that part of their activities out to trusted third parties, again in such a way as to make it extremely difficult to trace anything back to the supposed brothers. The Kerryman would fit in very nicely with that kind of structure. He's their ideal type of operator - nobody knows who he is, or where he lives, or who he works with. Claire Riley's semi-conscious mutterings have given us the first real 'insider' clue as to who his most recent employers have been. She could only have learned about him while she was sharing Sergei's bed. We need to build on that knowledge."

"So, presumably your calculation is that if the fake brothers are of 'White Russian' descent and inclined towards political meddling, they might be tempted to use some of their muscle to do serious damage to the Soviet Union's operations in this country, given the virulently anti-communist role of their fathers in the Russian civil war?"

"Indeed. Interesting, isn't it? These just might be the people we've been looking for."

"Well, some of the people. Theoretically, the kind of info they had on the Russian intelligence officers and their movements could have been obtained by their own people doing the necessary surveillance for them, but it is much more likely to have come directly from within the intelligence community. That's equally true with regard to our man who was murdered in Kensington Gardens. So, it's reasonable to assume that they're working with, or for, an as yet unknown intelligence agency, or rogue operatives within it. They could be simply the stooges, the people we're meant to think are behind it all. On the one hand, what could be more logical than a couple of second-generation White Russians seeking to carry on the civil war with the communists? But on the other, isn't that just a bit too convenient, a bit too like a mask someone really clever would use to hide their own role as the puppet-master behind the scenes? And presuming the fake brothers were the ones who hired the Kerryman for the murder of Tony Gregory, then if their motive for the church killings was revenge for the revolution or whatever, why would they be in the business of eliminating British intelligence officers as well as Russians when Britain is on the opposite side of the Cold War to the Soviets? It seems to me that if they are behind both the Kensington Gardens and the church murders, then they are more likely to be working for someone with a grudge against both the UK and

Russia than for themselves."

"Yes, I like that extra layer of analysis, it has a logic that we need to be aware of. What we have to do most immediately, of course, is find the evidence that will establish the exact role of the fake brothers and then who, if anyone, is behind them. We need to fill in the picture stage by stage."

"We could start by shaking the tree to see what falls out, perhaps?"

"Indeed. So, can I rely on you to do the initial shaking, and to prove the linkage between the Kerryman and the fake Stokowski brothers in the first instance?"

"Of course. I'll need the usual stuff - photos, known habitats, etc. And I'll need some detailed information on the Stokowskis' likely movements over the next two or three days, a phone-tapping team on call, a van with blacked out rear windows and the loan of three of your finest - of the hefty variety, preferably."

"Hm, that's quite a shopping list. Very well. Just this once, your wish is my command. I should really make you pay out of your fat fee for such wilful use of our assets, but on this singular occasion I accept that needs must. A suitable van will appear as if by magic outside your office tomorrow, on the assumption that it will be returned to us before the end of the week. Just let me know when you need the hefty chappies and what you require them to do. You'll find all of the information we have on the so-called brothers in the file inside this envelope. Let's call them by their real Russian names henceforth to avoid any confusion, by the way. Does that sound sensible?"

Gus nodded. Mr. One said,

"Good. Just one more thing. Files like this are not supposed to walk out of the office as you know, so I'm relying on you to keep it safe and secure. It may only be a copy, but our relationship would be compromised should it go awol and cause me unnecessary embarrassment."

"I shall guard it with my life."

"Excellent. Now the business side of things has been dealt with, I do believe I see our lunch arriving."

Back at the agency, Gus spent an hour sifting through the file on the fake brothers. At the end of the process he had a firm plan of action. As soon as Alice got back from a meeting at a client's house, he called her into his office.

"Alice, dearest, would George greatly mind if I borrowed you for one night to play the role of my wife? You would get a very nice meal in an excellent restaurant and all you have to do is enable us to blend in as an ordinary couple celebrating their anniversary, while helping me do a bit of crucial observational work. If George suspects my motives might be in any way less than honourable, he's welcome to have a table to himself on the same night, so that he can keep an eye on us. I'll stand him a slap-up meal."

"I very much doubt that George would worry, Gus, dear, he has an extremely high regard for you and a very sharp right hook should his opinion ever turn out to be naive. Would a black dress and matching patent leather handbag be suitable attire do you think?"

"For you or me?"

"How very witty. Who exactly are we supposed to be observing and when?"

"A gentleman who isn't who he claims to be, plus his henchmen. I've booked a table for seven-thirty tomorrow evening."

"Might I enquire if the job is dangerous? George is bound to ask and I need to have suitable words of reassurance."

"Well, the answer is yes and no. These people are lethal, so we need to avoid arousing their suspicions which, given our joint experience in such things, shouldn't be too difficult. The good news is that there will be very large gentlemen on hand should anything go awry. So overall, I would say that the risk to either of us is low."

"I shall put George's mind at rest then."

"Yes, tell it to put its feet up and smoke a fat cigar between his ears."

By the time Gus and Alice entered the restaurant on the following evening, everything was in place. A black van with a souped-up engine sat waiting a little further down the road. Inside were a very large driver and two even beefier heavies, watching the outside world through small observational spyglasses in the side of the vehicle. Gus and Alice had hardly sat down when Vladimir Polmonovski swept in with his wife and three grim

74

looking minders. He looked remarkably like a Transylvanian count, all in black, with thick, brushed back hair and a hostile frown that added another ten years to his forty-year-old face. His wife, in a sweeping white silk dress, had been beautiful, but her face now had the slight puffiness that came with the over-consumption of alcohol. Two of the minders sat at the table next to that of the Polmonovskis, while the third sat near the entrance on his own, watching carefully all who came in. At their table ten feet away, Gus and Alice had a good sideways line of sight of proceedings within the little entourage. Gus told Alice to keep an eye on the minder near the entrance and to let him know when his eyes were on them, so that he wasn't spotted when he was monitoring Polmonovski. He would watch everyone else, without, as far as possible, appearing to watch anybody other than her.

The background file had said that Mr. P, as Gus referred to him, was in the habit of coming for dinner at this very exclusive restaurant every third Thursday of almost every calendar month. Quite why he was such a creature of habit in this matter was a puzzle. Generally, his visits lasted no more than a couple of hours. He always remained as sober as the proverbial judge, but his wife was noted to partake liberally of wine or champagne, or sometimes both. The timing of their departure seemed to be tied to her continuing ability to stand upright. Mrs. P would be the one doing most of the talking, with her stone-faced husband nodding occasionally, but rarely saying very much. He seemed to be more interested in the food than anything else and he usually progressed through a series of generously portioned exotic dishes, washed down by a single glass of wine and some table water. Once the meal was completed, he would smoke his way through one and sometimes two large Cuban cigars, his eyes suggesting that his mind was in some far and distant land while the increasingly inebriated Mrs. P babbled on. Very occasionally, a third party would join them for all or part of the meal. He was presumed to be an intermediary between Polmonovski and some of the various criminal elements he dealt with. His exceptional talent for losing the tails sent after him meant that little was known about him or his movements. Mr. P had obviously chosen him well. Polmonovski also further secured his lines of communication through a series of telephone code words. Anyone ringing about a criminal operation would say no more than the relevant code and then hang up, leaving the phone tappers of Mr. One or the police with little to go on. If the matter required an urgent response, Polmonovski or one of his men would then go to a randomly chosen public telephone box and call a number - which always turned out to be another public telephone box - to discuss the matter in secrecy, given that there wasn't enough time for surveillance teams to get a tap in place on the public lines. This meant that there was no immediately obvious way for Gus to prove that Polmonovski and the Kerryman were in cahoots, given the care the latter took in avoiding the public gaze and the code-based system of untraceable phone calls used by the fake brother. He had therefore devised a simple but ingenious plan to short-circuit all of the protections that Mr. P had put in place and it was about to be put into action.

Half an hour after the Polmonovskis had arrived, one of the well-dressed heavies out of the back of the van entered the restaurant. Standing just to the side of the doorway leading into the dining room, he beckoned to one of the waiters to come over to him. He was out of the line of sight of the minders. He gave the man an envelope, asked him to deliver it to Mr. P and then hurried out.

Polmonovski looked at the envelope as if it was foul smelling excrement when the waiter presented it to him. He immediately dispatched one of his minders to see if he could detain the messenger and question him concerning the surprise delivery. His thick black eyebrows seemed to meet in the middle as he slit open the envelope and removed the single page of notepaper inside. The message was short and sweet. It said, "An urgent issue has come up. No time to wait until later/ring and use the code, etc. The Kerryman needs to speak now. He will be on the PT number below in ten minutes."

The number was a public telephone half a mile away, which was manned by one of the heavies from the van. It was also being tapped by Mr. One's people.

After a couple of minutes the minder returned empty handed, telling his boss that there was no sign of the man the waiter had described to him.

In composing the note, Gus had presumed that as Sergei's ex-lover, Claire Riley, had very specifically referred to 'the

Kerryman', that most probably was how the two fake brothers referred to him also. Watching carefully through the corner of his eye, Gus observed that his assumption appeared to have been correct. The deep frown on Mr. P's face seemed to indicate that he was taking the message seriously and ruminating on what the 'urgent issue' might be. He looked at his watch, thought for a moment, then gave the note to the minder who previously he had sent out in pursuit of the messenger. He whispered some instructions into his ear and the man then hurried out of the restaurant. As he headed off down the road, the black van followed discreetly at a distance. He went into the first public telephone box that he found and dialled the number he'd been given. The person at the other end picked up and said simply, "Yes?" He spoke with a carefully honed imitation of a Kerry accent. The minder said,

"If the Kerryman wants to speak, where's the code?"

Mr. One's heavy had already been informed that Mr. P had sent one of his flunkeys and would not be calling himself, so he was ready prepared for an answer. He said,

"I need to speak to the organ grinder, not the monkey. Now go back to Vladimir and tell him I need an urgent little chat with him and him alone. I will wait for ten more minutes and then I'll be gone. I'll leave him to clear up the mess himself if he doesn't come."

The minder cursed and said,

"No code, no conversation. If you were the Kerryman you'd know that. Your voice doesn't sound right either. If I find you, whoever you are, you're dead."

He threw down the phone and hurried off back to the restaurant to warn his master that something odd was going on. He'd gone no more than twenty yards when he was surprised from behind. A bag was pulled over his head and his wrists were handcuffed. He was relieved of his gun and bundled into the back of the black van, which then drove off at speed.

The heavy who had impersonated the Kerryman smiled as he waited for the van to pick him up. The minder may have rumbled him, but not before he had betrayed crucial information. He had confirmed that there was a direct code-based connection between Polmonovski and the Kerryman, a fact that the phone tappers who had been listening in to the conversation now had on record.

Inside the restaurant, Gus and Alice observed with interest Mr. P's increasing discomfort as the minutes ticked away with no sign of his minder's return. After a quarter of an hour he sent another minder out to see if he could find his missing colleague. He returned ten minutes later, shaking his head. Polmonovski's face now betrayed real alarm. He called for the bill and after paying, left in a hurry, with his inebriated wife complaining bitterly about having to abandon her sweet half way through. Gus and Alice finished their meal shortly afterwards. When they went out to their waiting taxi, they were somewhat surprised to find Mr. One sitting in the back seat with a beaming smile on his face. He said simply,

"Hole in one, Gus, old chap! Well played."

CHAPTER NINE

When Malone eventually awoke, he felt a certain sense of déjà vu. His view of the world was restricted by the fact there was a bag over his head. His movement was constrained by the ropes that tied his wrists and ankles to a chair. The boatman's rope round his chest, a tightly lashed binding that made his chances of escape even more remote, was very definitely the signature of the same unseen assailant who had flattened him when he returned the gun from the first murder. He wondered whether he'd been taken back to the same dark, mould infested terraced house that was the scene of his imprisonment then. The more he came to, however, the less likely that seemed. There was an aroma in the room and it most definitely wasn't the musty dampness of that previous house. It was strong enough to penetrate the bag and after a few seconds he recognised it as the potpourri that a past lover had installed in his apartment in her attempt to introduce a feminine touch. It was in a vase in his own dining room, so that was where he was. While he couldn't see any detail through the bag, he could at least tell that it was now daytime. He had no idea how long he'd been unconscious. His cuckoo clock let him know by obligingly singing out for nine o'clock. Its chirpy cheerfulness seemed entirely inappropriate and such was his mood of anger and frustration that he might well have thrown it across the room had his hands been free.

He appeared to be alone. There was no sound other than the ticking of the clock and his curses as he railed helplessly against the ropes that bound him to the spot. He wondered if he could gradually wriggle and wiggle the chair into the kitchen and then angle it so that he was able to pull open the knife drawer. He might be able to cut himself free and escape before anyone came back to do whatever it was that his captors intended. He started to shuffle and twist his way across the dining room floor.

His efforts came to an abrupt end after he had moved the chair no more than three feet. He heard the sound of the front door being opened and closed, followed by a single set of footsteps that entered the room and then stopped. He felt cold, helpless panic. Whoever it was said nothing. Malone heard the characteristic twang of the springs in the armchair that lived in the corner of the room, next to the drinks cabinet. The invisible guest still said nothing after sitting down, preferring to let him sweat. Control of his life had been ripped out of his hands during recent days and it now felt as if things were reaching their logical conclusion, the endpoint. Presumably, the job that the female assassin had failed to do in the hotel was now going to be completed by somebody rather more lethal, somebody who liked to inflict psychological suffering before firing the bullet that would shatter his skull all over the floor. After three minutes he could stand it no longer. He said,

"Who are you? Have you been sent to kill me?"

"Me? No, I'm merely the one who comes before, the man who smooths the ground on which the feet of one far greater will tread."

The accent was Irish, but the speaker was not the Kerryman. His voice was softer and his tone was vaguely flippant.

"What? So you're simply the guard - the man who makes sure I don't escape before my executioner arrives?"

"Am I? Now I always wondered what my role in life was. This executioner feller you refer to, can you tell me who he is or what he looks like? It would be handy if I could recognise him when he arrived. It wouldn't do if I thought he was the milkman or a meter reader, or even the parish priest now, would it? He might shoot me as well as you in revenge for the insult of my not guessing his profession and that would be entirely against me hopes and expectations."

"What kind of a joker are you? I just need to know what's going on. If I know at least I'll be ready for what happens."

"Well you look pretty ready to me, Mr. Malone, I must say.

Unless you'd prefer a different kind of a hat perhaps, something a little more dignified - what would you like, a bowler, a flat cap or a bearskin of the Irish Guards?"

"Do you enjoy making fun of the doomed?"

"The doomed indeed. Why sure, we're all doomed, Mr. Malone. That's what my boss always tells me. Every gravestone you trip over on your way home after one too many is testimony to that sad fact. If I'm making fun of the doomed then I must be having a joke at me own expense as well."

"For God's sake, stop going round and round in circles and just tell me what's happening. Why am I here and what happens next?"

"Well, the first question is an easy one with two possible answers. You're here because you're not there, that's the first thing that can be said. The second is that you're here because you came here and you'll know the reason for that much better than me by virtue of the fact that it's you inside your head and not me. So rather than asking me you'd be better asking yourself. As for your second question, now that's the difficult bit, for none of us can do more than guess at our own futures. I could say I'm just going to the shop round the corner and I'll be back in a minute. But then a passing bus could slide on a patch of ice or oil, mount the pavement and flatten me like a piece of cardboard. Or I could say that tomorrow I'll be in Dublin, but a storm wave that hit the ferry while I was on deck could bowl me over the side and down into the deepest depths of Davy Jones' Locker. So I could tell you what I thought was going to happen next in your case, only to discover that fate had something entirely different up its sleeve. I think it would be best for all concerned if we just skipped over that side of things for the moment and waited to see what the Almighty has in store for a man in your position."

Malone cursed in frustration inside his hood. No sooner had he done so than he heard the outer door to the apartment open and shut once again and a second set of footsteps made its way through the flat and into the dining room. He heard another Irish voice, this time one with which he was already all too familiar.

"I hope you've not been driving poor Mr. Malone insane with your excuse for a sense of humour."

"We've been having a philosophical discussion about this and that, with him arguing that this is more important while I'm much more inclined to come down on the side of that."

The Voice said,

"I thought as much, the man must now be as mad as a hatter. Go and deal with our other problem of the moment in Soho, and leave your comical face behind. That matter requires a very serious solution. I want a little chat with Mr. Malone on my own."

As the underling departed, Malone heard the twang of the armchair springs again when the Voice sat down. He felt a mixture of emotions - on the one hand relief that at least a familiar individual was in charge, but on the other, a deep, flesh-freezing fear that this was to be his final conversation on earth. The Voice said,

"Well, Mr. Malone, whenever we meet you seem to have a bag over your head. It's hardly the most dignified form of headgear, but then it does have the virtue of preventing you from seeing my face. I have to warn you that I'm a bit like the old phrase, 'see Naples and die'. Those who see me and register my face tend to have only a short path to travel before meeting their maker."

Malone drew the logical conclusion. He said,

"Does the fact I'm not seeing your face mean I'm being allowed to live?"

"Now that's what I like about you, Mr. Malone, your ability to see the wood for the trees. You might well conclude that you've at the very least a fighting chance of getting out of your current predicament alive. Which, I have to say, is a complete turnaround from the situation yesterday. You see, the wind has blown seven different ways at once and scattered the forces that wanted you dead. Not only that, but it is now blowing firmly in your direction, if you will but let it. Are you not intrigued to hear such news?"

"What's the catch? I wouldn't be trussed like a chicken unless there was a price to pay for my release."

"Ah now, I must apologise for the whack over the head and all the rest that my man did to your unfortunate self. You see, there was considerable uncertainty for a while about what exactly was going on, you having knocked for six the minder in the hotel and then making a bolt for it. So we had to presume the worst and incapacitate you while we did a little bit of the old investigation. Now we know the full truth of the matter, things for you are much improved. We know now that a certain Miss Riley misrepresented herself as being sent by me and then tried to kill you. And we assume that you believed her and fled for your life, knocking seven bells out of my man in the process. I'm happy to tell you that she was and is nothing to do with me at all."

"You say 'is'. Does that mean she's still alive?"

"Indeed it does. We know that she was not seriously wounded and that she has been interviewed by the gentlemen in blue. We also now know who really sent her."

"Who was it?"

"Well, the name needn't concern you, but, if you agree to what I am about to propose, I will leave you a photograph of the man who wants you dead and those who he will next ask to kill you."

"When you leave me photographs you always want me to kill the people in them."

"Well, let's just say I put the possibility of so doing into your mind, but the decision as to whether you follow through is always yours alone, Mr. Malone. As I keep repeating, you always have the opportunity to refuse, although that inevitably means that you become the fatality instead of the person you would have returned to their maker, had you chosen to accept the job offered you. Now, before you launch into yet another of your 'I'm not a killer' routines, let me just point out that, on this occasion, you are being given the opportunity of killing those who otherwise would kill you. You could almost see the whole affair as one of legitimate self-defence, so your famous conscience could take a rest for once and let your trigger finger loose. What do you say to that now?"

"Why does this individual want me dead?"

"It's a hazard of your new trade, Mr. Malone, your new life as an assassin. There are always people who want assassins dead, for this reason or that. So don't let such things trouble you. Just take the job and make the world a safer place, for you and everyone else he would otherwise have killed should his life have continued along its current path."

"And what then? Presumably my doing this job will benefit you or my creditors in some way as well, otherwise you wouldn't be so keen to offer it to me. If I do it will I finally be free, or is it merely the precursor to the next job and the one after that and so on, and so on, forever, into eternity?"

"Well, there's only one creditor that wants your continuing

services, Mr. Malone, but he is very insistent that you are now his for life. I spoke to him first thing this morning and he's very impressed with the way that you've handled yourself, despite being only a beginner. You disposed of two experienced killers in the church and survived the attempt to murder you in the hotel, putting your would-be assassin in hospital. You made light of your first job in Kensington Gardens as well. Had the police likeness of your face been in any way precise your usefulness would have come to an end, but the good news is that it is more like the newspaper seller at Kings Cross than you, so you will live to fight another day. There is yet more good news, I'm delighted to tell you. Your creditor is so pleased with your performance so far that in future he intends to pay you for your services. The payments start with this next job. You'll find a sizeable number of five-pound notes in the sealed envelope I've put on the coffee table. With wages like that you'll be able to pay your rent and keep hold of this impressive apartment. You'll be able to afford again the elegant young ladies you have such a taste for, something that has been a little out of your grasp since you ran up your disastrous gambling debt. Think about it, Mr. Malone, your new profession is your ticket to all of these things. You have, as always, the right to turn this offer down, but then your prospects return to the imminently terminal, I'm afraid."

"Why can't he just release me once this job is over? I'm not a professional assassin - if I were, I wouldn't have been caught out by your man with the mallet. I've done everything that's been asked of me. Every time I kill someone new, I feel as if I'm slipping further down into some great darkness. I have nightmares in which my hands are literally dripping with blood. Even though I've virtually no religious belief left, I have a recurring dream in which I'm being cast down into hell for the mortal sin of murder. I spend my every waking hour in a deep, death-black depression and a dread of what I might be asked to do next. It's not a life. I feel a lot of the time that I might just as well be dead, that I ought to refuse the next job and take the consequences, instead of just becoming a serial ender of the lives of people I've never met before."

"Ah now, it's the old Catholic guilt that's eating at your soul, Mr. Malone, it's your upbringing coming back to bite you. You don't know it, but your subconscious mind is hankering after the lure of the confessional, it's desperate for the chance to unburden itself of all your sins and enable you to enter heaven as a forgiven man. Now that might be a real possibility, or the whole idea may just be part of a mad religious fantasy that is more fiction than fact. Who knows? I've never been able to come to a definite conclusion on such matters myself. That's one of the reasons I never myself make the decision to kill anyone – I always make it the choice of others. You see, if there is a God, he may then view me with a certain leniency for having always left open the door for people to save their immortal souls, rather than throwing them away by firing a gun and killing a man. You'll need to make a choice, Mr. Malone. Do you believe in all that religious stuff? If you do, your best course of action is to stop killing now, make your peace with your maker and then accept gracefully the bullet that will return you to him. Or do you instead conclude that religion is nothing more than wishful thinking and that it makes more sense to live for the now? In which case you'll take every opportunity to keep on living that's given you. I'm offering you both paths. You must choose the one you want to take and then be man enough to live with it."

"You're mad, completely mad," Malone said.

"The world is mad, Mr. Malone, I'm merely a man who offers people choices about how best to navigate their way through some of the more perilous bits of the insanity. Now, knowing you as I do, I'm willing to predict that, despite all your usual protestations, you're going to take this new job and worry about the consequences later. So, I'm leaving the photograph of the gentleman in question on your coffee table here. You'll find also photos of the gunmen that are always at his side and who he'll next send after you. There is also a box, in which you'll find a service issue sub-machine gun. I know from my investigations that you had training in its use when you were in the army. You will need to assassinate all three individuals at one go and this is the best weapon for the purpose. I happen to know the rough time this afternoon at which they will be travelling down a nicely quiet country road with some very thick hedges in which you can hide. Their driver will sound his horn twice to let you know when they're about to round the bend where you'll be hiding. I've left a full set of instructions on the coffee table as to what you're to do once they arrive, together with the numberplate and model of the car in which they'll be travelling. You need to be in place an hour before they appear on the road in case there are any surprise alterations to the timings. A car will be delivered here at around midday. You will use this to get to the location where you will ambush our friends. You will bring it back here afterwards and one of my employees will pick it up. That is everything you need to know. Someone will drop in to cut you free shortly after I leave. Do not take off your hood until you have heard them vacate the premises. My advice to you is do the job and do it well – earn the money and regain everything you have been in danger of losing. Unless, of course, you would prefer to lose that most precious and irreplaceable of things, life itself. The choice is yours. Goodbye, Mr. Malone, until we meet again, as they say."

Sitting in the back of his chauffeur driven Bentley as it headed back to his Belgravia townhouse, the Voice chewed over in his mind the events of the last few hours. He took great care with the security of all his communications in order to avoid any of his clients knowing precisely who he was or where he lived. If Vladimir Polmonovski needed to contact him urgently, he knew that the only way he could do this was to send a car to a quiet street in Limehouse and for the driver to sound his horn ten times in quick succession, followed by four long blasts. Somebody unseen, in an unknown house somewhere in the street, would hear the simple code, providing they were in. They would then ring the Voice to let him know that Polmonovski needed a chat. The Voice would then venture out and ring him from a random public telephone box to avoid the call being traced to his home address. Polmonovski had his own code-related procedures in place as well, which added a further short delay before the two men could actually speak directly. All of those elaborate precautionary and protective measures had been rapidly implemented at seven this very morning. When the two men actually spoke, half an hour after the sounding of the car horn, Polmonovski was in an angry and highly focussed frame of mind. His trust of his fake brother had deteriorated to such an extent in recent months that he had infiltrated a paid informer into his house staff. The informer had just spilled the beans about Sergei, aka Jerzy, having despatched

Claire Riley to kill Malone. He'd also told him about the operation having gone badly wrong, with Riley, who was well known to be closely connected to Sergei, ending up in hospital, with the police intending to question her. Vladimir had already been highly concerned about Sergei's growing drugs habit and his worrying tendency to become indiscreet while under the influence. He'd been increasingly worried also about how Sergei was starting to engage in badly thought-out high-risk operations of various kinds, without any consultation with him. Individually and collectively, these various cack-handed killings, robberies etc. threatened to undo all of the careful work that Vladimir had put in place to distance the two of them from their criminal activities and minimise the chances of them ever being caught by the police. This latest disaster, with Claire Riley now in the hands of Scotland Yard, was a bridge too far. If she talked then she knew just enough about Sergei for the police to arrest him. If he was questioned at a time when he was high, then the risk of him letting slip details of activities in which he was involved with Vladimir would be unacceptably great. For all these reasons and more, Vladimir had now concluded that Sergei and his lieutenants had to be eliminated urgently. His fake brother had long outlived his usefulness and was now threatening Vladimir's life and liberty. Just a few details, carelessly revealed in a drug-influenced police interview, could be enough to send Vladimir and his men to the gallows. The Voice was sure that there were other, possibly even more serious worries underlying his client's desire to execute his partner in crime as well. He suspected that the people who had been paying the two fake brothers to organise the Kensington Gardens murder and the church murders were so powerful and deadly that Vladimir was terrified they would have him killed as well, if it became known that his partner had become dangerously out of control. Whatever the full truth of the matter, Sergei was now very clearly the proverbial dead man walking. As Malone had proved himself a surprisingly effective assassin so far, Vladimir wanted the Voice to give him the job of neutralising Sergei. He wanted the Voice to provide also his highly efficient body-disposal services, so that Sergei and co would quietly disappear without trace. With no bodies to find and with the murders carried out by someone who was several stages removed from Vladimir's personal chain of command, the whole operation should be as low risk as it could possibly be made. Malone also was to be given no details of who precisely had ordered the killings or why. The Voice had extracted a highly lucrative fee for his part in putting the plan into action and had succeeded in persuading Vladimir that it would be far better if Malone also was now actually paid for his services in order to give him an additional incentive for continuing to play ball. He'd stressed the importance of using carrots as well as sticks and Polmonovski, ever the practical man, had taken his point. From being a serious debtor with a lot of repaying in kind to do, Malone had turned into a highly effective hitman, with no criminal record to put him on any police list of possible suspects. He was, the Voice knew, a weak and malleable man whom he could be reasonably confident of twisting around his little finger with an appropriate mix of threats and subtle psychological manipulation. He was certain that, given a choice between damnation in the next life and his death in the present, Malone would always go for the option that put off the day of reckoning for as long as possible.

At midday precisely a set of car keys was put through Malone's letterbox and the doorbell rang. When he opened the front door there was no-one there, but a smart, two-tone Ford Zephyr sat ready and waiting in the street. There was a map on the front passenger seat which, when he opened it, showed the route to the ambush site marked in red. He stared at it as if in a trance for a good two minutes. He felt a dull, deep, dread that seeped out from his mind into his very bones. He couldn't get to grips with the fact that he was about to embark on his third assassination since coming under the dark spell of the Voice. At the same time, the fact that there had been an attempt on his own life and the knowledge that the people he was being sent to kill were likely to kill him if he didn't get to them first were creating a sense of panic and urgency within his confused brain that he was unable to resist. Since the Voice's visit in the morning, he'd been trying to find a way of psychologically adapting to his predicament, his loathing of the fact that he had become a killer and was too cowardly to end the cycle of murders by laying down his own life instead. In this one unique instance he could at least try and persuade himself that the situation was no different to when he'd been in the army. He'd been trained to kill before being himself killed, that was his duty as a soldier. Wasn't that a comparable imperative to the one that faced him now, wasn't he only acting in the same way he would have been expected to act in the army? Perhaps if he could imagine himself back in uniform, going out on an operation to confront and take out the enemy, perhaps if he could do that the whole thing would become easier to stomach. The fact that he'd never actually killed anyone during his uneventful national service was a slight problem, but one that his imagination should be able to overcome.

Looking at his watch he realised that he'd got just over ninety minutes to rush to the ambush site and get in position. The panic kicked in and started to drive him, while the device of imagining himself back in a military role gave him the excuse he needed to partially override the darkness and depression that swept over him every time he prepared for a murder. He had everything ready in the house - the box with the gun and ammunition in it, the Voice's meticulous typewritten instructions and all of the photographs that would help him identify the individuals he was tasked with eliminating. After depositing them on the passenger seat he jumped into the vehicle and simultaneously put the car and his mind into gear. There was no time to think about anything more than the operation he was embarking on. If he failed to make the ambush site on time his opportunity to save his own life by taking those of his intending killers would be gone. He doubted the Voice would give him a second chance. He had to get everything right first time.

The lonely country road he found himself on as the minutes counted down to ambush time was the same road that Claire Riley had travelled up on her unsuccessful mission to murder him. As per the Voice's instructions, he slowed down as he came to a sharp bend with two large oak trees on either side, their branches touching over the middle of the road to make an impressive ancient archway. Twenty yards past the bend he found the open gateway into a field where he was supposed to park the car. He drove in and hid it behind the large kerbside hedge. Hurrying over to the other side of the road, he found the tangle of tree branches that he was instructed to drag across the tarmac as soon as he heard the two parps on the horn that would warn him that the targets' car was forty seconds away. He inserted the magazine into the machine gun and fired three quick test blasts to make sure everything was working as it should. He then hunted for the small hole in the hedge that had been expertly cut for him to shoot from without being seen. Having found it, he slid the gun into it, ready for use, and then went back to where the branches lay, ready to slide them across the road.

After twenty minutes of increasingly nervous waiting, during which nobody at all came past on the deadly quiet road, Malone was shaken into action by the sound of the horn. He raced out into the single-track road with the branches and laid them out as instructed. He then went to his hiding place and held his gun in position, his hands shaking so much he almost fired it by accident. It was a bitterly cold day, but he was sweating profusely. His thoughts seemed to be frozen in his head, as if he had been taken over by a machine programmed to kill without question. The only emotion that registered within his brain was an anxiety to get the whole thing over and be on his way, to pretend that nothing had happened. The large black Daimler in the Voice's photograph rounded the bend and braked hard to avoid colliding with the branches. The driver got out to move them, as the Voice's instructions had said he would. Malone could see his three targets clearly in the back of the vehicle. They were all in his sights. Almost without any prior thought his finger pressed the trigger and the gun started rat-tat-tatting in ear splitting fashion. The earplugs he was wearing reduced the noise significantly and it was almost as if he were watching the action as a spectator in a cinema. He hit all three with his first shots, but one of the minders was still able to make a grab for the gun he kept in a holster inside his jacket. His hand didn't actually make contact with the weapon, because he was soon sliding down the seat dead as Malone's bullets continued to shred the car's window glass and rip through the rear passenger door. It seemed like he kept firing for the eternity that his victims had just been plunged into, but finally he emptied the magazine and an unsettling silence followed. The driver, who had run a good twenty yards away from the car to be sure of not getting hit in any crossfire, was watching anxiously, clearly afraid of a double cross in which he would be the next victim. The Voice's instructions said he was to be untouched and Malone saw no reason not to honour them. He had a spare magazine and loaded it just in case the driver had any ideas of trying to shoot him. The mistrust was mutual. After a minute or so, the driver cautiously walked back to the car with his arms raised. Malone stayed silent and hidden, watching. The driver moved the branches out of the way, got in the car, and then, with shaking hands and a face as white as the death that filled the back of the vehicle, slowly drove off. His instructions told him to take the car to a disused quarry ten miles away, where it would be set on fire and then buried under enough earth and rocks to flatten it and 'disappear' the remains inside.

Once the bullet riddled Daimler had vanished into the distance, Malone put the gun back in the box and walked unsteadily back to the Ford Zephyr behind the hedge on the other side of the road. He threw the box into the boot as instructed and lowered himself gingerly into the driver's seat, almost unable to move due to a sharp pain in his back where nerves had become temporarily trapped as a result of the state of shock that he was in. He was aware that he should feel some sense of relief at having eliminated a pressing threat to his own life, but only a general numbness registered in his brain. His hands were cold and clammy and gripped the steering wheel as rigidly as if rigor mortis had set in. The guilt that he had felt after every killing suddenly swept in as if from nowhere, together with the deep blackness of a depression that made him feel as if he were as dead as the people he had just murdered. Despite a dissolute life, in which he'd felt entitled to all kinds of things that he hadn't earned, including, from time to time, sexual favours from other people's wives, he'd come to realise that he did have one fundamental value that he was loathe to compromise and that was the sanctity of human life. His belief in God had long been at best tenuous, but nevertheless he worried that the scale of the bloodshed he'd now inflicted through his various assassinations - the taking of six lives - was something that might weigh so heavily against him, should that God indeed exist, that he might as well give up any idea of being forgiven when he died. But with or without a judgmental creator awaiting him after his own death, Malone found it difficult to see how he could ever forgive himself for the killings and that in itself was a recipe for a life of sleepless nights and self-loathing. These uncomfortable and depressing thoughts gnawed at the back of his mind as he sat unmoving in the vehicle that was supposed to be his means of escape and he knew that if he didn't act quickly, he'd freeze, have some kind of a breakdown, he didn't know what. He needed some means of urgently pushing all of these fears and worries into his subconscious mind and kicking his brain back into gear. He concentrated on the threat his most recent victims had presented to him and, as he'd preferred to see it, his right of self-defence. As when he had set off from his apartment, he told himself that this was just like a military operation in which he'd had the duty to kill before he was killed, to preserve himself as a useful asset. He wasn't sure precisely what 'use' he was, given the many completely useless things he had done with his life, but wisely he avoided dwelling on that. He tried to focus also on the money that was waiting for him on the coffee table back in the apartment, how it might enable him to start putting some sort of a normal life back together. But that part of the equation didn't seem to quite fit, it was difficult even to imagine what a 'normal' life might look like now. However, he didn't let that throw him back into freeze mode, he'd managed to get just enough thoughts of a more positive nature into his mind to hold the darkness at bay for the moment. He turned the key in the ignition and listened to the engine ticking over for a minute or two. When he felt able to just about hold himself together, he turned the vehicle slowly round, and drove through the gateway and onto the road. Then, with his hands still shaking and his eyes like those of a ghost, he drove back the way he had come, trying to leave the secret of what he had just done behind him.

In and around the ancient oak trees, where some winter robins had been chattering earlier, there was a deep silence, broken only by the occasional faint barking of a guard dog on a distant farm. In the roadway, a night black crow stood in the middle of the shattered glass from the car windows. It pecked morosely at the sparkling shards, as if searching amongst them for the lost souls of the slaughtered. A desolate, freezing wind came from nowhere and the bird shuddered, before sailing up and fleeing, far away, into the bleak mid-afternoon sky.

CHAPTER TEN

Alice said,

"Mr. One or Sir Arnold Bentley?"

"What?" Gus enquired vacantly, as he perused the inside pages of the Times in his office.

"If I was to weigh their bags of gold, whose would be the heaviest?"

Gus looked up at his assistant, who was standing in the doorway with a quizzical look on her face. He said,

"That is a very Alice type of question, deliberately forcing me to fill in the gaps in its meaning. I presume you're referring to the size of the fees that the two gentlemen are paying us?"

"Spot on Sherlock."

"Well, since you ask, if we were to take the present cases that we're handling for each, then Sir Arnold will be paying us rather more money than Mr. One, should we deliver what he wants. But if you look at things over the longer term, then the quantity of work that Mr. One sends our way means that we will earn far more from one year of his kind favours than we will ever do from the one-off fee payment of Sir Arnold."

"But Sir Arnold's gold is nonetheless an extremely useful contribution to our current income?"

"Indeed."

"Then perhaps we should make an extra special effort to make Sir Arnold feel that he's had value for money, wouldn't you agree?"

"I might if I knew what you had in mind."

"Oh, nothing too dramatic. The freelance you told me to hire to do the initial legwork has found where he thinks the son is living under an assumed name - Harris Willis. Perhaps I could nip down there on my way home this evening and establish matters beyond all doubt - using appropriate subtlety, of course, so as not to create any unwanted problems. Such a speedy wrapping up of Sir Arnold's case may even cause him to recommend us to others in his circle."

"What you mean is you're itching to get out in the field and do a bit of hands-on investigation, instead of spending most of your time in the office. Alright, as long as I don't get an earwigging from George for keeping his delightful spouse working all hours."

"Don't you fret, Gus, dearest, I have George well and truly under my thumb on such matters."

"As you do me apparently," Gus said, with a twinkle in his eye.

When Alice arrived at the Soho apartment block where Bentley's son was believed to live, she was able to slip past the uninterested and half-asleep concierge with ease by sailing in on the coat tails of a macabre looking middle-aged man, who resembled a funeral director going home for his tea. Her information was that Bentley junior lived in Apartment B on the top floor. The rickety lift blended in with the rest of the building, which seemed filled with the remnants of a splendid 1930s' past, now gone to seed. She shook and rattled her way upwards and then went hunting for the correct door. When she found it, she was startled to hear the sound of a woman screaming coming from inside. Instinctively she knocked on the door and shouted,

"Is everything alright in there?"

There was a sudden silence and she wondered whether she should stick around for an answer, or play it safe and go straight back downstairs to call the police. She didn't get the opportunity to decide. The door was flung open and an angelically smiling muscular man in his twenties stood staring down at her. She was concerned by the fact that the messages from the eyes and the smile were radically at odds with each other. He said,

"Are you the new girl? You're an hour late if you are and I've already got a replacement due at eight."

The question took a second or two to register while Alice

mentally confirmed to herself that the individual in the photograph supplied by Sir Arnold and the man standing in front of her now were one and the same, Charles Bentley. She had at least accomplished the purpose of her visit. By the time her mind was ready to answer his query his patience had gone, along with the angelic smile. He said,

"Well, are you or aren't you and if you're not what the hell are you doing knocking on my door?"

She said,

"Oh, sorry, I was just passing and I thought I heard a scream coming from your apartment. I must have been mistaken."

He said, curtly,

"Yes, you must, mustn't you. Goodbye."

Before he could slam the door shut the author of the scream stumbled into view behind him, a half-naked young woman with a bloodied lip and what looked like a rapidly developing black eye. She looked as if she was about to collapse and said,

"Help me, for God's sake help me."

The scowling ex-Etonian hunk looked momentarily panic-stricken. He then grabbed Alice by the arm and pulled her into his apartment. Before she could scream, he had one arm round her neck and a hand firmly over her mouth. He said,

"You would be nosey, wouldn't you? Just like a bloody woman. Let's see who you are."

Keeping the back of her head firmly welded to his chest with the oversized hand that he was holding over her mouth, he opened her shoulder bag and rummaged inside it. Unfortunately, one of the first items he pulled out was the agency's business card. He said,

"Well, well, a little private detective. How quaint. Let me guess, my father hired you to find out where I was living? No doubt he spun some yarn about wanting us to become reconciled. You're looking at the real reason over there - I'm in the prostitution business and daddy would really like to find some way of stopping me before I ruin the hallowed family name forever. Well little lady, that's not going to happen, I'm making much, much, too much lovely money. See what's happened to her? Take a good look. She got it into her head that she could switch her services to a rival pimp. I was in the process of giving her some very good reasons for thinking that's an extremely bad idea when you stuck your nose into my affairs. If you so much as even think of telling daddykins that you've found where I live, you'll end up like her times ten - and that's if I'm in a good mood, which is extremely rare. That pretty little face of yours will look like it's been run through a wringer and carved with a corkscrew. And if I'm in a really bad mood you'll end up taking a parachute jump without a parachute. Here let me show you the basics."

He yanked her over to the sash window at the far end of the lounge and opened it. He pushed her half out to the point where she thought he was going to let go of her. With her head spinning and her mind frozen with terror, she couldn't even force out a scream. The prospect of plummeting head first onto the concrete pavement far below had gripped her by the throat so fiercely that her vocal chords were unable to function. Then, just at the point where she thought he was going to let her drop, he pulled her in again and shut the window. He laughed in her face and shook her violently. She could smell so much whisky on his breath that it made her want to retch.

He said,

"That's what terror really feels like and you're going to feel a lot more unless you forget ever having come here. If you call the police she'll be out of here long before they arrive and I'll deny everything. Nobody on this floor will confirm any story about hearing her screaming because they've all got too much to hide and I know more about them than they do about me. If I even sniff that you've told anything to my beloved father then all that I've threatened you with will come to pass before you can say Jack Rabbit. I'm about to make a move that will give me control of all the prostitution businesses in this half of Soho, baby, and I don't want irrelevances like you getting in my way. If you do, you're a dead girl walking. Have I made myself clear?"

"Absolutely," Alice said, trembling.

"Good, well in that case it's time for you to go home to mummy, isn't it? And don't forget, I know where to find you."

Alice was very aware of the fact that he'd told her much more than wisdom suggested he should have done, particularly about his activities in the prostitution racket, due to his state of considerable inebriation. She was praying that he would throw her out of his flat before he realised that he'd been a little too free with his words. To

96

her relief, he duly obliged and she was literally hurled out of the apartment by the scruff of her neck, landing in a heap in the corridor, but somehow undamaged. As the door slammed shut behind her, she scrambled to her feet as quickly as she could and made good her escape.

When she told Gus what had happened the following morning, he was both deeply concerned for her welfare and outraged. He said,

"Sir Arnold seems to have been somewhat economical with the truth concerning his thug of a son. I really don't like people who lie to us and knowingly put our staff at risk. It might be safer if you spent the rest of the week at home while I eradicate this Old Etonian Nastiness's ability to even contemplate carrying out any of his threats."

"Eradicate?" Alice said. "That sounds vaguely terminal. What exactly are you planning to do about this nauseous hunk? I don't want you risking your neck on my account."

"I don't make a practice of risking my neck, given that I only have one of the things. I intend persuading others of a habitually pugnacious disposition that it is very much in their interests to do the job for me."

"How very clever of you, Gussie, dear. I suspect that means another outing for the East End hat and coat?"

"Indeed," Gus replied.

"Well, while you're busy sorting all of that out I'll hold the fort here. If I go and cower under the kitchen table for a week I'll lose my nerve to do this job, so I intend coming into the office as normal. You've got a lock on the outer door that wouldn't look out of place in Fort Knox, so I'll use it every time you're out of the office and only let pre-booked appointments into the inner sanctum."

Gus said,

"And if I instructed rather than asked you to stay at home for your own protection?"

"You'd have about as much luck as George does when he tries to instruct me, poor man. Being politely told to sling his hook really doesn't do his self-esteem any good."

Gus smiled wryly and said,

"Indeed. Poor George."

Fate and good fortune had already provided Gus with an opportunity to deal with Bentley's rogue son. He'd previously arranged to have lunch with Tasty Harry in an eatery seven doors down from his East End office to discuss another matter, so he decided to add this new problem to the agenda. He arrived at the café just before twelve and was unsurprised to find that Tasty had already ordered and was busily demolishing an over-filled plate of egg and chips. As he sat down Tasty snapped his fingers and pointed to Gus. His prearranged signal was picked up by a waitress on the other side of the room and within less than a minute a matching plate of still sizzling egg and chips was delivered to their table by a young woman with a smile as warm as the food.

"That's my cousin's gal," Tasty said as she hurried off to take another order. "She's very generous with the helpings where family and friends are concerned."

"If I eat all of this, I'll need a crane to lift me out of my chair afterwards," Gus said.

"Go on, get it down you me old china, it'll put hairs on your vest as well as your chest. So what is it you want to ask me?" Tasty said, getting straight to the point.

"Well, before I get onto that, something else has come up that you might be able to help with."

"Depends what it is, but fire away."

"I think we have a couple of things in common, one of which is a profound dislike of chaps who are violent towards women."

"Too right," Tasty replied. "There's more than one villain round here with a permanent limp that they didn't have before I found they'd been beating their gals. It's a point of principle with me, a line that shouldn't be crossed."

Gus explained what had happened to Alice and the badly beaten prostitute that she'd seen in Charles Bentley's apartment. As he did so, the scowl on Tasty's face became so pronounced that his eyebrows met in the middle. He said,

"So, you'd like me to give him a good doing over?"

"No, no, it's very kind of you to offer Tasty, but I wouldn't want you to bruise your knuckles on somebody as worthless as him. Among his drunken ramblings he let slip that he plans to muscle in on other gangs in the same line of work and take over their Soho territory. I thought you might know some people who would take violent exception to those ambitions."

Tasty's frown was replaced suddenly by wide-eyed laughter, with fragments of half-eaten chips hurtling in Gus's direction.

"I like it, I like it, you are a clever boy, Gus, me old mate! I do indeed know some villains who fit the bill. Of course, if you want this gentleman permanently removed, there is your old mucker, the Kerryman."

"I thought nobody knows who he is, or how to find him?"

"Yeah, that's right, I've no idea where you'd find him, he's the original unfindable villain, but people like me know how you contact him through a third party. I can see that he finds out if you've got a job for him."

"You didn't say that last time we spoke."

"You didn't ask. But knowing how to contact him is as far as it goes with that geezer. He has so many protective walls in place that you'll never get to find out who he is. The contact will merely pass the message down a long line of go-betweens and then tell you whether a contract has been accepted or not. If you wanted someone rubbed out, the Kerryman's the safest way of doing it because he takes such care to make sure nothing is ever traced back to him or his clients."

"So who's the contact?"

"That's one of the questions you don't ask, Gus, me old china, trade secret as they say. But I can ask him things on your behalf. Do you want me to find out if the Kerryman will arrange a permanent farewell for this happy chappie?"

"No, it's just useful to know that you can contact him if necessary."

"That knowledge comes with a health warning. It's only safe to contact him if you want a job doing. If he thinks you're trying to discover a way to find him that's a very bad idea. You might as well pick your favourite spot in the graveyard and dig the hole ready for his boys to chuck you in."

"Thanks for the warning. I'd be perfectly happy for now if you'd simply let the relevant rival gangs know that Bentley intends taking over their territory in Soho. To be more precise, I believe his ambitions currently extend to their territory in the half of Soho in which he lives."

"No sooner said than done. I'll spread the word this afternoon.

You have the address for Mr. Bentley I presume?"

Gus wrote it down on a piece of paper, saying as he did so,

"He's using an assumed name by the way, Harris Willis."

Tasty laughed raucously and said,

"Change the last 'i' for a 'y' and he's got exactly the right name for his line of business.

Gus smiled wryly and handed over the piece of paper. Tasty scrutinised it and said,

"Just what the doctor ordered. Speaking of doctors, I'll let you know which hospital this schmuck ends up in, should you wish to send him some flowers."

The following afternoon saw Charles Bentley, aka Harris Willis, heading towards his most profitable brothel to check the takings for the week. He was surprised to find two unfamiliar bouncers with biceps like whisky barrels blocking his entrance. The larger of the two turned to the anxious looking madam in the doorway and said,

"Is that him?"

She nodded, being careful to avoid meeting Bentley's gaze. The bouncer said,

"Sorry, no entry. The premises are under new management."

Bentley said,

"What do you mean? I am the management."

"You need to discuss it with the gentleman in the car over there."

Looking behind him, Bentley saw a large black Rover with a sharp-suited minder leaning against the side, smoking a cigarette. He marched over in high dudgeon to give whoever was in the car a piece of his mind. Looking in through the back window he saw his own bouncer sitting on the back seat, bound and gagged. Before he could say or do anything, his arms were yanked behind him and improvised handcuffs slipped onto his wrists. He was then bundled into the back of the vehicle, which drove off at high speed.

With his afternoon already having got off to a bad start, Bentley soon discovered that things could only get worse, very much worse. He was taken to a disused warehouse near the docks, bundled upstairs and invited to sign a document handing over the ownership of his various properties to the McFalmack brothers. He had already consumed half a bottle of whisky before leaving his apartment and was full of fire and fury. Unfortunately for him, so were his kidnappers and they, unlike him, did not have the disadvantage of having their hands cuffed behind their backs. Being as stubborn and as violent as a disgruntled mule, he still tried to fight his way out of the derelict top floor office to which they'd brought him. With well-aimed kicks to the private parts of two of his kidnappers he bought himself enough time to make a run for the fire escape at the end of the corridor outside the office. He made it to the top rickety and rusted iron stair before one of the two uninjured heavies managed to grab hold of his left arm. He whirled round and attempted to aim another kick to free himself, but lost his balance and found himself plunging and rolling down ninety bone-cracking steps, before landing heavily and awkwardly on the concrete floor below. When the heavies reached him, he was hardly conscious, with an ominously large head wound and an inability to move his legs.

After a brief conference among themselves the kidnappers went through his pockets and found a cheque with his signature on it in his wallet. Agreeing that they could use it to help forge his signature on the legal transfer documents, the gang decided to uncuff him and leave him to die. They took his wallet with them to make it difficult for him to be identified.

Once they'd driven off, his one and only piece of good luck came when a lorry driver who'd lost his way wandered along the deserted side road by the warehouse, trying to work out where he was. Spotting Bentley's prone form, the driver got out to investigate and then hurried off to phone for an ambulance.

It was just after ten o'clock the next morning when Gus received a call from Tasty. As always, his food-loving friend didn't identify himself over the phone and spoke half in riddles, but by the end of the conversation it was clear that the threat to Alice from the psychopathic Mr. Bentley was over. Gus called her into his office and said,

"I've just had some news which is extremely bad for Charles Bentley but rather good for you. He seems to have toppled down a rather long staircase and lost half of his wits and his ability to stand upright in the process. He'll need a nurse for the rest of his life apparently. Perhaps you could ring Sir Arnold and give him the address of his son's apartment and his current residence, which I'm told is St. George's Hospital. He'll need to arrange for the care of his offspring when he is eventually discharged - and to pay our bill. We've done everything he asked. I think we should add an extra £200 to our fee as compensation for the violence inflicted on you by his son. I'll put the money into your bank account as soon as we get it."

Alice smiled, but looked a little concerned as well. She said,

"Have we acted properly in sorting out the Charles Bentley problem, Gussie, dear? I know the man's a swine, but I'm a little uneasy about the extreme nature of what's happened to him."

"All his own work apparently," Gus said. "I didn't get a lot of detail, but I gather that his over-fondness for the demon drink left him a little unbalanced at the top of a fire escape."

"Hm, I suspect there might be a little more to it than that, but I know better than to take issue with Robin Hood."

"Indeed. We did get a bit of a boost during my discussions about how to get the good Mr. Bentley off your back by the way."

"Oh?"

"Mm. We now have a means of contacting the famous Kerryman. I just have to decide when and how to use it without lining myself up for a bullet in the back of the head."

CHAPTER ELEVEN

With every new sunrise Malone felt only deeper gloom. The fresh dawn of others was for him another dusk in disguise. He was back in the considerable comfort of his luxury flat, his rent was paid in advance, thanks to his new earnings, nobody had any immediate intention to kill him and in theory he could afford to resume his pursuit of expensive, attractive women ten years his junior. But this happy state of affairs was overshadowed by the deep stain of the guilt he felt for the various murders that had been committed by his own very reluctant hand and an overpowering dread of those yet to come. He was a man haunted by dreams of the next call to action. He was full of terror for the next time he would hear that softly lilting, Kerry voice, the caster of spells that would lure him into the commission of unthinkable acts against people he had never met.

A fortnight had now passed since he had sent Sergei and his henchmen to their doom, plunging head first into Hades for all he knew. He was almost beginning to wonder if he had been forgotten, or if a new, much better hitman had been found for the kind of jobs he'd been given, someone who wasn't plagued with guilt and an inconvenient loathing of killing. He began to hope that he'd become superfluous to requirements, that the Voice and his client would simply leave him alone and that, gradually, he could begin to crawl out of the deep pit into which his life had fallen and make some effort to reclaim at least a few fragments of a normal existence. But then, what he dreaded most came to pass.

The phone rang early on a Wednesday morning. His blood turned to stone as he heard an all too familiar voice at the other end. It said,

"There is a park about half a mile away from your apartment. At the far end there is an old Victorian shelter, an attractive shade of deep blue I believe. Go and sit there and wait at noon today. Don't be late."

There was a click as the receiver was replaced at the other end. So no, Malone hadn't been forgotten. Now he was a paid employee he seemed to merit few words. Gone were the rambling conversations, the discussion of the choices confronting him, of compliance or oblivion. In their place were simple instructions. He had taken the King's shilling and had spent all of his wages for the last killing. The Voice knew very well that he would continue taking the money rather than choose to die, he knew precisely how every cog within Malone's mind interacted, one with another. Malone knew all of this as well and he could only despair at his own weakness. At half past eleven he put on his coat and set off for the park.

The shelter was an ornate piece of ironwork, divided into two identical halves, with a dividing wall separating each. Unsure of which side he was supposed to sit on, he opted for that which faced forward into the park, rather than backwards towards the north gate. There was a cold, bleak, snow wind that was strong enough to deter anyone else from venturing out amongst the sleeping winter flowerbeds and the damp lawns full of unrecovered bare patches and muddy hollows. After a while he floated off into a trance in which his mind achieved some sort of temporary peace by thinking of absolutely nothing at all. Then, the bird-free silence was broken by two heavy thumps on the other side of the iron dividing wall. Malone jumped and then cautiously rose and peered round to find out who was there. He saw only a tall, muscular figure in a black coat and hat disappearing at a rate of knots towards the gate. On the seat he found yet another box. Gingerly opening it, he discovered inside a familiar set of contents - another Luger, a box of ammunition, two photographs and a set of instructions. Looking around to make sure nobody had seen his delivery, he closed the box, tucked it under his arm and walked uncertainly back to his apartment. As he did so, he pondered, in a rambling kind of way, the nature of the Voice's strange organisation. He wondered if, like him, the courier who had delivered the box was someone who had started out by paying off a debt. He clearly didn't want his own face to be seen and Malone wondered if he had ever seen the Voice's face. The man who had guarded him when he had been bagged and trussed in his own flat clearly was allowed to see his boss's face, the two of them had spoken directly in front of him. He wondered how many people were similarly favoured and what it took for them to earn such a level of trust. He'd been told that if he were to join the select group who'd seen what his manipulator looked like that would be as good as signing his own death warrant, so he was a thousand miles away from this privileged inner circle and the access they enjoyed. He wondered how many others like him had become forced operatives within the organisation, forbidden from seeing who was commanding and controlling them. Perhaps he was but one of a large network of debt-ridden, army-trained, anonymous gunmen, all unknown to each other and unaware of the identity of their controller - a regiment of nobodies commanded by an invisible man.

When he got home, he found that the two photographs were not of individuals whom he should kill together, as in his most recent job. Their journeys to the graveyard were to be separate but swift. The first hit was scheduled for the evening of the next day, while the second was to be completed during the afternoon of the day after. He scrutinised the photographs carefully. Both men were in their mid-thirties. One looked quintessentially English, somebody who'd been a junior officer during the war perhaps. The other was harder to categorise, he looked as though he might be anything from an insurance salesman to a boxer in his Sunday best. Malone wondered what they'd done to merit assassination. He tried to distance himself from them as people, to tell himself that they must be killers in their own right, and that those who lived by the sword must expect others to want to skewer them before they did any more damage. He tried to persuade himself that he might well be making the world a safer place by reducing the number of violent men in it, that he was in a way a positive force whose actions benefited others, those who were saved from being killed by people like these two. He wondered if the logic of this train of thought was in a way quite reasonable and if he ought to stop beating himself up about all of the people he was sending into oblivion. Maybe that was what they deserved. Around the edges of these thoughts, he had a nagging suspicion that they might be a little too convenient, a way of making him more comfortable with all the money he was now earning - in particular the thick wedge of five-pound notes that sat at the bottom of the box. But he didn't let that possibility trouble him too much. The idea that his work might actually be in some way justifiable made him feel a little better. It didn't get rid of the lead weight of Catholic guilt that sat permanently on his shoulders, or of the frequent nightmares, but it gave him just enough relief to make his days bearable. It gave him the degree of lift that was necessary to put his mind into military operations mode, that other coping mechanism that he'd developed since the Voice had taken over his life. Looking at his watch he decided that was the frame of mind he now needed to be in, because if he couldn't switch his brain into gear by using that previously effective device, he might not be ready in time and miss the opportunity to take out the two specified individuals as required. And if he failed to deliver the deaths of one or both of them, then his own demise would be the next item on the agenda of the Voice's client. That cold, steel-hard realisation was what continually sat at the back of his mind and drove everything else. He'd tried talking his way out of this unwanted 'angel of death' role that he'd been dragged kicking and screaming into, but his efforts had got nowhere. He had been given no opportunity of discussing the matter in this instance and from that he concluded that the talking was over. He was now in a situation of do or die in its most literal sense and that was going to keep recurring on a week-by-week, month-by-month basis for the foreseeable future. He was on a treadmill that he couldn't get off and unless he wanted to go mad or kill himself, that was a reality he needed to learn to live with.

He started reading the rest of his instructions which were, as always, to be burned on completion of the jobs. He would be supplied with a car with false number plates for both assassinations. The first killing was to be done at a country house ten miles outside London. The occasion would be a party for the great and the good at which the target would be present as a guest.

The Voice's client had someone on the inside who would prepare the ground. At eight o'clock in the evening precisely the target would be told that there was a telephone call for him. Guest phone calls were always taken in the study. The French windows would be unlocked by the insider, ready for Malone to slip in and hide behind the massive red velvet floor-to-ceiling curtains ten minutes or so before the target entered the room. He was to make it look very much like a professional killing, with one shot to the back of the head and one to the front. He was then to exit the way he had come, running back down the tree-lined side-path that ran parallel to the long front lawn and then over the estate wall, out into the road, where his car would be waiting for him to make his escape. It all seemed so clinical, so military, so neutral.

The second job was an outdoor affair. He was provided with a map location and photographs of the site. It was a woodland copse, four hundred yards away from a quiet country road. A small, fake bird box, nailed to an old oak tree, was used as a letter box for secret communications by the target. He was known to be going to the site to make a collection and Malone was to be waiting for him. Reaching the box required a short climb up the tree and during that time the target would be at a maximum level of vulnerability. It was then that Malone would shoot him.

A racing green MG sports car was delivered overnight, while Malone was fast asleep, and the keys pushed through his letter box, along with a note telling him that his 'tools' for the second job were in the boot. He opened it the next morning to discover a large black briefcase, inside which was a rifle in two sections, with sights fitted to facilitate his aiming from a concealed location, some distance away from the target.

At around five o'clock in the afternoon he set off for his first destination, leaving himself enough time to scout out the site and most particularly, his entrance and exit routes. He arrived in good time and after driving round the perimeters of the grounds a couple of times to establish the scale and peculiarities of the location, he parked by the estate wall, four hundred yards from the entrance, as instructed. From his observation point he could see expensive cars rolling up the long drive to the sprawling Victorian mansion from around six o'clock onwards. At seven-thirty he clambered over the wall and after making sure that no-one had seen him, hurried along the tree-lined side-path that ran parallel to the long, ornamental lawn. It was unguarded and the trees prevented anyone inside the house spotting him. He hid behind a large clump of exotically manicured bushes that sat near the French windows he was instructed to use as his means of entry and bided his time. At ten minutes to eight, as had been promised, he heard the windows being unlocked and they were left slightly ajar. After checking that nobody was outside to see him, Malone pulled a balaclava over his head, hurried across to the house and slipped inside. As instructed, he hid behind the floor-to-ceiling curtains and cut a small hole at eye level for viewing and shooting purposes.

In the ornate, gilded ballroom of the house a large cross-section of the upper- and middle-ranking members of the British elite were busy networking within and between small groups of superficially convivial guests. Under the surface, the main motives at work were naked ambition and powerplay. The over-supply of expensive alcohol was being consumed liberally by those who were nervous, or simply liked fine wines, while those who thought that the business of the evening would be best achieved if they kept their wits fully about them were notably abstemious. In the centre of the room a tall, elegant looking man, in a dinner jacket made by the Duke of Edinburgh's favourite tailor, was involved in deep conversation with a senior civil servant from the Admiralty. One of the house staff suddenly appeared at his side and whispered in his ear. He nodded and apologised to the Admiralty man, before following the messenger to the study. Once inside the room, he picked up the phone that was lying on the desk near to the window. He was about to speak when a bullet hurtled across the four feet that separated him from the curtain and hit him straight between the eyes. He was knocked backwards onto the floor by the force of the impact. Malone emerged from behind the curtain and tried to blank from his mind the horrific destruction that the bullet had caused. Shaking and feeling faintly sick, he nevertheless continued with his instructions. He once more tried to play the mental game of pretending this was another military operation, in which he was simply taking out a man who would have gone on to kill others if he'd been left alive. He pushed the body over and fired a second shot into the back of its head. He felt even shakier than before and turned desperately towards the French windows, his lungs screaming for fresh, cold air to calm him down. As he did so, the study door opened and a security guard peered in to check that everything was okay. Seeing the body on the floor and the killer in the process of fleeing, he immediately went for the gun inside his jacket and instructed the would-be escapee to freeze and raise his hands. Malone had wondered and worried about just this kind of possibility while he'd been waiting in the car earlier. He'd decided that he didn't want an endless list of bodies on his conscience and that, wherever possible, he'd try and neutralise pursuers rather than killing them. The fact he was wearing a balaclava meant they couldn't see his face, so there was no practical need to send them to kingdom come. So while pure terror and his instinct for self-preservation drove him to react within a split second, the nature of his action was deliberately non-lethal. He shot the man in the thigh before he was able to reach his gun, causing him to fall to the floor, immobilised by the pain. He then ran out of the house and across the lawn as if the devil were on his heels and scrambled over the wall. He was racing away from the scene in the MG within five minutes of the shootings, his heart hammering away inside his chest, his clammy hands gripping the wheel like vices.

When he got back safely to his apartment he collapsed on the sofa, numb, depressed and totally exhausted. The gathering at the house had been so obviously high profile that he assumed the shootings would automatically make the headlines. After a restless nap he switched on the late radio news to find out whom he had assassinated. As always, the Voice had given him no details beyond an identifying photograph. The name of his victim was indeed revealed, although little was said about him other than that he was a distinguished war hero who had undertaken a number of highly dangerous and extremely successful secret missions into German occupied territory. What was curious was that he was stated to have died simply from a brain haemorrhage. The explosive fact that this had been caused by two gunshots wasn't mentioned in the brief report that was slipped in towards the end of the bulletin. Malone's depression moved from the foreground to the background of his immediate consciousness as his mind focussed on what seemed to be an attempt to disguise the true nature of what had happened. He had had little previous interest in politics and great matters of state, due in no small part to the fact that his main preoccupation had been with his presumed right to live the good life, with as little effort as possible on his part to pay for it. But the vast change in his circumstances that had resulted from the negative consequences of that preoccupation was starting to take his mind in new directions. He attempted to join the dots in what had been said in the report. The man had been an undercover operative during the war, possibly in intelligence rather than the regular army. Nothing was said about the nature of his recent employment before his death, presuming that he needed to work for a living. Might it just be that he was still involved in the intelligence services and that was why misinformation had been put out concerning his death? If that supposition was correct, then maybe an admission that the victim had been shot would have had damaging consequences for the intelligence unit he worked for, or some project or other that they were engaged in. Malone thought back to the church murders. Both of those individuals had been Russian, so maybe they also were spies of some kind. The man whom he was supposed to assassinate next seemed to be doing something that a spy might do, in terms of collecting information from a drop box. So, putting all these things together, was he being used as some kind of tool in a shooting war between intelligence agencies? He couldn't even begin to fathom what the point of such a conflict might be, or why it needed him to assassinate people from two different sides, but his mind latched onto it in his ever-present attempt to find ways and means of justifying his role as a hitman. If he was part of a war, didn't that legitimise his killings? Wasn't he just the soldier he kept trying to imagine himself to be and weren't soldiers allowed to kill, particularly if the war was a just one? His mind started to waver a little with the introduction of the idea of a just war - he had no idea whether this possible intelligence war was just or not, he had simply no information. But mightn't it be reasonable for him to presume that it could be until told otherwise? He knew that he was stretching the logic underpinning all these speculations to absolute breaking point and beyond, but he didn't let that stop him from holding onto the hope that he might have found a new and better way of dealing with his guilt - and of trying to push back the depression that accompanied it. A little comforted and consoled in his new life of otherwise continuous misery, he sloped off to his bed to try and get a good night's sleep, ready for the next lap in the seemingly endless marathon of death that he was running.

At precisely noon on the following day, Malone eased the MG out onto the road and set off on his second mission of the week. The military metaphor was very much at the forefront of his mind and he had fully immersed himself in the role of a special operations soldier, fighting a war being run and justified by others. After a ninety minutes' drive he arrived at the spot where he was instructed to conceal his car. He drove it through an open farm gate and parked it out of sight, behind a large roadside hedge. He donned his balaclava and removed the briefcase and its deadly contents from the boot. Crossing to the other side of the road, he walked back thirty yards, then vaulted over a low fence and headed towards the copse. The target was expected there at some time between two thirty and four o'clock on the basis of the information that the Voice had been given.

As Malone walked onwards, he was conscious of the excited 'happy chatter' of winter birds in the branches high above. It seemed oddly out of place in relation to the grim reality of what he was about to do. The sun was painting the ground with long tree shadows and he distracted himself as he walked along by trying to step out of them into the intervening patches of unbroken light. He recognised the old oak tree as soon as he saw it, with the fake bird box about four feet above his reach. He scoured the surrounding area and found the ideal spot that had been suggested to him in the instructions. At its centre was a gnarled, dead and very wide tree trunk, with a convenient split where it had been hit by lightning, about five feet above the ground. It would completely conceal his presence, while simultaneously providing an optimum shooting point. He had a clear view of the fake bird box through the split in the trunk, which provided also a firm resting place for the gun barrel while he took aim. He opened the briefcase and removed the sections of the rifle. Having assembled the weapon he aimed a couple of shots at the tree, just to ensure that everything was in order and that there were no surprises in terms of how the weapon recoiled when fired, etc. All he had to do then was wait - and worry.

As the minutes ticked by the sun faded and was replaced by a rolling band of thick, grey cloud. His morale sank as the light dimmed and he imagined it to be some kind of omen, a sign of the disapproval of the gods, fate, whatever. There was a short, very heavy shower, after which a strong, damp earthy smell rose from the ground all around him. It seemed he could taste it, almost as if he was within the soil himself, a corpse perhaps, staring blindly into the mud that encased his rotting flesh. He shuddered and tried to push his mind back into military mode, but it seemed to be frozen in a state of deep apprehension. He only snapped out of it when he heard the sound of a car pulling up on the road, followed by the slamming of the driver's door. He slipped the gun into the V-shaped incision in the tree trunk and lined it up directly with the letter box. He heard the snapping of twigs that indicated the target was getting near and then suddenly he walked directly into Malone's line of sight. He was about thirty-five, with blond hair and a face that looked as though it had been involved in some fierce fisticuffs during the past few years, with a once broken nose that was not quite as straight as it should have been. He tripped on a fallen tree branch and cursed. Malone recognised the accent immediately as Russian. He was about to fire when he heard a second car door slam, indicating that the target hadn't come alone. A sense of panic now set in and he hesitated, wondering whether he should wait until both parties were in view and then shoot them. He could then avoid the danger of the second individual hiding at the sound of the gunshot and hunting him down. In the end his decision was made for him by a wholly unexpected random factor. A large Alsatian dog ran into the copse and rapidly detected his scent. As the target was climbing the four feet of tree trunk that separated him from the letter box, the dog started barking ferociously and hurtled towards Malone's hiding place, determined to flush him out and grab an arm or an ankle with its teeth. It was most definitely an attack dog rather than a pet. Transfixed with fear, Malone decided that he would have to shoot the dog before it did him serious damage. With the animal's head clear in his sights he fired two quick shots and it collapsed to the ground in mid-flight. Alerted by the rifle fire, the target slithered back down onto the ground and, while reaching for his gun, attempted to dash for cover. Malone by now had him firmly in his sights and three quick shots rang out. His heart hammered so fiercely as he fired the gun that he thought he was going to explode, but his aim remained steady and the target was dead before he hit the ground. At the precise moment he fired the first shot a young woman appeared. She too was armed and when she saw her colleague fall, attempted to jump behind the nearest tree. Malone aimed for her right shoulder and, despite his growing sense of panic, managed to hit it, sending her flying onto the ground. Banging her head on a tree stump, she lost consciousness. He grabbed the rifle and the briefcase and started to run as fast as he could back to the road. Vaulting over the fence, he ran past the target's parked car and retrieved the MG from behind the hedge. He swung it round and fled back onto the road and away, with his foot forcing the accelerator down as far as it would go.

By the time Malone had left the vehicle in a car park near the Royal Festival Hall, as instructed, he could hardly remember how he'd got there. His thoughts had been in semi-frozen mode as he headed back to London and it seemed almost as if he'd been driving on automatic pilot. After he'd wiped his prints off the large briefcase and its contents, he locked everything in the boot and then headed for the nearest tube station. As he hurtled through the tunnels in the train, like a squashed sardine among the rush hour crowds on board, he felt wholly insignificant. Looking at his reflection in the carriage windows he saw a slightly dodgy-looking, unshaven man with crumpled clothes and muddy boots, someone who seemed to attract little more than disdainful stares from the smartly dressed commuters around him. When he emerged out of the station nearest to home it was dark and he felt under-dressed against the cold. With his nose running and a slight feeling of feverishness, he decided to take a short cut through the cemetery to get back to the warmth of his apartment. As he hurried past the tombstones, some of them monumental in scale, his over-active imagination created an irrational sense of terror within his mind. He began to feel that all the spirits of those he had killed were rushing after him, anxious to scream and roar their rage into his bleeding ears as they tore the flesh from his body and snapped off his bones, limb by limb. What had begun as a fast march through the long, winding, unlit cemetery paths ended as a panic-stricken run to and through the far gates, back into the safety of the street lamps. Panting and short of breath, he finally stopped as he got to the road leading up to his apartment. With his hands on his knees he bent over, trying to recover enough to reclaim his mind from its demons and find the energy to drag his increasingly feverish body back home.

Once he was back inside the apartment he felt utterly exhausted as well as feverish and collapsed onto the sofa. He fell asleep almost immediately and didn't wake up until nearly three hours later. When he did so, his mind momentarily was blank, but then everything came back to him, together with the deep darkness of his feelings of guilt. He tried as before, by now so many times before, to push back against it by telling himself that it was a war he was involved in, in which killing was part of the process, and it was legitimated by the fact that the people he was shooting would probably have killed him in similar circumstances. They were all most likely spies and death would be a familiar weapon as well as a risk for them. But then his mind began to ask more questions than he was prepared for, almost as if it were operating as an intelligence independent of his own brain. If they were all spies, why was he being instructed to kill British intelligence officers as well as Russians? Whose side were the people who were directing him on? Might the British officers actually have been double agents, traitors, perhaps even working for the Russians? Was he being used to eliminate some kind of conspiracy against the British state? Or was there something much more devious going on?

Then the phone rang. He picked it up and heard once more the soft, lyrical voice of his new master.

"Mr. Malone, I trust you're enjoying a well-earned rest. I just thought you'd like to know that my client is extremely pleased with the work that you've done for him during the past couple of days. You'll find a very tidy little bonus included with the payment for your next job. I'll be in touch with the details soon. Enjoy the rest of your evening."

Malone attempted to ask for answers to the various questions that had been running through his mind, but the Voice had put the telephone down before he could say a word. He was left staring into space, with the receiver still held to his ear and his mouth opening and closing soundlessly, as if he were a fish. The cuckoo clock behind him sang out its celebration of the hour. He turned, grabbed the bird within his fist and wrenched it from the casing, before stamping on it repeatedly. Then he sat down, his eyes vacant and unfocussed, and the room was returned to a silence that felt like death itself.

CHAPTER TWELVE

"My, my, what an absolutely gorgeous office. And aren't you a pretty thing? Where's the boss, is he in his inner sanctum?"

The questioner was a thirty-something vision in a black dress and a matching hat with a veil. From her manner she seemed to think Alice was a junior clerk. Keeping her cool, Alice said,

"Mr. Benedict is due in shortly. Would you like to take a seat and I'll see if I can fix you up with an appointment?"

"Oh, no, don't bother yourself, honey. Gus and I know each other from way back. I just can't get over what a swell little suite of offices he has here. I must take a peek at his little hidey-hole in there, this is all so very British."

The vision's accent was that of the East Coast American elite. She had powered her way into Gus's office before she could be stopped. Alice hurried after her, saying,

"Excuse me, that's private. Would you mind waiting in here, please, if you want to see him?"

She was relieved when Gus suddenly arrived, dripping with rain from a surprise downpour outside. She scurried over and said, sotto voce,

"There's an American woman who's materialised out of nowhere and planted herself in your office before I could stop her. She claims she's known you for years."

Gus raised his eyebrows and nodded, hurriedly taking off his hat and coat and then going into his office. The vision had her back to him while she surveyed the view of the city from his window.

He stood in the doorway and coughed to attract her attention. She turned round, took off her hat and veil and smiled, looking him up and down in a deliberately 'undressing' manner. She said,

"Well there you are. Hello, Gus, long time no see."

He looked startled, but quickly recovered, saying,

"Well, well, the spy with an angel's eyes. I thought you'd gone back to Washington for higher things."

"Oh, I had a few years back home, a few in Moscow and now I'm back here. With my favourite British spy still around how could I resist when they offered me another London posting?"

"Your favourite retired British spy," Gus said. "I left the service some time ago and turned my hand to upmarket private detective work, as you can see."

"Nice cover story, baby blue. From what I hear you're still very much in business. You and Aberdeen Angus are stuck together like glue, or so I'm told."

"Angus is my former boss, an old chum who likes to reminisce on past cases, particularly the ones where we made a difference. He likes to think the service helped make the world a better place and to an extent he's right."

"What a charming bedtime story, one might almost believe it was true. You could never retire, Gus, sweetie, you've got the service in your blood. But you always were a good storyteller. Perhaps you might like to tell me a bedtime story tonight?"

Gus hastily shut the door. She surveyed him archly,

"Afraid the girlie next door might hear our pillow talk Mr. Bendy Benedict? How touching, I do believe you're blushing."

"Our pillow talk was a long time ago," Gus said. "I seem to remember it ended when your very impressive bedroom athletics failed to deliver me as Uncle Sam's little mole in the hole in British intelligence. When I declined your kind offer you became suddenly unavailable. The next thing I heard was that you'd disappeared back to Washington."

"Oh that had nothing to do with you, Gus. Just like a man, you do overestimate your own importance at times. There were far higher forces at work than you or me, or moles in the hole. My very specific talents were needed for something much more important back home at the time. So then I was gone and now, guess what, I'm back again. Don't tell me you're not pleased to see me."

"What exactly is it that you want from me, Jennifer?" Gus asked pointedly.

"How about a roll in the hay, or two, or three? I seem to remember we were pretty good at it. It would be a shame not to share our athletic talents while we have the opportunity."

Gus smiled wryly. He said,

"Well I'm sure I'd love the opportunity, what man wouldn't? The question is, would I be getting the real you, or just a highly polished bit of play acting while you worked away at your real purposes? You're not trying to tell me this is just a social visit?"

She smiled and drew an imaginary circle on his desk with her finger. She said,

"No, it's not, but the business end of things is the now. What I'm talking about is the flip side, the time to come, this evening perhaps? The bit that's pure pleasure for pleasure's sake, no strings attached. We're adults, we can separate the two, can't we?"

"Let me think about that. I'm only just getting used to the fact that we're back in the same room together. Tell me what's on your mind business-wise first."

"OK, why don't we do that."

She sat on Gus's desk, crossed her legs and gave him a come-hither smile that would have caused a regiment to lay down its arms and swoon. He knew her too well not to be aware that it was the precursor to some hard-boiled politicking, the hint of good things to come if he was receptive to whatever it was that she was about to put on the table. The smile subsided and she said,

"OK, so here goes. I'm here on one level because we've been noticing quite a little spat going on that seems to involve the British and the KGB. First a British intelligence officer gets killed, then two Russians. Then another British officer is terminated, followed immediately by the assassination of one KGB operative and the wounding of another - and all right here in little old England. It looks to us like there's a war going on that we've not been told about. So we asked our counterparts in the British intelligence services what the hell's going on and they said, 'You tell us.' That makes us think that London believes we're maybe just a little bit gullible. So we do a little digging and we find that Angus is the guy tasked with handling all of this as far as the UK end of things is concerned, and we have a look at all the information we have about where his enquiries might have been leading him. And then it gets interesting, because yours is a name that keeps coming into the picture. So we figure that you're a man who knows and I know you. So here I am. No subterfuge, no trying to pretend my business agenda is anything else, just a plain, straightforward statement of the facts as they stand. Why am I being so upfront? A, because I know you too well and you'd smell a rat fifty blocks off if I tried to bullshit you. B, because I don't want to mess up on the flip side of our relationship, which I'd rather like to resume. The offer for tonight is still on if you'd like to take it."

"Well I'm a man who knows alright, I know Angus and I know you. But that's as far as it goes, I'm afraid. I have no information on any turf war or whatever that may or may not involve the KGB. I'm retired from all that, as I told you."

"Of course you are, you poor old thing, you must be all of thirty-five. It's a miracle your hair hasn't turned white or fallen out completely - and how you can stagger around without your walking stick beats me. There's just one teeny-weeny snag with that charming little fairy tale. You see, we know that your little private detective agency is, in effect, part-financed by the service. You were too damn good a spy for them to completely let go, Gus, honey, so they came to an arrangement with you whereby they'd use you as a freelance, on a case-by-case basis, subject to your consent. And that consent was crucial for you, wasn't it, because a leopard doesn't change its spots. You felt uncomfortable with some of the things the service was involved in and that was the reason you wanted out. So they never ask you to do things that they know you'll hate, only the stuff where you and they share a common view. And this little war is one of those things you both agree on. You want to put a stop to it before it gets out of hand and goes heavens knows where in terms of its consequences. And you'll be thinking of the families of the men getting killed, like you always do. You'll want to stop this before there are any more widows to add to the regiment of mourners still lonely after the war. Remember, I know you like the back of my hand - and the top of my thigh."

Gus laughed and said,

"Did you dream all that after three vodkas too many and then wake up thinking it was reality? Do you remember that Edward G. Robinson film where he dreams of being involved in all kinds of plots, mayhem and murders and then wakes up to find it was all a nightmare? It sounds like you and the character Ed was playing have a lot in common. Angus will be very amused when we next meet to discuss old times."

"The only dreams I have are of you, honey pie. Which is why I was quite jealous when I saw you in that spectacular restaurant with the pretty little thing in the office next door - until I realised that you were just playing a couple for surveillance purposes. And I thought who amongst all these rich, sleek stallions feeding at the trough could old Bendy Benedict be keeping his beady eye on? And then I realised, you were there because Vladimir Polmonovski was there. You didn't see me I know, but then you weren't expecting to and I was very well disguised. So, to return to the main plot of the story, back at Uncle Sam's brains factory we asked ourselves why Vlad the Impaler might be of interest to the Brits and we wondered if it's the Russian dissident émigré connection. We wondered if you guys suspect that rather than there being any KGB people behind the killing of your intelligence officers, the old Russian dissident diaspora are the real culprits, creating a bit of mischief which they hope will play badly for the Soviets. Then we notice that one of Vlad's lieutenants mysteriously goes missing from outside the restaurant and we hear a rumour afterwards that you guys have him holed up for interrogation in a safe house. So that seems to add substance to our suppositions. Then we notice that Sergei has mysteriously disappeared as well and we wonder what's going on there. But then we have a really big think about all this and realise it sounds more like the stuff you'd get in a spy novel than the real world and that what you Brits are doing is telling Uncle Sam a fairy story to distract him from what's actually going on. So you see, Gus, in some ways, I really am the girl in a dream, I could be your Alice in Wonderland."

"Well, that's certainly a very creative interpretation of what you saw on that evening, Jennifer, dearest. Yes, I did note that Mr. Polmonovski came in while we were having dinner. Unfortunately for your burgeoning web of unlikely intrigue, Alice and I were there for entirely different purposes of a much more mundane nature. We were indeed on a little observational exercise, but our concern was with a philandering husband wining and dining his floozy, and not some imaginary Russian émigré plot. I'm sorry to be such a disappointing bore."

She laughed, saying,

"Gus, honey, you are never a bore. I do so enjoy sparring with you, just like old times. Listen, I have to go, I have a bit of surveillance of my own to do today. Would I be terribly unwelcome if I dropped by at your apartment at around seven tonight?"

Gus smiled. He said,

"Let's agree on tomorrow night. Eight will be fine, if that's OK with you? I'll make you dinner."

"How sweet, just like the old days. Eight's a date, I won't be late. Oh, by the way, don't forget any of the details of what I've just said when you pass them on to Angus. He may be a little more cooperative when he realises just how much Uncle Sam knows."

She smiled mischievously and gave him a little wave as she opened the door and left.

Bursting with curiosity, Alice wandered into Gus's office with a cheque that conveniently needed signing. As she did so she said,

"Well, she was a steamy package. Did dear old Gussie know her before his fling with me, during it, or afterwards I wonder?"

Gus smiled wryly and said,

"My, what big ears you've got, as the goblin said to the elfin queen."

"Oh, I didn't hear very much," Alice said. "I wasn't earwigging with a jar wedged against the wall or anything. I just couldn't avoid hearing a word or two before you closed the door. But being possessed of superior talents in such matters, a woman can put two and two together even when she's got no more than one to count with, so you might as well spill the beans."

"Well, if it will satisfy your curiosity, my fling with Jennifer Marquis was before we got together, if fling it was. With that very able lady you're never sure where her professional life ends and her private life begins, or if the two are in any way really separate at all."

"And now she wants you to fling again?"

"That's none of your business, Alice, dear, you're a married woman with a full-time job making sure that poor old George doesn't go astray, without having any time to keep an eye on my dalliances, or lack of them."

"She does, doesn't she? Want a fling I mean. You've got a slightly hunted look in your eyes."

Gus said,

"The main point of Miss Marquis's visit today was purely business, or more particularly, the business of trying to get information out of me and sending a message to Mr. One. Which has nicely disrupted my previous plans for this morning and requires that I arrange a meeting with One for lunch, always presuming that I can get hold of him."

"She's CIA, isn't she?"

"Well, given that she's as good as got it written across her forehead, yes. Like your good self, she's a very bright and very persistent character and poor old Mr. One is not going to be in the slightest bit delighted when he hears how much she knows about things he thought she didn't."

Three hours later, Gus found One sitting at a secluded table at the far end of the largest lounge in his club. He did not look a happy man. As Gus sat down and ordered a whisky, One said,

"So, the wicked witch has been a-calling. According to your file, the two of you were lovers for six or seven months during her last London posting. Am I to regard that as good news or bad?"

"If you mean did that compromise the confidentiality of the service's affairs, then there is no bad news. She tried to recruit me as Uncle Sam's fly on the wall, but failed. She had another little go this morning, but was really just going through the motions. The principal purpose of her visit was to send us both a message about how much she knows concerning our enquiries."

"To what end?"

"She thinks the British know more than the Americans are being told about the spate of killings of intelligence personnel and is letting us know that they're watching our every move. She wants you to know that they'll find out pretty damn soon if they're being kept out of the loop and the consequences of that, by unstated implication, are that Uncle Sam will not be happy and as a punishment may well put some limits on his preparedness to cooperate with the British intelligence services. That's on top of the current limits of course, bearing in mind past scandals."

"You've always been good at reading unstated implications, Augustus. How did she find out about our continuing relationship with you?"

"Well, my suspicion is that, having failed with me last time she was over here, she's found somebody else who will be the mole in the hole. Whoever it is clearly doesn't have access to the full picture, otherwise he or she would have known that when the Americans were told that we didn't as yet have an answer as to what precisely was going on, they were being told the truth."

"Interesting. I have a pretty good idea who the leak-prone individual might be and will deal with him tomorrow," One said. "This is all down to the Burgess and Maclean affair again, isn't it? Our American friends still think we're riddled with holes full of Soviet moles. They may even suspect that I'm a KGB double agent, God knows. Forgive such an intrusive question, but did Miss Marquis express any interest in starting up her relationship with you again?"

"She did indeed."

"And what did you say to her?"

"I invited her round to my flat for dinner tomorrow evening."

"Good. It's hardly a savoury sentiment to express, but there are always possibilities that intimate relationships in one area may improve fractious relationships in another. She will of course have a business side to things, as you are aware from your past dealings with her."

"Of course. I'll try and engineer the business part of the equation in our favour and she will try and engineer some benefit for Uncle Sam. It should be an interesting sparring match. She enjoys that kind of thing."

"Excellent. Now, if I'm to get full value for the money we're paying you, I wonder if you might care to give me one of your famous strategic assessments?"

"Of what?" Gus asked.

"Of precisely what the Americans suspect is really going on."

"Well, from the extent of their probing of what the British are up to, it's clear, as I've said, that they think something highly significant is being hidden from them. Given their anger when the

Burgess and Maclean scandal broke and their continuing conviction that the British diplomatic and intelligence services are penetrated by the KGB, I'd infer that they think this shooting war is the result of London having discovered one or more new Soviet moles. Their logic could run in several different directions, but knowing the way Jennifer's mind works, I'd suspect they might be thinking something like the following: the British intelligence officer killed in Kensington Gardens had seen or heard something that would be likely to expose the mole, so had been assassinated by the KGB before he could share his information with you. The mole then set up a meeting with his handlers in the church, but by then he'd been rumbled and was followed. When the Russians arrived, the little tea party was surprised and a firefight broke out. The mole got away – he's the chap seen by the people outside the church as he made a run for it. Your man was either wounded or killed in the firefight, along with the two KGB men, and was spirited away afterwards before the police arrived. The KGB retaliated for the death of its intelligence officers on a tit-for-tat basis and killed a high-ranking British operative. Your people are keen to keep the true nature of what is going on from Uncle Sam, because they know he would be furious if he realised that another mole had been allowed to burrow his way into the UK establishment and imperil Western security. So they put out a story about the MI5 officer having died from natural causes to try and cover up the true scale of the very un-British shooting war that has been going on. The mole then broke cover and arranged a second meeting with the KGB, this time out in the middle of nowhere, but the Brits got wind of it and arrived mob-handed in the middle of the tearful reunion. Another firefight ensued, during which one of the Russians was killed and the other wounded. The mole was spirited away and currently is holed up in a safe house somewhere under interrogation. What the Americans want to know is who he is, how much information he has given to the Soviets and, in particular, how much that is specifically damaging to their interests. They think that we've been trying to cover our tracks by appearing to investigate a Russian émigré plot led by Vladimir Polmonovski, whereas in reality, this is just a red herring to distract them from what's really going on. Jennifer told me the last bit herself by the way."

"What makes you confident that your analysis is so near the mark?"

"Well, I'm not saying that it's correct in every detail, but what I am sure of is that the CIA is thinking something that's at the very least similar to what I've just told you. They're paranoiac about possible KGB penetration of the service and the UK government in general. Within their current mindset, the kind of shooting war that's been going on only starts to make sense if you fill in the gaps in the way I've just done."

"OK, you've convinced me. You have a history of being right in such things, but how very alarming. We really have to get to the bottom of what is actually going on if we're to get them off our back as well as the Russians. What a nightmare."

Gus nodded and took a long draught of his double whisky. He said,

"So what's the plan, what do you want me to do?"

"Well, as you know, we're not completely without leads. We know that the killing of the Russian intelligence officers has not been authorised by the service or any section of the British government. We know that the Russians deny being involved in the killing of our people and so far, we have no reason to doubt their word. We suspect that Polmonovski may be behind some or all of what's going on, either on behalf of some Russian émigré political grouping that isn't yet on our radar, or on behalf of a party unknown. We know that he has a working relationship with the Kerryman and there are grounds for suspecting that our Irish friend might have been behind at least one of the killings. So, our only current options are to put the squeeze on those two parts of the chain and see what results. I can persuade the police to pull Polmonovski in for questioning about the disappearance of his fake brother. The cover story about him having fled the country for reasons unknown doesn't stack up and we know the two of them had fallen out quite seriously at the time Sergei went awol. I'll then secure access to him while he's in custody and apply the old thumbscrews. It's amazing what you can do with a bit of bluff and menace."

"Except when you're dealing with a man who's all menace and no bluff," Gus said pointedly.

"Maybe, but let's just see how things pan out. I've got a bit of a track record in interrogations that you're maybe not aware of, old man. Now, further along the food chain we've got the Kerryman. From what you told me a few days ago you've got a source who knows how to get in contact with him."

"Well, yes and no. If we were to say that we required somebody to be sent to kingdom come, then we could hire our friend through my source. But if the Kerryman were to even half suspect that my purpose in contacting him was to try and find out who he was, then I would be the one that would be biting the dust. So, there are some practical limitations on the usefulness of this contact information."

"Practical limitations have never stopped you before. I suspect that you've thought of a way round them."

"I think that a cautious yes would be my answer. My source is a likeable rogue and I don't want to put him in any danger. He is also extremely useful and reliable and would be difficult to replace. So I've been trying to think of a way that I could use him to help us get to the Kerryman without him - or me - being put at risk."

"How typically noble of you, Gus - and practical, of course. So?"

"I'll need three of your best fieldwork people, characters who, unlike me or my source, aren't known around the East End."

"To do what precisely?"

"To start a hare running and then to follow it. I'll arrange a meeting with my source and ask him if we can go for a walk asap to wherever the character who is a contact for the Kerryman lives or operates. I'll ask him just to give me the nod when we get there so that I can see who it is. Last time we spoke he said that details of the contact were a trade secret, but if I tell him that lives depend on me knowing it, I may be able to change his mind. If he agrees to play ball, I'll then pass the details on to your chaps. I'll need one to approach the contact with an urgent request - that he asks the Kerryman if he'll be prepared to carry out a contract killing for him and how much he would charge. We'll need to have a credible cover story as to who our man supposedly is and how he knew where to find the contact. The other two of your chaps must then keep a close eye on the contact to see what he does and where he goes."

"What if he goes nowhere, what happens if he simply rings our

Irish friend from a phone our men can't even see? The whole process might well be completely invisible and then we've wasted our time getting nowhere."

"I don't think he'll use a phone. The Kerryman wouldn't give anyone a number that could be traced, he's too meticulous and too cautious. He is someone who will only ever use random public phone boxes for business purposes and as he is unlikely to live in a phone box, our contact won't be able to get hold of him that way. It'll be a walk to a dead letter box, or a word in someone's ear, a someone who then goes and passes the message on to somebody else, who in turn passes it on to yet another link in the chain. It will be anything other than a phone call. We need to see what happens and to follow the contact wherever he goes and then follow anyone who he appears to pass a message on to. Given that our chap will have said that he needs an urgent answer, hopefully events will move quickly. We follow things as far along the chain as we can. If we're really lucky, we get to the end and find our man. But even if we get only part way there, we can pull in and interrogate the last link in the chain that we manage to follow and see if we can get him to divulge the identity of the person who picked up the message from him - providing he knows it, of course. If we can find that person, we can in turn interrogate him and repeat the process, until we get to the end. At the moment it's our one and only hope of getting to the Kerryman."

"Not quite, Polmonovski may decide to give him up when I interrogate him."

"Powerful as Mr. P is, I would very much doubt if even he knows who our Irish friend is or where to find him. You told me that the bodyguard you pulled in and interrogated claimed that the two men only ever communicated by public telephone boxes and dead letter boxes. You thought he was lying, I don't."

"Alright, we'll give it a whirl. Let me know as soon as you've identified this contact chappie and we'll start the ball rolling. I'll get things moving with our constabulary friends so that I can give Mr. P, as you call him, the third degree."

"What happens if he won't play ball?"

"Something very nasty, I'm afraid. We'll have to let the KGB know that we suspect he is behind the killing of their men. They'll be rather less gentle with him than we are and I suspect if we don't get the answers we need, they will. If he doesn't talk, I'll dangle that chilling possibility in front of his eyes. That's one of the reasons I'm reasonably confident that he'll tell us at least something of what we need to know."

CHAPTER THIRTEEN

The silence of the deep pile carpeted corridor outside the apartment was lacerated by a piercing scream. It was followed by a long, low moan.

These unnerving utterances had been preceded, a good minute earlier, by a woman's energetic cries of, "Whoopee! Yeeha! Ride 'em cowboy!"

Inside the apartment, the cowboy, or rather cowgirl in question, was sitting naked astride Gus, who looked very much like a man who had just been electrocuted. Then, after punching the air while shouting, "Yeeha! Yeah!" she eased herself down onto the bed beside him and said,

"I hope I didn't frighten the neighbours."

"I wouldn't worry too much about that, Jennifer dear, they're very old and very deaf."

"Just as well. You really do bring out the Texan granddaddy in me, Gussie baby."

"Your habit of pre- and post-coital whooping you mean? I thought your family were traditional Boston old money, through and through?"

"My gran's side yes, but she liked a bit of Texan exuberance to put some colour in her cheeks. So she married against her family's wishes and chose a man who could whoop with the best of them. She was a very frank lady. She told me that he whooped when I was conceived and he whooped when I was born, so it's hardly surprising if I keep up the family tradition. Have you never thought about whooping Mr. Bendy Benedict, or is that all too much for your English reserve?"

"I think I prefer to be a spectator rather than a participant where whooping is concerned."

"How very English of you. But you know, England is the old world and America is the new, haven't you heard? If you were to spend more time with me, I could show you how to become an American and then you'd be a whooper too."

"I'd be quite happy to spend more time with you and help you to whoop for England, but I'm afraid I could never whoop for America."

"You're never going to agree to become my little mole in the hole, are you? Uncle Sam would be so very grateful and you'd be working for the people who are making the future, not the stuffy old British stuck-in-the muds with their feet bogged down in the past."

"But, if I were still in the employ of the British intelligence services, which of course I'm not, would I want the kind of future that Uncle Sam dreams of and what makes you think Britain hasn't got a future of its own?"

"Listen, honey, look at Rome, Venice - great empires in their day, but now just cities in Italy, museums for tourists to visit to see what the past looked like. That's Britain's future. Your empire is half gone and it will have vanished almost completely within ten years. The forces for change are too great and too expensive to resist. Your obstinate delusions of grandeur have caused you to miss taking the leadership of the existing European community and the proposed new ones that will soon grow into a superpower around you - and you'll never get a second chance. The future in Europe now is France and Germany. The Germans have buried the Nazis for good and with the British throwing their chance away, they're all set to become the heart of a new democratic Europe when it emerges, as soon it will. It's only you Brits who can't see what's coming. You think that when the negotiations begin, you'll be able to undermine them and water down the European integration that's being proposed. Your people are chasing fool's gold, honey. This is a land of the past, exiling itself from the real world. You hang onto America's coat tails to help protect you from a Soviet superpower, but America would have preferred you to accept the new realities and to grow closer to Europe. We'd be very happy if you were our best bosom friend within the emerging European communities, not some tired old relic in a threadbare coat, dreaming of long-lost glories and an empire that's setting with the sun."

She licked her finger and running it gently across his lips, said,

"You see honey pie, apple of my eye, World War Two may have been your point of greatest triumph, but it was also the start of an unstoppable decline. That's the bit you dear old British have missed. You never see the writing on the wall until it's written all over you. You just ain't got the dough in the bank anymore pal, as my boss would say. You're a tiny little island in a world that's going to be run by the guys with the big territories in the future - the Russians, soon the Chinese, the Europeans, but most of all us. Without a place in Europe, little old England's going to become a stranded seal, bobbing about in the ocean. So, Gussie baby, where your own future is concerned, why work in the last gasp saloon when you could be working for us, helping build a new world in which democracy is the dominant force, the communists kept in their place and the old oppressive empires are kicked over the horizon and out into space?"

"Well that's a very glitzy view of a rather less virtuous reality. The American future is a different kind of empire, but empire it is. Your people are simply smart enough to know they can control territories through economic power and that's the new kind of world that you're building. It's no less oppressive a system than the old European empires, it's just that you use money and arms deals instead of armies. Armies are only necessary to keep the communists out of your new kind of empire, as in Korea and Europe. And you can hardly preach the virtues of spreading American style democracy when your people still don't give African-Americans the full rights to which they're entitled. I hardly agree with everything Britain stands for, but its values are the closest to my own of anywhere on the planet, so my loyalties are not for sale I'm afraid."

"Spoken like a true Englishman. You'd have been the man of the moment in the nineteenth century, Augustus Benedictus the Great, but in today's world you're yesterday's guy. Sign up with me and you could become Captain Future, my new all-American superhero! Look, Gus, if I can't persuade you with the geopolitics of all this, how about if we consider the financial options? I know all about the goody two shoes stuff you're doing, the way you donate some of your hard-earned dough to worthy causes and don't get me wrong, I admire you for all of that. But think how much more you could give to the needy and deserving poor that you so care about with all the extra dollars that Uncle Sam would be pouring into your bank account in return for your services. Whatever the Brits are paying you would be peanuts by comparison. Don't you owe it to the guys you're trying to help to at least think about it?"

"Well, if I were still working for British intelligence in some capacity, freelance or otherwise, there would be a very short answer to that question and it would be no. Uncle Sam's interests are Uncle Sam's, not theirs, so helping him would not necessarily benefit them. But as I explained yesterday, I'm a private detective now, I no longer do any intelligence work."

"And pigs might fly in a purple sky. I thought we'd done that particular fairy tale to death."

"Oh dear. I suspect that my answer will mean no more rolls in the hay, but that's a price I'll have to pay."

"What did I say yesterday, Mister Frowny Pants? Business and pleasure are two separate agendas. I don't let one mess up the other. The messy part is that after all the big hints I sent to Angus, I'm still getting the same bullshit about the Brits not knowing what's going on with the spy war that's been playing out here. And then there's my never, ever, ever, ever being able to persuade you to give me a feed on what's really going on within that relic from deep antiquity they call the British state. Or even to admit that you're still part of it, despite the fact I know you are. But there is a good side to all of this and that is here and now, in this very bed – and if I'm not mistaken, Mr. Bendy Benedict, I feel another big fat whoop coming on and by the look of things, you do too ..."

In another, less salubrious part of the city, Canon O'Leary was pouring himself a small glass of the whisky that an appreciative parishioner had given him, a golden thank-you after a midnight visit to his dying mother to give her the last rites. He'd taken no more than a sip when the telephone rang. Worrying that it might be another sick member of his congregation needing his attention, he answered straight away. What he heard was a familiar Irish voice on the other end of the line and his heart sank. The Voice said,

"Good evening Seamus, are you enjoying your nightly tipple?"

"Padraig, how kind of you to ring. How is it that you know my nightly habits? I think at times you must be watching me through a window."

"And that I might, although not tonight you'll be pleased to know. I like to see my brother when I get the chance, I always feel it brings us closer."

"Closer? How can that be when you haven't let me see your face for twenty years?"

"Oh, you've seen it Seamus, it's just that you didn't recognise it. I'm much altered. Time, weight changes and life's accidents and worries can make an entirely new face for a man as the years roll by."

"If you've been so close, why haven't you said hello at least? I feel at times as though you're on another planet."

"That's exactly it, Seamus, I am. You and me, we live in different universes. You disapprove of me I know and I never go where I'm disapproved of. But I like to keep in touch over the airwaves, as they say, I like to know how you're getting on in your very different world."

"Well, I'm as alright as a man with a rheumatic knee and an invisible brother can be. I would be a much happier man if I didn't feel always that there is a certain darkness in your life, a shadow that in turn keeps you in the shadows, away from my gaze. It seems to me you must have something to hide, something that makes you anxious that nobody should be able to recognise your face as it is now, something that causes you to keep even your address secret from me, your own brother."

"I have nothing to hide from you Seamus, I just like things the way they are. It's one of my eccentricities, of which there are many, as you must surely remember."

"Then tell me who you work for. Who do you serve?"

"Who do I serve? I serve no-one. The only thing I serve is my curiosity."

"That's a fatuous answer, as you well know Padraig. Explain what you mean and stop playing word games."

"What do you think this is - a conversation between brothers, or some ill-advised attempt to hear my confession? You know very well that I don't have time for your medieval beliefs and all their sacraments and penances, Seamus. It's a penance simply listening to you when you start to go on about all that guff."

"I'm asking what precisely do you mean when you say you serve your curiosity."

"The human mind is curious about all sorts of things, Seamus, when it's freed of the shackles of the Church. For example, I'm curious about people's notions of right and wrong, about how they choose between them and how far they will go to justify doing wrong, when the costs of doing right are too high for them."

"That's an interesting choice for your 'example'. What kinds of wrong are we talking about Padraig, are we talking about the taking of lives here?"

"What makes you think that?"

"I've always thought you capable of killing a man Padraig. Ever since we were children, I've felt I could see it in your eyes, hear it in your voice. So that might be a topic that would interest your curiosity, the killing of a man."

"I've never killed anyone, Seamus, not a single soul."

"With your own hands perhaps."

"What's that supposed to mean?"

"I think you're a man who orders deaths Padraig. I think you're a hard case, a gang leader or some such. I remember the way you used to strangle rabbits back on the farm, with a smile on your face and a fascination as to how long you could make the process last. You're intelligent, ruthlessly ambitious and you take pleasure in killing. Those three things are likely to take men in dark directions in my experience. Why else would you be so keen to remain invisible?"

"Rabbits for God's sake, I was a child, man. Children can be cruel little monsters, but that doesn't mean they remain cruel when they grow up. Our daddy knocked all that out of me. I'm simply a man who gives people choices, Seamus. I get paid large amounts of money to give people choices. That's all I do, the beginning and the end of it."

"And what kind of choices might they be?"

"The choice of doing a terrible thing or a good thing. It's as simple as that."

"You're playing games with me Padraig, aren't you? On the one hand acting the innocent and on the other dropping provocative hints that you may be entirely the opposite, purely for the purpose of baiting and mocking me."

"I'm doing no more than answering your questions, Seamus, as I always do. I'm sorry that you find my answers provocative."

"Of course you are Padraig. So what are the costs of refusing to do the terrible thing? That's what you want me to ask next, isn't it?"

"It depends on the individual and their circumstances. For some it's simply the case that they don't get the money they otherwise would have been paid. For others it can be quite terminal."

"You mean they get killed?"

"Indeed, but not by me, so you needn't worry your priestly head. And if they do get killed, it's only because they've decided to do a good thing instead of a terrible one, so in your religious view of the world, that must surely guarantee them a passport to heaven mustn't it?"

"And you're telling me you have nothing to do with the ordering of these killings?"

"I told you Seamus, I simply give people choices, I don't order anyone to do anything."

"I think you have the devil's tongue, Padraig, and his diabolical slipperiness with words."

"Well you would Seamus, but I think in truth the tongue is mine alone. Now, if we've finished with our little word games, I'd like to get to the main point of my call. If you'd care to take a little walk into the hall, you'll find a small package has been posted through your letterbox this evening"

The canon did as requested. On opening the package he gasped. He picked up the phone again, his hand shaking with a mixture of shock and rage. He said,

"What is the meaning of this? There's five thousand pounds here. Are you going to tell me that this is another donation to charity?"

"It's a donation to the charitable work that you're doing Seamus, yes. The previous amounts were smaller because they were speculative, I wanted to see how well you used them. I was impressed, so now I'm giving you a larger amount."

"But this is the devil's money. You've more or less admitted that, one way or another, you're in the killing business and you're asking me to use some of the proceeds to do God's work. You must know that I can't accept such money."

"I didn't say I was in the killing business, Seamus, I said I was in the choices business - and I even said that I've never killed anyone. And as you said yourself, I do from time to time succumb to the temptation to bait my oh so holy brother. You were doing as you always do and trying to hear my 'confession', so maybe I simply invented some hints at fictional sins for you to get your teeth into. So there is no reason whatsoever for you to reject the money. If you do, you're as good as stealing from the mouths of the poor, you're taking away from them something that would be of great help. As a priest, you can't do that Seamus. You must accept the money and use it well, as I wish."

"I don't understand you. I don't understand you at all. Why does a man as evil as you give me money to help the poor? Why should someone like you care?"

"Perhaps because I'm not evil, Seamus. Has it never occurred to you that your priestly view of the world might be a little too black and white? We were both poor when we were children back on the farm, back in Ireland. Our father was often too ill to leave his bed and we had to do most of the work in the fields ourselves, just to put enough food on the table. We're where we are today solely because of the money our New York relative left us in his will when we were in our teens, the key that opened the door to possibilities that previously we could only have dreamt of. That money gave us the education that turned you into a priest and me into someone with the confidence and the skills to make his own way in the world. I'm a man of great wealth now, Seamus, I have far more money than I need. Why shouldn't I want to use some of it to help the poor that I see in this city? It gives me satisfaction, Seamus, to help people who have a similar plight to ours all those years ago, when we were children. And whatever our differences, I trust you with the work that you're doing, I know you'll do the right thing by them. Is that a crime?"

The canon was lost for words. After a pause, he said,

"I don't know what to say Padraig, you are a most confusing man. Is this all about power? Is it that you relish the power to condemn one man to death - as I'm sure you do, despite all your denials - and the power to give another a new life through your charitable acts? Is that what you really enjoy, to be able to demonstrate that you have power over life and death? Or is this some kind of hedging of your bets, good deeds to counterbalance the evil ones, so that if there is actually this God you don't believe in, you'll not go to hell when you die?"

"Well, if you would but listen, I don't know how many times and in how many different ways I have to tell you, but I do not kill people. As for your speculations about the afterlife, there may be truth in some of that, who knows, Seamus? Life is a strange and mysterious thing, but death is stranger still. I often think about it. When I was younger, I even tried to have the belief that you have. Perhaps we all hedge our bets to a degree. But all of that's irrelevant. I'm giving you the money purely for the sake of what you can do with it and that's the beginning and end of the matter. Now, I have to go, Seamus, I have another call to make. Enjoy the rest of your whisky. We'll speak again and you can tell me how you've used the money. Goodnight."

The line went dead. The canon said to the silence,

"You are the most confusing and confused of men."

Back in Gus's apartment building, on the other side of the city, a loud cry of "Yeeha!" cut through the deathly quiet of the plushly carpeted corridors for the third time in an hour. In some respects at least, the fabled and often exaggerated British-American special relationship seemed to be in fine fettle.

CHAPTER FOURTEEN

Gus met Tasty Harry at noon on the following day. After their usual animated lunch, for which Gus, as always, paid, Tasty agreed to make a one-off exception to his rule of not revealing trade secrets. He made it clear that he only did so because lives were at stake. He then took Gus on a mile-long route march to the pub which the Kerryman's London contact patronised, the Fox and Squirrel. As it came into view, Tasty said,

"I'm going to take you in, but in no way must you look directly at our man - although I hardly need say that to a geezer with your 'hush hush' history. We'll buy a drink in the bar and you can see him and precisely where he sits in the wall mirror above the whisky bottles. He drinks alone at a table in the corner between twelve and two every lunch time. He's a middleman for a couple of villains, so people who want to do business through him will come and see him there. You can't miss him. He wears a black hat and never takes it off. It must be glued to his head or something. He's a man of few words and if he doesn't like the look of someone, they'll be told to scarper smartish or else. So your man had better have a good story as to how he got to hear about him and his Kerryman link. You say he's going to ask him to get a quote from Mr. K for a contract killing?"

"A fictional killing to be precise, the details of which will be in a sealed green envelope. If he takes the bait, we just want to follow the envelope's trail and see if it leads us to the Kerryman."

"Well, I don't want to be a wet blanket, but good luck with that

Gus, me old mate. Mr. K will have thought that one out well in advance, otherwise he wouldn't still be the original mystery man. He'll have some way of throwing the hounds off the scent."

"The hounds in this case will be pretty damn good."

"So is Mr. K."

Standing at the bar as they chatted away three minutes later, Gus observed his man closely. He was almost as large as Tasty, with a face that had been made with a chisel. He appeared to be preoccupied with his copy of the Daily Mirror, but noted everyone who came and went. After a couple of minutes a tall, wiry man, with a suit that looked like it had shrunk in the rain, approached him. After a brief conversation he was sent packing and Gus noted that a nod from chisel face was the signal for a bull-built villain at the other end of the bar to leave in pursuit of the thin man. He could see why Tasty emphasised the need for a good cover story.

After he'd passed the information on to Angus, the next stage of the operation was activated. The man that was sent to the Fox and Squirrel was good. With a wrestler's build and a chin that might have been used to hammer nails into coffins, he looked the part. After a short interrogation, chisel face told him to sit down. He agreed to pass on the message to the Kerryman, but said he charged a fee for doing so for all new clients. Fortunately, Angus had anticipated this and the two hundred pounds that he had given to his man was enough to smooth things through. Hammer chin slipped the money under the table in a plain brown envelope, which chisel face pocketed.

After Angus's man had departed, Mr. K's contact remained at his usual seat until precisely two o'clock and then left. As he walked quickly down the road he checked constantly to see if there was anybody following him. His two pursuers were so skilled in their art that he didn't spot either of them at first. He got as far as Covent Garden market, but then clearly noticed at least one of them. He suddenly turned round and walked back the way he had come. He stopped to buy a copy of the Sporting Life from a street vendor and then went into a coffee bar. After ordering a cake and a drink, he sat down in a window seat and started to read the newspaper, periodically checking the street outside to see if he could spot anybody watching him. The game continued for the rest of the afternoon and into the evening, until he went home to his flat around eight, following another couple of hours spent in the Fox and Squirrel. Angus's men had to call in for replacements after midnight, on the correct assumption that they had been spotted and that new faces were needed.

At precisely ten o'clock the next morning chisel face emerged from his apartment block, checked out the faces on both sides of the road and then set off back towards Covent Garden. As before, he surveyed everything and everyone around him in search of tails. When he arrived at the market, he went over to a group of truanting boys who were hanging around outside, smoking and sizing up potential wallets that they might be able to separate from their owners. He picked out a boy he clearly knew and gave him something crucial. It was the sealed green envelope that Angus's man had passed to him containing the details of the fictional contract killing he needed pricing. That confirmed to the men tailing him that the message to the Kerryman was finally being sent. He gave the boy some instructions and then disappeared into the crowds milling around the flower and fruit stalls within the market. The boy hung around for five minutes or so, laughing and joking with his fellow miscreants. It was notable that he made no attempt to open the sealed envelope and that none of his chums seemed inclined to express any curiosity as to its contents. That confirmed to the watchers that the boys had been left in no doubt that its opening would have deeply serious consequences. Suddenly, without any warning, the courier ran off at speed, weaving in and out of the bustling crowds of buyers and sellers in a manner that left his pursuers flat footed. By the time they made it out of the market he had vanished from view and their only option was to wait for his return, grab him and try and persuade him to tell them where he'd taken the message.

Their wait was a long one. It wasn't until after midday that Mercury reappeared and headed back towards his waiting chums, who were just about to leave in search of a more profitable location for pickpocketing. Neal, the tail nearest to Mercury, grabbed his arm before the other boys spotted him and pushed him behind a stall. He said,

"Five pounds for telling me where you took that green envelope. Here, look at it, a nice crisp fiver - and very nearly yours. All you have to do is tell me where the envelope went."

"Five pounds for something that could get me killed, mister? No ta."

"OK, ten, that's my highest offer - and the information must be accurate or I'll come looking for you with a lead-lined cricket bat."

"My life's worth more than ten quid, mister. Even my old man would tell you that and he thinks I'm worth less than nothing, drunken old git."

"Twenty."

"Na. Not worth the risk."

"Thirty - but that's your lot - and remember what I said about being accurate."

Thirty seemed to be the magic word that unsealed Mercury's lips. He said,

"I took it to Hadblinder's Yard. I was told to stand there with my hands behind my back, with the green envelope clearly visible. Someone would come up behind me and say, 'Thank you mailman.' They'd then take the letter out of my hands. I wasn't to look back at them and I wasn't to let go of the letter unless I heard those words. That's it, mister, now how about my thirty quid?"

"So you're trying to tell me that you didn't let your boundless curiosity get the better of you - that you followed your instructions exactly and didn't get even a half look at the man who took the envelope?"

"I know which side my bread's buttered on, mister. I don't go looking for a knife in my back if I can help it. I didn't see a thing. I only heard him."

"And what did he sound like - what was his accent like?"

"He was trying to speak posh, but wasn't. He had a gruff voice, like he had a sock in his mouth."

Neal concluded that he had got the most that he could out of Mercury. He gave the boy the money and let him run back to his chums. Turning to his colleague, Wright, who had been watching the proceedings, he said,

"Angus isn't going to like this. The trail ends in Hadblinder's Yard with the envelope being taken by an invisible man. The Kerryman remains exactly where he was before we set the trap, completely out of our reach."

Wright said,

"Why don't we nab the bloke in the pub and see if we can

persuade him to be nice and talkative and fill in the gaps as to where the envelope went?"

"Because he won't know. I recognize the set-up that's being used here. This kind of messenger system relies on each separate part of the trail only being known to those running the message on it. Only the Kerryman will have the overall picture. Because we missed the second part of the trail, we've lost all chance of knowing where the envelope ended up. That's it, end of story, we've messed up old man."

Meanwhile, deep in the Kent countryside, the next part of the operation was well underway. Mr. One had persuaded the police that there were sufficient grounds for arresting Vladimir Polmonovski and taking him in for questioning regarding his business partner's mysterious disappearance. Mr. One would then use that operation as cover to interrogate him about the killings of intelligence officers while he was in custody. What he hadn't anticipated was a phone call from the team staking out Polmonovski's country mansion informing him that a helicopter had landed on the back lawn, out of their sight, in the middle of the morning. It had left with three passengers with their hats pulled down over their faces and it seemed very likely that the target of the operation was amongst them. These suspicions were confirmed when the police arrived in force at midday, only to find the house empty of everyone bar its staff, who were busy covering the furniture and shuttering the windows. They had no idea of where their boss had gone, or when he might be back. It seemed highly likely that someone had tipped him off.

The following morning saw Gus arrive at his Mayfair office shortly before Alice. He was just hanging his hat and coat up when she arrived, saying,

"Well, well, the wanderer returns."

"I've been tied up at the other office and doing some surveillance for the McHaligan case."

"And frolicking around in the reeds with the lady in the lake?"

"I can't imagine what you mean."

"You know very well what I mean, Gussie, dear. After she rang the other day, I noticed a definite spring in your step and a gleam in your eye - yes, I can see it now, it's still there. You're positively glowing."

142

"Perhaps I'm radioactive."

"Talking of cases, if I may, what do you want me to do about Lady Witchfield's barmy investigation? I've used a freelance for a solid week's surveillance and there's absolutely nothing untoward to report in the behaviour of Canon O'Leary and Sister Agnes. They're both clean as beans, the original little goody two shoes, as they're supposed to be. Do you want me to wrap it up and send her a report, plus the bill?"

"No, not quite yet. Lady W's groundless persecution of the poor canon does maybe require a little penance, as his religion would see it. I think that the addition of some extra costs to our fees should do the trick nicely, so I'll go and interview the canon, without letting him know precisely what I'm about of course. That should add a tidy little extra amount to our bill, as well as clearing his name once and for all, then we can send it. I will of course be donating a chunk of Lady W's fee to the canon's work with the poor, in the agency's traditional Robin Hood fashion."

"Dear oh dear, you are a one, Gussie. I'll await your final report and then send her the bill. Presumably the awful Lady W will then demand we start a new investigation into rumours that the canon and Sister Agnes have been running a brothel for delinquent clergymen and one-legged funeral directors?"

As she was speaking the outer door burst open and Mr. One charged in like an express train that had come off the rails. Pointing to Gus's inner office he said,

"One needs a private word, pronto, if you please, Augustus."

Gus nodded and took him into the inner sanctum, closing the door after him. Mr. One sat down in the comfortable leather armchair provided for clients, with a frown so deep that it seemed to swallow all light within it. He said,

"We have a leak. Polmonovski was given notice of the police raid a couple of hours beforehand and escaped in a helicopter with his minders. We've no idea where he is."

"Well it's not me, you didn't give me any information about it. How many people knew other than you and the police?

"The three people above me in the service and the Americans."

"The Americans?"

"Miss Marquis, to be precise. She's been badgering me on and on with this American paranoia that we're just using Polmonovski to distract them from the truth - this nonsensical idea that the supposed shooting war between us and the Russians is the result of us having found more Russian moles. I told her that we were picking up Polmonovski at midday and she was welcome to sit in on the interrogation so that she could see we were serious about him. It seemed to be a good way of calming our American friends' anxieties."

"Well, I've had the same line from her about our interest in Mr. P being no more than window dressing, so it's difficult to see how she would have any motive for leaking our intentions to a target who is of no apparent interest to her. What about your three illustrious superiors? Do you have any grounds for suspecting one of them?"

"None at all. I only told them at a meeting at around eleven am on the day of the raid and none of us left the room until the operation was well underway."

"And what of our constabulary friends?"

"As far as the police were concerned, we wanted Polmonovski detained for rather less exotic reasons than our real ones, so they weren't aware of his suspected link to the killings of the various intelligence officers. It's always possible that there is a corrupt officer who he pays to provide information, someone who gave him a warning that he was likely to be hauled in over a suspected murder charge. That's the only possibility I can think of at the moment regarding the police."

"So the leak isn't at your end and the only other possibility seems to be our constabulary friends?"

"Not quite. What we don't know is if your American lady friend told any of her colleagues about the raid before it happened. She may well have reported the information to a superior or somebody she was working in harness with. We need to know if that was the case."

"Which translates as you want me to find out?"

"Exactly. Consider the matter something for your pillow talk."

"What makes you think we're back under the same sheets?"

"Passers-by have noticed that you have a very noisy apartment in the evenings, or so I'm told, Augustus."

"Passers-by in the sense of one of your chaps who just happened to be 'passing by'? So, you've been tailing her?"

"I couldn't possibly comment - and that is a matter that's strictly not for your pillow talk."

"Well I can't guarantee that Jennifer will be my guest again any time soon, she's very much a free spirit and I'm fairly certain I'm not her only port of call in London. I'm a bit puzzled as to why you think anyone in the CIA might have been interested in warning Polmonovski, unless you have information suggesting that he is important to the Americans for other reasons. If they've seen him as some kind of asset they could use against the Soviets, someone they would want to keep out of our grasp in case we discovered what they were up to, then that's another matter."

"I have no such information, Augustus. I'm merely allowing for the fact that there may be games and motives that we haven't thought of so far and that, for all the protestations to the contrary, they might actually involve the Americans - or some of them at least. I need you to find out whom she told so that we can put a tail on them, just in case. We already have one on her, as you have correctly guessed. When you're in a position of dangerous ignorance it's essential to follow as many leads as possible to see what they turn up. In the meantime, the police have been left under no illusion as to their responsibility to try and find out precisely where that helicopter went."

"I wouldn't hold your breath. Mr. P is probably out of the country by now."

"And he may not be. He has rather too many fingers in profitable pies in London to want to be too far away. Now, moving swiftly on, we're at a complete dead end with our attempts to locate the Kerryman. Our men fluffed it I'm afraid and they won't get a second chance to use the same ploy. I need you to come up with some alternative ways of getting to him - and fast."

Gus sat back in his chair and scratched his head. He said,

"Well, it's a bit of a long shot and it may all come to nothing, but somebody at the centre of one of my other cases told me something a while ago that just might have a bearing on Mr. K. It didn't strike me at the time, but the more I think about it the more what he said sounds interesting. It was in a conversation we had before he became the subject of an investigation. I intend having a chat with him this afternoon, so I'll see if that leads somewhere or nowhere and get back to you."

"I think I'd prefer somewhere rather than nowhere - and pronto. I'll hear from you by the end of today then. Right, that's it for now. I've got two more sets of ears to bend before lunch. I'll show myself out."

With that, Mr. One departed, a rush of nervous energy that swept past Alice as if she didn't exist, almost bowling her over in the process. As Gus wandered out of his office, deep in thought, she said,

"That man could do with a lesson in basic courtesy and good manners, starting with the need to acknowledge that the female of the species actually exists and merits civilities and greetings - something as simple as hello and goodbye would do to start with."

"Mr. One still thinks he's back in the war commanding a regiment I'm afraid. For him, only officers merit his attention and those he regards as foot soldiers are merely allowed to salute."

"Well, this foot soldier is sorely tempted to use her feet for purposes other than marching and give him a jolly good kick up the btm. But fear not, Gussie, dear, as you know, I am a model of self-control. Now, while I have sight of you, there's a Colonel Solomon who would like to discuss a potential case with you in person asap. Can I pencil him in for some time this afternoon, or has One-With-No-Manners already nabbed you for something else?"

"I have indeed been nabbed, so tomorrow morning is the earliest time I'm going to be free - you can pencil him in any time then. I'll be busy killing two birds with one stone round at Canon O'Leary's freezing cold presbytery after lunch."

"Why two? What has a second little feathered friend done to so deserve meeting its maker?"

"Well, in addition to my original reason for seeing the canon in pursuit of a final answer to Lady Witchfield's barmy allegations, I now have another of a rather more sane and sensible nature. Whatever the very strange Lady W might suspect about him, he may turn out to be the priestly goose that lays the golden egg - an offering that may cause that rarest of things, a word of gratitude from Mr. One."

"Why settle for one kind word from One? You could go for broke and see if he could manage two - and maybe even throw in a friendly smile as a bonus. Now there would be an amazing transformation of a chap ..."

CHAPTER FIFTEEN

"Through this single, magical device you can see the complete pointlessness of all vanity, ambition, greed, hatred, jealousy, envy - every venal trait in human nature is made laughably, risibly, so infinitesimally small that its total and utter irrelevance becomes apparent with a clarity that blinds you more fiercely than the sun. It is a true wonder of scientific invention and I am permanently in awe of everything it shows me."

Gus had found Canon O'Leary in an almost bare upstairs room of the presbytery. He was sitting in a faded old armchair, cradling a large brass astronomical telescope, which he had just finished polishing. Grace Grogan, the elderly housekeeper, placed a cup of tea on a small table beside the chair and asked Gus if he would like one as well. He politely declined and she departed with a smile. The canon, a lithe, red-faced man in his early fifties, continued,

"A parishioner left it to me in his will. I'd always admired it when I went round to visit him and was astounded the first time that he let me look at the night sky through it. All that vast expanse of space - of stars, planets, galaxies and heavens knows what dark, unseeable matter in the huge distances between them. For some in my profession such moments are an affirmation of faith, but for me it was something more - a seismic revelation in which I realised in an instant just how utterly, utterly tiny I and everyone else in this unfathomable, infinite strangeness we call the universe really are. This wonderful, precision instrument has the power to bestow in an instant true and lasting humility, one of the greatest gifts that anyone or anything has ever given me. I thank the man who left it to me every night and every morning of my life."

He smiled at Gus and touched something within him deeply. He felt as if the ever-present memories of the horrors of Hitler's brutally murderous war, the terrifying phantoms that wandered among the darker shadows within his mind, suddenly had been exorcised.

The canon said,

"It's Mr. Benedict, isn't it? You're the gentleman who made a kind and considerable donation for the poor of the parish a couple of months ago. That money has done wonderful things, wonderful things. I remember, you're not a Catholic, are you? And yet you are more Christian in your kindness than all the wealthy Holy Joes and Joannas of the parish who label me a communist for preaching charity, God bless them and God save them. Tell me Mr. Benedict, why do you do such kind things for people of a religion you don't believe in?"

Gus said,

"Their religion is irrelevant. You are someone who is looking after people who have fallen through the net, and you do it well. Very well from what my enquiries have told me. That's all that matters. That's why I'm here to give you some more money."

The canon looked quietly amazed. He placed the telescope delicately on the floor beside him, got up and said,

"Come on, we'll go downstairs, it's warmer there and there's actually a chair for you to sit in. If you'll not have a cup of tea, perhaps I could offer you a whisky, if it's not too early in the day for you?"

Gus, whose hands had turned blue in the freezing cold room upstairs, was relieved to see a briskly burning fire in the grate of the presbytery parlour. Mrs. Grogan had just finished stoking it up. She drew the curtains a little to block out the fierce, low glow of the afternoon sun, smiled welcomingly again at Gus and then shut the door behind her as she left. The canon produced a whisky bottle and a glass from a little cupboard on the wall. He said,

"It may seem impolite my not joining you, but I only have a dram after supper. I've seen one or two in my profession grow a little too fond of the bottle with the pressures of the job and am trying not to fall into the same trap. Mind you, I'm sure Satan has many other little traps he'd like me to fall into instead. You might not believe it, but there are people within the parish who have been spreading rumours that I and Sister Agnes are in some kind of forbidden relationship. I think you met her last time you visited didn't you, she was telling you some of the uses we would be putting your donation to then?"

Gus nodded as he poured himself a small whisky. He felt guilty about having anything larger, noting that the cupboard was bare of additional bottles. The canon continued,

"Well, you'll have seen that Sister Agnes has arms like a wrestler and a fierce look in her eye, even when she's smiling. She is a devout but very formidable lady. Should I have ever even half-suggested something of an inappropriate nature to her she would have boxed both my shell-likes so firmly that I'd look as if I was wearing cauliflower ear muffs. And yet one of the wealthiest among my flock is still peddling the same nonsense. The whole idea is so hilarious that I've long ceased to be annoyed. Please, sit down and make yourself comfortable."

Gus made a mental note of what the canon had said concerning the formidable nature of Sister A. Now it had been pointed out he did indeed remember such fearsome attributes as had been described to him. He would ask Alice to find a suitably diplomatic way of phrasing the point in the final report to Lady Arabella. He went on to explain how much money he was now donating and the two men then spent almost an hour discussing the best ways in which it could be used. When they had devised a plan that was agreeable to both the canon said,

"You cannot imagine the pleasure and relief I feel as a result of your act of kindness. The donation is extremely generous and will make a real difference to the lives of struggling people. And I know it comes, untainted, from a reputable source. I may have mentioned last time we met that I have one other donor of similarly significant amounts. He is a man of darkness and violence I fear, whose generosity is purely self-interested. I think he is hedging his bets in case there really is a God, even though he has no active religious beliefs. My suspicion is that he thinks he can wipe his spiritual slate clean every now and then by carrying out a series of spectacular charitable acts - and then go on to commit more crimes, and so on. I feel that, because I am so certain of the contaminated nature of the money that he gives to the poor of the parish, I should refuse it. Yet, because I have no hard evidence of his wickedness, I cannot turn it down. I feel deeply compromised, as though my hands are dirty just through touching his money."

"I think you told me last time that the man is your brother."

"Did I? That's more than I should have said, perhaps, but it's true. We grew up on a farm in County Kerry and were inseparable for years, yet I haven't seen his face for a quarter of a century, at least not knowingly. I've tried looking for his name in telephone directories and every other form of public record I can think of, but with no success. Whatever name he has been going under, it's not his real one."

Gus felt a cold shiver run through his body, as often happened whenever his instincts told him that he was onto something dangerous and incredibly important. He said,

"Do you have any photographs of your brother, from the time when you last saw him perhaps?"

"I did and that is a curious thing. We never had a camera back home on the farm, we didn't have the money for such a thing. But when we were in our late twenties, he agreed to have his picture taken with me after my ordination. Even though he had long previously lost his faith in God he came to the ceremony, as a matter of brotherly solidarity I suppose. I had the photograph framed and kept it on my bedside table for years and then, one afternoon, about five years ago, I received a call to visit a sick parishioner about a mile or so away. When I got there, I found it was a hoax and that she was healthier than I was. It was Mrs. Grogan's afternoon off and the house had been unattended while I was out. When I got back, I found the back door had been forced. My desk drawers had been ransacked, but nothing in the house appeared to have been taken - apart from one thing. The photograph. The thief even left the frame behind, undamaged, in the same spot that it had stood before. I'm certain that it was him. It must have been at the point he decided to eradicate everything that could possibly identify him. He'd suddenly remembered that I had the photograph and had made arrangements to get me out of the way and the photograph removed and probably destroyed. So now I have no pictures of him at all."

"Could you describe what he looked like to an artist, a good artist, someone who could reproduce his likeness from what you told him?"

"Vaguely, but not precisely. It's so long since I've seen even the photograph that my memory for the fine detail is less sure than it was. But even if I did that and your artist reproduced his likeness from way back, from when I last saw him, it would give me little idea of what he looks like now. He said an interesting thing when he last rang me. He said that I'd seen him recently but didn't recognise him. He presumed I didn't know it was him because his face has changed so much - as a result of age, illness, accidents, heavens knows what. But if I have indeed seen him and couldn't recognise who it was, then the change in his appearance must indeed be great."

"But he does speak to you over the telephone?"

"Yes, but never from a number I can trace. The first time he rang he said he was ringing from a public call box and that he would always do so. It was as if he was telling me straight away that if anyone ever wanted to try and find out where he was ringing from, it would be a waste of time. It's all these various things that first convinced me that he is involved with people and activities that are seriously wrong, evil, criminal, call it what you like. Anybody who goes to that degree of trouble to prevent people tracing him has some very dark secrets to hide in my experience. And whenever I've challenged him about it, he resorts to word games, he always has a clever answer to keep me guessing. But some of his comments have been quite tantalising - he has, on occasion, half-confirmed that he is involved in deeply evil things, but then backtracked so quickly that it's almost as if the half-admission had never been made. He's always enjoyed teasing me, but I think this present teasing has a firm underpinning in dark and solid fact. You told me when we first met that you run a private detectives' agency. If I had the money, I'd hire you to try and find him, to let me know what it is he really does for a living and where all this money he donates comes from."

"You don't need any money," Gus said. "I'll make enquiries for you without charge. What's his first name?"

"Padraig, although, as I said before, it's very clear he goes under another name now."

"Is there any regularity to his telephone calls, or does he just tend to ring out of the blue?"

"I never know when to expect them. Sometimes it can be weeks between calls, then suddenly he'll ring me when I'm least expecting him to. He seems to know often what I'll be doing when he rings, as if he sometimes observes me, through a half open curtain or whatever, who knows? It's a slightly weird feeling - as if he wants to see how I look, how I'm getting on, without ever giving me the pleasure of reciprocation. He asked on one occasion if my cold had got better. He'd been in the congregation for the main Sunday morning mass the week before, when I was sneezing and coughing all over the place, a man who long ago said he'd given up going to church. He'd been there obviously just to observe me and how I was. I suppose it might be a sign of some remaining good in him, as may the donating of the money, who knows? But it's very frustrating when he won't allow me in turn to see him. There are usually around three hundred people at that Sunday morning mass, so he had the ultimate protection, two hundred and ninety-nine people to hide among."

"If he observes you from time to time, both during the day and in the evening - and at weekends - it seems pretty clear that he is most likely to be living in London. Has he ever mentioned any favourite places, parts of London where you think he might aspire to live once he had become wealthy enough to be so generous with his gifts, as he is being towards the poor in your parish?"

"Now you mention it, he has always been an admirer of Georgian architecture. He loved some of the old buildings in the Georgian quarter of Dublin and I'm sure that taste will still be with him in a city with so many eighteenth-century buildings as London. He may well be in one or other of the Georgian parts of the city."

"OK, so the fact that he often observes you suggests that he may be living quite near, perhaps even within walking distance. I could be quite wrong of course, given how quickly the tube connects even quite distant parts of the city, but it's worth considering the possibility that he may be close by. I can get my assistant to identify all the Georgian buildings within a three-mile radius that currently are being used either as apartment blocks or private residences in their own right. He still has his Irish accent, as you do, I assume - he hasn't tried to modify it or disguise it as far as you know?"

"He always sounds exactly the same as he did when we were back in County Kerry."

"Good. That means there is a reasonable likelihood that if he has chosen another name for himself, it will be Irish. Again, I could be completely wrong, but it is a strong possibility worth considering. If he's thinking of a new identity, in the depth that he seems to consider all things that might help keep him unrecognised, he's likely to look for consistency. So an Irish name to go with an Irish accent is a good possibility. I'll ask my assistant to identify all of the local Georgian places of residence that have owners or tenants with Irish names. I'll get someone who does the kind of artistic recreations of faces that I suggested before to come and see you. Even though the face you describe may have changed over the years, there should be enough of its original features in your brother's present face for us to spot the likeness. The people who will be looking for him are very experienced in such matters. All being well, the number of wealthy Irishmen in the immediate locality shouldn't be too high, so my people should be able to identify them and visit them fairly rapidly. They're very good at innocent questions that can cause even the most cautious of individuals to give up just enough information for us to begin to piece together an idea of who they really are. The picture will be an additional useful aid with identification. I can't guarantee success, but it's all worth a try don't you think?"

"I do, most certainly I do. But this is extraordinarily good of you, what you suggest will take no small amount of time and effort. I feel quite uncomfortable in so far as I have no means of paying you even a fraction of what such an investigation would cost."

"Don't worry about it. My people can do it in between doing other things. It will be an interesting exercise and a useful test of my deductive skills."

As Gus hailed a cab to take him back to his Mayfair office, he felt more than a little guilty about not having told the canon the truth about his interest in his brother. If he did in fact turn out to be the elusive Kerryman and if Gus's various hunches did indeed enable him to locate his prey, then he would have to come clean to the priest about the real nature of his interest and apologise for misleading him.

It was nearly five o'clock when he got back to the office. Alice said,

"Well, did the priest and Sister Agnes confess and throw themselves upon your mercy, or do they both now have a clean enough bill of health for me to close the case and send Lady W the price of her unwanted curiosity?"

"You can close it for all eternity, I think. I have a fairly cynical view of clerics, having found several that I've encountered to be as full of the human vices they preach against as any sinner within their congregations, but Canon O'Leary is one of the good guys. I'll draft you an appropriate paragraph about my interview with him, which you can include in your report."

"Okey-dokey, I've written up my bits of the report already, so as soon as I get your paragraph, I can finish the thing and get it sent off. Let me know how much you want to charge for the interview and I'll type up the bill. Oh, and you have a telephone message by the way. Mr. One from the Land of No Manners will be dropping by at five, which is exactly one minute hence I note."

"Will he indeed? Angus will be coming to claim his pound of flesh no doubt."

"And do you have it for him? You do seem to have a natural talent for all things fleshly at the moment, Gussie, dear."

"Hm. I think somebody is on a fishing expedition again."

"Oh, just innocent curiosity."

"People with guilty faces don't have innocent curiosity. Hello, I think I hear the patter of tiny feet."

No sooner had he spoken than Mr. One's silhouette appeared against the frosted glass of the outer door. A cursory knock was followed by the usual human whirlwind of an entrance. Gus said,

"My office?"

Mr. One nodded and they disappeared inside. One said,

"I'm hoping you've got good news for me."

"Indeed. I have a promising lead."

Gus explained everything he'd learned while at Canon O'Leary's presbytery, together with his plan of action for identifying and locating Padraig O'Leary, a man who sounded very much like the elusive Kerryman. When he'd finished, Mr. One said,

"Well, even by your usual high standards, this is excellent work, Augustus. So, if I understand you correctly, you will be setting Mrs. Harding to work first thing tomorrow to identify likely buildings that our elusive friend might be living in and then you want me to use some of my resources to identify all of the wealthy Irish male residents of said buildings. I then send some of my people to do the necessary doorstepping to see if we can flush the rabbit out of its hole."

"Exactly."

"Good. An excellent plan. We'll set the ball rolling first thing tomorrow."

"I wouldn't get your hopes up too high yet, one or more of my assumptions might turn out to be wishful thinking. If I'm wrong, we can easily modify our strategy and try something else. But the downside to that is it will take a lot longer if I'm wrong - and that could lead to some additional deaths of intelligence officers while the Kerryman is still on the loose."

"We'll cross that bridge when we come to it, Augustus. For the moment we have a name and we have a plan to try and locate him, neither of which we had this morning. That's the first bit of good news I've had all week. We're still no closer to locating Polmonovski. I'll be in touch tomorrow morning. Let's hope this gets us somewhere."

With that, Mr. One was gone, sweeping past Alice with the nearest she had ever seen to a smile on his face. As Gus wandered back into her office to tell her what needed to be done the following morning, she said,

"It looks like you made a grim man almost happy - he didn't quite get there with a smile, but there was a definite flicker at the sides of his mouth. And just to add to the general sum of human happiness, somebody left you a message while you were having your confab."

"Not Lady Arabella I hope."

"Indeed not. It was a certain somebody asking you to ring her back asap."

"By 'a certain somebody' and the mischievous look in your eye, I take it you mean Jennifer Marquis?"

"Your lady of the night, indeed. Perhaps she's hoping you'll be her gentleman of the night this evening?"

"We're keen chess players, perhaps she wants a game."

Alice laughed and said,

"Fibber!"

Gus said,

"You may think so, but you have to remember that my lady of the night, as you refer to her, works twenty-four hours. Any romantic liaisons and pretty much all her general friendliness has a second dimension - she's always after something, whatever she's doing, she's always foremost an intelligence officer. She's constantly trying to get information out of me and I'm always trying to get it out of her. So, you see, when I say we're chess players, I'm being entirely accurate."

"Oh dear, you're never going to find the one true love of your life are you, Gussie, dearest? Just think what you're missing - you could have a nice, predictable and totally boring home life like George and I and yet you always go for the women who'll let you down, like yours truly, or the ones who just want information."

"I just like the excitement of the ride. When it's over I simply wait until the next one comes along. I'm not like George, I'm not cut out for the long game. Now, if you have the number that my chess playing friend rang from, I'll find out which variation of the Queen's Gambit she'll try when I ask her a difficult question or two."

"You think she might sacrifice a pawn?"

"I think Jennifer would sacrifice her own grandmother in the right circumstances."

"Oh dear, you do pick 'em, Gussie, dear."

CHAPTER SIXTEEN

Jennifer Marquis sighed and asked,

"Did anyone ever tell you that God created men to give women something to laugh at?"

Gus said,

"I thought we were created to be annoying rather than amusing."

"That too," she replied. "He's certainly hitting the ball over the line on both of those counts for me."

He followed her eyes to a bespectacled, studious looking man in his early twenties, who was seated alone at a table on the other side of the plush Savoy bar, reading a book while drinking. She said,

"If you look closely, you'll see that the book is upside down. He probably doesn't want to turn it right way up because he knows I'm watching him and he'll feel an idiot, which, of course, he most certainly is."

"And how does he know you're watching him?"

"Because he's watching me, that's why he didn't initially notice that he had the thing the wrong way up. He's one of British intelligence's finest and has been following me around for the last couple of days. I'm just trying to read the title - it's not easy to see from this distance. Is it 'Evolution' do you think? Surely, he's not brought Charles Darwin in for a bit of light reading at this time of night? Or maybe his thumb is over the 'r' and the actual title is 'Revolution'? Something by Marx do you think? That would be very appropriate reading for a third-rate functionary of a British state that still seems to be riddled with Soviet spies and double agents."

"Ouch," Gus said. "Is the CIA really so convinced that there's a mole in every hole in government buildings? You're going to tell me next, for the umpteenth time, that you believe the whole Polmonovski thing was just an attempt to distract you guys from the discovery of more Russian double agents."

"No, not just yet, I'll do that in a minute or two. For the moment I just want to wave at my friend over there and say hello. Waiter, could you take the gentleman at the table in the corner a large whisky and charge it to my bill? Tell him it comes with the compliments of the United States of America if you will - he'll understand. Thank you."

The waiter nodded and went off to do her bidding. Gus said,

"What if you're wrong? If he's that incompetent an observer perhaps he's more likely to be a shy, besotted admirer who's been following you in the hope of acquiring enough courage to ask you out."

"Oh sure, when I'm very obviously with another guy and a pretty damned handsome one at that. Do me a favour, Gussie baby, let's just admit that the Brits have lost the plot somewhat where intelligence is concerned at the moment. I mean, that guy's hardly out of short trousers. He hasn't been trained properly and he sticks out like a sore thumb. That's the beginning and the end of the story. Oh look, that was quick, his drink has just arrived."

The recipient of the gift looked across at her furtively as the waiter told him who had kindly ordered it for him. Jennifer Marquis waved at him vigorously and blew a kiss. He tried to look puzzled and, in his confusion, decided that it would be best to return to pretending to read his upside-down book. Before Gus could say anything, she had zoomed across to the embarrassed man's table. Smiling sweetly she said,

"Hello, let me help you with that."

She leaned down and gently prized the book from his hands. Turning it the right way up, she returned it to him, saying,

"There, that's much better. That will save you having to stand on your head to read your book."

Then, after blowing him a kiss, she returned to Gus, saying,

"Come on, time to go to your place. I feel the need for a bit of rodeo."

As their taxi passed Gus's Mayfair office on the way to his apartment, she closed the communication window between driver and passengers and said,

"It's kind of strange how the good Mr. Polmonovski disappeared just after I'd agreed to sit in on his interview, once your friends had reeled him in, don't you think? I suppose his whereabouts are now completely unknown and I'll be told what a terrible shame it is that I wasn't able to see for myself just how honest and accurate your guys had been concerning his role in the killing of the various intelligence officers."

"Well, as you know, I no longer work for the people you call my friends, so I only hear what little they want to tell me by way of social chit chat. But I did overhear something that leads me to believe they're very close to tracking down Polmonovski's current location, so you'll no doubt still get the interview you say they promised you. I'd say they're no more than a couple of days away from finding him. Of course, that's just my interpretation of what I heard. If you want to confirm it then it's best to go to Angus and get it straight from the horse's mouth."

Gus had had no such information, but had decided on the spur of the moment to invent it and see where it led. If Mr. One was right about the CIA possibly having some kind of hidden role in what had been going on with all the killings, then it would be interesting to see whether his bogus news had any impact on what they did next. If they, or a faction within the agency, had been responsible for Mr. P's surprise evacuation shortly before the police raid, then the news might panic them into moving him again. With rather more skilful and experienced people on their tails than the gentleman in the Savoy bar, one or more of them might actually lead straight to the fugitive crime boss. Even if Jennifer was not involved in any such covert plot, she would undoubtedly pass his news onto her colleagues and superiors and if any of them were implicated, then that might be enough to set the ball rolling. For now, he'd lit the fuse and would have to wait and see whether it simply went out like a damp squib, or whether instead it sent a rocket hurtling across the sky to wherever it was that Mr. P was holed up.

Things thereafter moved quickly. After a night of strenuous

athletic and operatic practice in Gus's bedroom, the extremely energetic Jennifer Marquis departed just before six am. Gus's telephone rang half an hour later, with an instruction to meet Angus at his club for seven o'clock in the evening precisely. The caller as usual was anonymous, speaking on an untraceable line, but the code word was correct. Gus had a hectic day, but managed to leave the office in good time. He arrived on the dot for their meeting and found Mr One already seated at a table with his salmon and boiled potatoes and a small glass of wine laid out before him. He invited Gus to sit down and told him he had already ordered his dinner for him. Gus wondered if there had been a choice in the menu, but such fine detail was obviously not of concern to his host. Mr One said,

"I'm told that Miss Marquis appeared to be having singing lessons in your apartment last night. At least that was what it sounded like from the corridor, apparently."

Gus grimaced and said,

"With so many ears listening in to my affairs you probably know more about my private life than I do, Angus."

"I'm not interested in the private bit, Augustus, old chap, I just want to know what useful information you learned from your CIA bedfellow."

Gus told him about his ruse relating to the supposed imminent locating of Polmonovski. Mr. One's reaction was that of a sun rising from a deep horizon. He said,

"Brilliant, Augustus, absolutely brilliant - and at precisely the right moment. I had another piece of good news shortly before you arrived. The base from which the helicopter that rescued Polmonovski came has been identified. Our chaps should be on site to look out for any take-offs in half an hour. I've a hunch that your little ruse might provoke some activity. We've already tapped into the communications system there, so we should get advance word of everything that happens to enable us to decide which flights might relate to our target and which don't. The RAF have an asset in place ready to follow and observe any flight. They can do that from a high altitude, so they won't be spotted. If our friends try and move him by helicopter again, we'll know when and where they move him to."

"My bogus information for Jennifer was purely speculative in terms of its premise of American involvement," Gus said. "You sound as if you're certain that it was the Americans who moved him last time."

"I am indeed. I was told that the helicopter is a CIA asset with a civilian camouflage identity. I've no idea as yet as to precisely what's going on, but we do know now that, for reasons unknown, the CIA - or a faction within it - has taken it upon itself to keep Polmonovski out of our reach. I intend that we get him back. I've no evidence as yet that Miss Marquis is a knowing participant in all of this, but clearly her reports back on our attempts to take Polmonovski into custody are being picked up by people who want to stop that from happening. We've got tails on all the likely players and that may give us some further clues as to who precisely is involved and what exactly is going on."

"I hope the tails are a little better than the amateur that Jennifer humiliated in the Savoy last night - or the two clots who made such a mess of following the trail of our message to the Kerryman."

Mr. One came closer to managing a smile than ever before. He said,

"Young clueless in the Savoy was merely a decoy to distract Miss Marquis from the serious tails. He's actually a very bright young man, but tailing is definitely not one of his strong points. I use him only as a diversionary tactic, so that the tails who actually know what they're doing can remain unspotted while persons of interest spend all their time focusing on him. As for the two who made a mess of things in Covent Garden, I've sent them for retraining. There was no excuse for that level of incompetence. The people I'm using at the moment are the best, so we should get some results."

"And the people you're sending to look for the Kerryman, they're all top notch as well?"

"As soon as your assistant has identified the most likely locations for his place of residence, I'll be putting our best spotters on the job. It's belt and braces in every respect now, Augustus. I intend that we haul in both of our big fish and find out just what's been going on. Once we've got some usable information, I'll arrange a cosy little fireside chat with my CIA counterpart and see what he has to say for himself."

"Are the Soviets still prepared to hold their fire?"

"I've had a word in the appropriate ear and they now know neither too little nor too much, just enough to persuade them that we have matters under control and that the killing of their people was nothing to do with us. They equally are entirely convincing when they say that they had no hand in the killing of our people."

Early the next morning, in another part of the city, Malone was on his hands and knees, counting the money that he had retrieved from under a floorboard in his bedroom. It was the sum of the various payments he had received for recent killings, minus the rent, coal, electricity and food bills that he had paid off using his new-found savings. He had begun his little accounting exercise after realising that he hadn't been given any more murderous jobs to do of late. He wondered if finally this was it, the end of his soul-destroying stint as a reluctant hitman. If so, he needed to know how much longer the money would last before he would have to find a new source of income. He'd thumbed his way through three quarters of the grubby bank notes when suddenly the phone rang. He jumped, almost as if he'd been kicked and an ice-cold chill slithered down his spine. He picked up the phone and the voice at the other end froze the air around him. It said,

"Good morning, Mr. Malone. There is a public telephone box around the corner from where you live, outside the post office. Go there immediately and wait for my call. You won't have to queue - you'll find an out of order notice on the door."

The line went dead. Grabbing his hat and coat, Malone hurried out of the apartment and ran to the telephone box in an unthinking panic. He'd managed to achieve something resembling calm during the past few days, bolstered by a groundless belief that things might somehow get better, that he would find some way of jumping off the treadmill of death that the Voice had forced him onto. Now all of that had been lost instantly in the fog that wrapped its icy arms around him on this cold and damp morning. He felt once more like a headless pigeon, plummeting blind and brainless into the middle of another deadly nightmare.

The telephone box was indeed labelled out of order. Almost as soon as Malone opened the door the phone rang. He picked it up. The Voice said,

"Well done, Mr. Malone, a very prompt response. I'm glad you haven't become unfit during your little rest. You will need all of your energy for the next job I have for you. When you get back to your apartment you will find that a car has been delivered to you. It is a black Riley. You'll find the keys on the mat in your hallway. In the boot you will find a suitcase containing a high-powered rifle in two pieces, plus telescopic sights, together with a submachine gun and ammunition. With them there is a map showing the location of a large country house ten miles from Dover and how to get there by road. If you choose to take this job, you will need to set off within the next half hour. I should tell you that it is an unusual assignment. If you terminate the target, you will finally have won your freedom, should you wish to claim it. If you'd prefer instead to continue earning your living as a hitman, now that you've seen how well paid the job is, you can work directly for me and I will pay you on the basis of your results. I say directly for me because, of course, until now I have been simply an intermediary, acting for the people that you got into serious debt with. One of them is now dead, killed by you, on the instructions of the other. Another contract has been placed with me this morning and it is for the life of the last remaining man who owns you, yes, the gentleman who used you to kill his partner in crime. Business is business - the client has impeccable references and is paying an extraordinarily large fee, so I have accepted the contract, subject to finding someone who chooses to carry out the assassination that has been requested. You are the most readily available name on my list of candidates and you equally will stand to benefit most from the contract's successful execution. Not only will you get an extremely generous payment, but, as I say, if you want it, you can have your freedom and leave your life as an assassin behind you. I am a man of my word, Mr. Malone - there are no strings attached. Now, time is short, so I must have your reply immediately. Do you wish to take this job? If not, you must drive the car to another address that I will give you and leave it there for someone else to pick up."

Malone could hardly think. On the one hand, the chance to regain his freedom was irresistible. But on the other, the thought of having to carry out yet another killing was causing a sense of panic mixed with deep fear inside him. This would surely be the most dangerous of all the jobs that he'd done. The man who had been moving him about on his chess board as a mere pawn would be sure to be well protected with hired guns. And how was he to know whether or not he could trust the Voice's word, how could he be sure that he would really earn his freedom? Patience was quickly running out at the other end of the line. The Voice said,

"Your time is nearly up, Mr. Malone. Yes or no please. Now."

As always, Malone buckled under the pressure. He tried desperately to focus only on the bright side, whether or not it really existed. The Voice might be being straight with him, this might indeed be a genuine chance to reclaim his freedom. The man he was being asked to kill was a killer himself, using pawns like Malone as his executioners, so why should he have any conscience about killing such a man? Perhaps the impressive amount of artillery he was being given would be sufficient to enable him to outgun the target and his bodyguards, no matter how well equipped they were, so maybe he had been overplaying the risks. But, most of all, he was terrified of hearing the click of the receiver being replaced at the other end of the line and then facing the uncertainty of what the Voice might choose to do with him. He almost shrieked,

"Yes. I'll do it. I want my freedom."

"Good man. You have my word. Carry this through successfully and you shall have it. Now, you need to be at the exact spot shown on the map by two o'clock this afternoon. From where you will be standing, you will be able to see the rear of the house where your target is hiding. At around two fifteen you should see him walk out onto the back lawn with his two bodyguards, ready to board the helicopter that by then should be hovering overhead, ready to land. You can watch them using the binoculars that you will find in the suitcase. Using those and the photograph of the target that is in the binoculars' case, you can identify your man. My client wants you to terminate him first, followed by the other two. Instructions telling you precisely how the weaponry is to be used are in the suitcase - you must follow them to the letter. Once the three men are down, the helicopter will simply fly away. You must then approach the targets, using the trees at the back of the house as cover. You must shoot them all again when you are within a hundred yards of the house. You should then go right up to them and make absolutely certain. My client wants nothing left to chance. Unless one of them is only wounded and manages to attempt a shot at you, you will not be in any danger. They will be the only people on the premises at the time. On the back of the map you will find details of your escape route and where you are to leave the car. There is a spot on a lonely country road marked on your escape route. When you get there, stop and burn the map and all other documentation, most particularly the photograph. Make sure that they are all completely destroyed before you move on. When you get back to your apartment, you will be a free man, to the extent that your recent past will allow. You made the choice to save your own life by becoming a killer, so now you will need to find a means of coping with the consequences of that choice. Until you do, you will not feel fully free. Believe me, Mr. Malone, I know these things. You will have all the time in the world to decide how you might deal with the burden of guilt that so obviously plagues you. Everyone in your position has his own means of living with the nightmares that being a murderer brings to a man who has some semblance of a conscience. Who knows, you might run despairingly back into your old religion and beg the forgiveness of the God you were taught to fear. It's up to you. Your future is between you and Him, if He exists. If you decide He doesn't, you will have to invent your own solution to the darkness that will embrace you whenever you remember the deaths you have occasioned. I, at least, will not be adding anything more to your burden. You have said you want your freedom, so you will not hear from me again. You will find an envelope on your coffee table with your final payment when you return from your assignment. That will be our last transaction. Goodbye, Mr. Malone."

With the click of the receiver at the other end, the line went dead. Malone stood there for almost a minute, in a deep trance, terrified of the task that he had been set, yet simultaneously gripped by the apparent prospect of his imminent escape from the treadmill that had been his life since that first, hope-draining call from the Voice, the single event that had set all of the killings in train. His contemplations were interrupted by someone banging on the door of the telephone box. He turned round to see a fierce looking man with the build of a house staring at him. He opened the door to leave. As he did so, the house said,

"I've been wanting to use that phone all morning and didn't

because of the notice. How did you know it was fake? Did you put it there?"

"No, no," Malone said, squeezing delicately past. "I just thought it looked a bit home-made and tried the phone to see if it was in fact working. It is, it's fine, be my guest, I've finished now."

His questioner was in two minds as to whether he believed him or should instead give him a punch on the nose, for he was most certainly a punching type of a man. His hesitation gave Malone the opportunity to slide quickly away and he hurried back to his apartment, where he found everything as the Voice had said it would be.

Half an hour later he was on the road, heading towards Dover at some speed. When he arrived at his destination, he snuck the car in between a bunch of towering elms at the side of an overgrown farm track. The track ran parallel to the crumbling, salt-whitened high brick wall of a slightly neglected country estate. At its centre was an eighteenth-century country house that rose like a grey stone marriage between a bank and a truncated Greek temple some two hundred metres away from where he stood. He could see it clearly through the hole in the wall that his written instructions told him would be there, a perfect spot to line up his rifle, ready for his final assassinations.

He hauled the suitcase out of the boot of the car and took it over to his firing spot. After going through the written instructions a final time and checking again the photo of the primary target, he assembled and loaded the rifle and laid it down beside him, ready to use. After loading the submachine gun, he checked his watch. It was nearly time. He had neutralised all of his usual, recurring qualms by telling himself continually during the drive down that he was merely killing killers, doing a social service even. He almost half-believed himself, which was enough to steady his determination. The nervous excitement he felt at being so near to being liberated from his unwanted career as a hitman gave him the remaining motivation he needed to carry things through. His terror of what might happen should he miss any of the lethal targets made him determined to get everything right first time. His army training kicked in also. He was, at that moment, the deadliest opponent the three unsuspecting criminals could face.

He pulled the binoculars out of their case and trained them on the rear of the house. While it was not a huge distance away from where he stood, he wanted to be absolutely certain of identifying the primary target. As he watched, he heard an approaching, throbbing roar that told him the helicopter was nearing the estate. As predicted by the Voice, three men came out of the house and walked towards the lawn where they expected the aircraft to land. Malone was quickly able to identify Polmonovski as the middle figure. He rested the high velocity rifle on the crumbling brickwork and took careful aim through the telescopic sights. He had placed the submachine gun next to the rifle, ready to switch from one to the other as his written instructions told him he should. As his key target stood absolutely still, staring up at the helicopter, Malone fired two shots, one at the head and one at the body. Polmonovski crumpled instantly. Before his bodyguards could react, Malone grabbed the machine gun and sprayed them with bullets, not stopping until both were motionless on the ground. As the Voice had promised, instead of landing, the helicopter rose up into the sky and started to head back the way it had come. He concluded the crew must be part of the set-up for the hit, their role being simply to lure the targets out into his sights. He reloaded the magazine and eased himself through the hole in the wall. Then, again following his written instructions, he ran towards the three fallen figures, firing the machine gun at them as he did so in mortal fear that one might still be in a condition to pull a gun on him. There was no return fire. When he arrived at the spot where they lay, he checked fearfully to see if there were any unseen gunmen, or just plain ordinary house staff watching him from within the building, but he could see no-one. As instructed, he checked the pulses of each of the men and established that they were without any signs of life. He ran into the house, fearful still that there might be witnesses who would be able to identify him in any subsequent investigation, but there was no-one. As he ran from room to room, in the quick but cautious manner he had been trained in for close contact urban fighting during his army service, all he could hear was the sound of his own footsteps on the cold marble floors. The whole building had the atmosphere of a mausoleum, something that seemed uniquely appropriate, given what had just happened.

When he was finally satisfied, he heaved a sigh of relief that was so deep and profound that it echoed back to him from all of the monumental walls, ceilings and alcoves within the dark and lifeless building. It seemed to embrace him with the final breath of death itself. He felt a piercing cold shudder ripple through his body as if something malign and ethereal had solidified into the form of a knife and sliced him in two from head to toe. Panic again set in and his focus switched now to his escape. He ran like a madman, back through the house and out across the lawn to the hole in the wall. He eased himself back through and then hurriedly but carefully collected up as many spent cartridges as he could find, packed the guns and the binoculars back into the case and loaded it into the boot. After checking his escape route once more, he eased the car onto the track and then headed back towards the road and his promised new life of retired hitman.

It was the reliability or otherwise of that promise that most preyed on his mind during the drive back to London. He'd half expected that, after he'd done the primary dirty work, a second assassin, hidden within the house, or somewhere within the woods of the estate, would then have killed him. That would have left no loose ends. But the more he thought about it, the more it seemed that there were in fact no loose ends to leave. Even if he had been caught, he couldn't have identified the Voice. He'd never seen him and he had no idea who he was or where he lived. His only contact had been via the man's voice, an Irish voice and there must be hundreds, thousands of those in London. He remembered how the Voice had told him that he would be safe as long as he never saw his face. So perhaps he would be left alive after all. Perhaps even the promise to release him from his new and unwanted trade would be honoured. Maybe the Irishman had meant exactly what he said, that his word could be trusted.

Mixed in with these frantic musings were other undercurrents of thoughts and emotions that made it hard to concentrate on the road. Several times he nearly failed to stop at junctions and on one occasion didn't see a car that was pulling out in front of him until the last moment. Feelings of immense guilt flashed through his head like momentary migraines. He tried to dismiss them by diverting his thoughts back towards the likelihood of the deal he had been offered being honoured. He couldn't remember if it was from Hamlet, or some other Shakespearean play he had studied at school, that the idea came from of somebody being despatched without any allowance for 'shriving time'. That half memory was the next worry to slide crazily towards the front of his mind. It collided head first with his long-lost Catholic upbringing. He wondered for a second or two how the possibly existing Almighty might view his having sent so many people down to hell without any prior chance to redeem themselves through last minute repentance and confessions. That thought he quickly tried to slide into a parking lot at the back of his mind, but it still slithered drunkenly around the perimeter of all his other musings. Then there was a nagging voice asking him how he was going to be able to pull himself together and resume some kind of a normal life if he was indeed now free. The initial euphoria that such freedom would bring would soon evaporate and all of the nightmares and other crippling traumas that the Voice had hinted at would come into play. He could be skipping out of the frying pan into the very hottest part of the flames beneath it. Those thoughts also he tried to park, but they too refused to play ball and weaved in and out of his mind as he drove robotically along.

When he had finally delivered the car, as instructed, to a pub car park in Camden, he headed for the nearest tube station. From the lethal hitman of the early afternoon, he had now been transformed into an unremarkable, anonymous figure, one more statistic in the early evening rush hour crowds that he joined as he boarded the train. As his stuffy carriage rattled and swung its way along the line, he was filled with a growing sense of apprehension as to what he might find when finally he got back to his apartment. He had been left alive so far, but now, with the car and guns safely back in the hands of the Voice's men, they might decide it was safest to kill him and remove the only person who could tell the police what had really happened to Polmonovski and his bodyguards. All of his earlier reassuring thoughts that he might be safe because he knew nothing about the Voice collapsed into an untidy heap within his mind. They were trampled on relentlessly by the simple realisation that it was not a matter of how he thought the Voice might really view things. The only thing that counted was how the Voice himself viewed them - and all of his words of reassurance in the morning might well turn out to be lies. He almost didn't get off the train when he came to his stop, wondering whether it would be safer just to keep going, to get a connection to a mainline station and try and disappear into somewhere like Cornwall or Scotland, places where there were large empty spaces to absorb him and give him a cloak of invisibility. But in the end, he did get off. He followed the small crowd of commuters that bustled off the train and up the escalator to the darkness and uncertainty that lay beyond. He decided that it was time to leave things to fate, that if he started running now, he might never be able to stop. And what he wanted most of all was to stop the fear that had been driving him since that first phone call from the Voice. If the only way to do that was by being killed, then so be it. The fate that previously he had tried so desperately to avoid now seemed to be entirely in the lap of the proverbial gods. He could return home and see what was waiting for him. If it was death, he could do as little about it as all of the people he had assassinated. He had returned his weapons and was unarmed. But on the other hand, there was just a chance that the Voice might have been straight with him in the morning. It might turn out that he was now safe, with no hitman waiting or coming and with the chance to try and rebuild something of a normal life, albeit one haunted by the ghosts of those he had killed. And if he ran, even to the remotest part of the country, someone as determined as the Voice would have him found and killed if he did in fact want him dead. If that was his real intention, then he was probably already having his every move followed. There would be no escape, so why bother.

As Malone hurried down the final stretch of road towards his apartment, the fear became almost unbearable. He kept looking over his shoulder at the various people he could see walking in the same feebly lamplit street, wondering which, if any of them, had a gun or a knife with his name on it, hidden within a pocket. Nobody looked suspicious or in any way out of the normal, to the extent that he could see them in the semi-shadows, but then that would be the hallmark of a truly professional killer. It would be the man who looked the least likely to kill him that would do so. He got as far as the front door of his apartment, but still there was no-one who seemed to be specifically following him. But the fear didn't subside. He began to worry now about who or what might be waiting for him inside, hiding in the kitchen, a bedroom, the bathroom, ready to kill him as soon as he closed the door behind him. He turned the key in the lock and went in.

Once inside, he scrambled feverishly to turn the living room light on. There was no-one visible, no sound other than his own breathing. He moved slowly and cautiously towards the first bedroom. Again there was no-one. He checked under the bed, inside the wardrobe, behind the curtains, but the only face he saw in the room was his own, in the dressing table mirror. He checked the second bedroom, the dining room, the kitchen and the bathroom, but again, found no-one. The only thing that was different from when he'd left in the morning was the fat envelope that sat on top of the coffee table in the living room. He approached it cautiously, half expecting it to contain a small, touch-triggered explosive device, or even something wild and exotic, like a scorpion. But its only contents were several hundred five-pound notes, more than he had ever seen before, his final payoff as the Voice had promised. He collapsed onto the settee, with the money falling all over his knees and onto the floor. The thought occurred to him that this was not just the price of three men's lives, but that of his own soul. He almost felt guilty for still being alive when he had taken so many lives of others, irrespective of whether they were good, bad or in-between. But that was a guilt to be felt and confronted much more deeply and more keenly on another day. For the moment, his fear returned. In placing the money on the coffee table, one of the Voice's men had entered his flat so easily that he had left no trace other than the envelope. This was the second occasion on which such an entry had been made. If the Voice's men could come and go so easily, they didn't need to be lying in wait for him, they could come for him at any time, when he least expected it. The money that they'd left might just be to give him a false sense of security. Once he had been killed, it could be taken back as easily as it had been delivered. He still wasn't safe.

These fears remained and multiplied throughout the next fortnight. Every evening, Malone barricaded the front door with the heavy settee and left things around the living room and dining room that he hoped any intruder would fall over, alerting him to their presence. But the only person who did trip over them was him, when getting up to fetch a glass of water in the middle of one night. He had no visitors, not even the postman. The phone didn't ring and the only voices he heard, other than when he ventured out shopping for food, were those on his radio.

Finally, on the morning of the fifteenth day after his 'retirement', he began to accept that the Voice had really meant what he said. If he'd wanted him killed, he would already be dead. He was not a man to procrastinate on such matters. If he'd have wanted the money back, he wouldn't have allowed him so much time to bank or spend it. If he'd wanted him to do another job, he would have rung by now. It seemed to Malone that the outcome that he had most hoped for but least expected had become a reality. He was finally free.

Outside, the early morning sun was causing the frost on the pavements and nearby trees to glisten and its hope-inducing light bathed the entire street. Wearing only his dressing gown, Malone opened his front door and stepped out into the icicle air and breathed it deeply, like a man surfacing from the depths of the ocean. Only a day or two previously he would have feared that so exposing himself to a dangerous world would have been the occasion for a single bullet to hit him straight between the eyes and send him plunging into oblivion. Now, he felt only relief, so much so that he hardly noticed the cold. He looked up at the clear, blue winter's sky and wondered for the first time in weeks what promise life might still hold for him. But, like the carrion crows that so favoured the surrounding trees and rooftops during the summer, dark, winged creatures sat menacingly at the back of his mind, watching over his thoughts, ready to tear any optimism to shreds with their razor claws. He had yet to work out how to come to terms with all that he had done and how to find forgiveness and someone or something to seek it from. His guilt sat on his shoulders, wearing a black cloak of death, a judge waiting to pronounce sentence. Before he could move on, he had first to confront the enormity of his crimes, his choice, as the Voice had put it, to save his own life by taking those of others. All of his attempted self-deception about being on 'military operations', of doing simply what he would have done in the army, now fell away. It was a long time since he had been a soldier and he had acted without any military or moral sanction to do what he had done. He had taken the lives of several people - the various intelligence operatives - who, for the most part, he knew nothing about and from whom he had nothing to fear. The killings had all been purely for his own sake, in his own interest. There was no escaping that. As he turned back and went into his apartment, his momentary hope had vanished. He had a much bigger nightmare now to deal with and this was only the beginning of the process.

He shut the door on the light, while he stared at the darkness inside.

CHAPTER SEVENTEEN

Gus was in his office, reviewing Alice's research on the Kerryman's most likely places of residence, when the outer door burst open and Mr. One steamed in without even a knock. Alice was drinking a coffee and was so startled by his explosive entrance that she dropped the cup, spilling the contents all over her blotting pad. She said,

"Oh good God, must you do that?"

Her angry words fell on deaf ears as the man on a mission marched regardless into Gus's office, slamming the door behind him. His bodyguard opened the outer door a discreet six inches and said, sotto voce,

"Don't let him get to you, he's even worse behaved with me. He thinks he's in the nineteenth century, charging about on his horse at the head of the dragoons. He's got twice his normal cobb on today, so he's crashing through doors as if they were the enemy, waving some bloody great sword in the air."

He smiled at Alice and then gently shut the door again, resuming his watch over the corridor.

In Gus's inner office, Mr. One had thrown his hat and coat onto a chair and was pacing up and down with a frown so deep that Gus imagined it might cut his forehead in two. He said,

"We didn't see it coming, Augustus and we should have done. We just didn't see it coming."

Gus waited with interest to learn what hadn't been seen. Mr. One paced up and down a couple more times and then said,

"You were absolutely right to feed Miss Marquis the false information that you did. It did its job and provoked an immediate reaction. The problem was that I and all of my team failed to grasp how radical that reaction might be. And now we've lost one of our best potential leads, dead as the proverbial bloody door nail."

"Are you referring to Polmonovski?"

"Absolutely. The man's been machine gunned to mincemeat along with his bodyguards. There isn't a one of them left alive to interrogate."

"Do we know who's responsible? Does it look like a CIA hit?"

"What it looks like is a bloody great mess, Augustus and the most annoying thing is that was exactly how it was planned to look. The RAF followed the CIA helicopter to the place where they had Polmonovski holed up, but it never landed to pick him up because somebody had already shot him. Even the nature of the hit was designed to maximise our confusion - a high velocity rifle mixed in, would you believe it, with a bloody submachine gun. Tell me, which of the security services - the KGB, CIA or whatever - which of them would carry out such a muddle-headed attack? It's almost as if Chicago mobsters had been imported to do the job. That's what convinces me somebody on the American side was behind it. It was made to look like a gangland hit, so that we would think it was purely the result of rivalry between competing crime bosses, with Polmonovski being taken out of the picture by people who wanted his territory. But how did they know he was there? Not even we knew where he was. The helicopter was sent, an obviously American intervention, but the crew appeared to be surprised by what they saw and turned back, making it look even more like the CIA wasn't involved in the killing. But here's the rub, I think they were involved, or rather someone within their ranks was, not necessarily acting under local instructions. I believe that particular someone had rather a lot to lose if Polmonovski talked and wanted him silenced rather than simply moved to another place of safety. So they initiated an operation of their own to have him killed before the helicopter arrived - and to create the maximum confusion as to who was most likely to have been behind the hit. And I think that this person or persons unknown cut out the middleman - for the simple reason that they had to. Previously they'd been using Polmonovski as their cover, paying him to persuade the Kerryman to do their bidding. Then the chance of their Russian friend talking became so great that they sent instructions to the Kerryman direct. I think they used him to terminate the very man who previously had been ordering the killing of others on their behalf. We didn't see how that particular transaction was carried out and who was involved, so last night I authorised the seizure of the Kerryman's contact in the Fox and Squirrel. I'm having him squeezed until the necessary information pops out onto my desk."

"That's if they used him," Gus said. "They may have had another route, something a little more direct perhaps."

"Possibly, but my suspicion is that if there is such a route Polmonovski kept it pretty close to his chest. I think they would have had to use the Fox and Squirrel man if they wanted their own line of communication - he's well known as the Kerryman's gatekeeper among the underworld. My people have checked him out, following the fiasco in the market, and everyone has to go through him as the first point of access. Only a very favoured few get to speak to the Kerryman direct and even then, it's only ever over a public phone line."

"OK, good luck with the grilling. What would you like me to do?"

"While we're waiting for the results of the interrogation, I want us to get moving as quickly as possible in the hunt for the Kerryman himself. It's our belief that his contact won't have much idea as to how to find him. We think the communication route is a long and convoluted one and that he knows little more than how to send messages off on the first stage of their journey. So I need to know how you've been getting on with your research."

"I've just been looking at the work Alice has now finished, with her customary efficiency, which, as always, is excellent. You really ought to try congratulating her on the way out, Angus, you do rather tend to steam straight past her as if she's little more than a skivvy."

"Yes, well, I'm not much good at dealing with women, Augustus, never have been. Too many years in the army, too many years out in the empire. I only really know how to command men. Perhaps you could have a word, tell her I'm grateful, something like that."

Gus raised his eyebrows, but didn't respond. Mr. One said, "So what is it that Mrs. Harding has found for us?"

"To be precise, no less than ten possible locations where our target may be residing. I've been studying the information she's dug up and I'm pretty certain you'll find him in one of these."

He showed Mr. One the paperwork spread out across his desk. After examining it closely for a few minutes, the commander of men said,

"Excellent work. You can tell her that. If you can put all of this into an envelope file, I'll take it with me and I'll get my men hunting straight away. As soon as we've got some kind of a result from the interrogation I'll be back in touch. If Miss Marquis is in any way implicated, I may need you to help me set the trap that will catch her - that's if you're not too personally involved?"

"I always keep my private and professional lives in separate boxes, Angus, you know that. If she's involved then she has simply been using me and I shall have absolutely no compunction about helping you reel her in."

"Good man. This is all going to get very complicated, with the Americans supposedly being our closest ally and all of that stuff. But if they've been working against our interests on our home turf, we'll have to put a stop to it one way or another."

Gus had been busy inserting Alice's research into a file while they spoke. He handed it to Mr. One, who said,

"Thank you, Augustus. We'll speak again shortly I hope."

He then grabbed his coat and hat and hurried out. As he passed the fiercely frowning Alice he said,

"I believe Augustus has something to say to you. Good morning Mrs. Harding."

With that he swept out of the room. Alice looked startled. As Gus emerged from his inner office she said,

"Am I imagining things, or did Mr. One just acknowledge my existence, no, more than that, did I actually hear him say good morning to me?"

"It's what he didn't say that's more interesting," Gus said. "He told me to congratulate you on excellent work in identifying the various possible residences of our Kerry friend."

"Well hit me with a kipper and tickle me under my chin," Alice said. "That must be a first in anyone's book - Mr. One actually paying a woman a compliment."

"Well, you can do what you like with the kipper, but I think I'd better leave the chin tickling to George if I'm not to get a black eye," Gus replied.

By lunchtime, Mr. One's hunters were at work, using a variety of cover stories to try and prise information out of the neighbours of the Georgian residences that had been identified. They avoided knocking on the doors of the ten shortlisted target houses, on the assumption that if any of them was the Kerryman's residence, it would be one of his minders that opened the door rather than him, leaving them little the wiser as to whether their suspect was inside. Rather than risk alerting him through such a direct approach, they wanted to see if the artist's likeness rang a bell with any of the neighbours first. If it did, the order would then be given to move in and seize him. By four o'clock it was clear that six addresses could be wiped off the list. By the following morning they had narrowed their search down to a single address sitting in the middle of a quiet terrace of large Georgian townhouses. Gus was mulling over a file from a new, potentially very lucrative case when Alice knocked on his door to tell him that Mr. One needed to see him urgently and had sent a driver to pick him up.

Twenty minutes later he arrived at what was believed to be the Kerryman's house. Mr. One was standing on the steps outside with a look of exasperation on his face. As Gus got out of the car he said,

"I can't believe it, Augustus, this man is like a ghost. One of the neighbours recognised him instantly from the artist's impression that we showed him and we've been watching the house since eight-thirty. He'd been seen leaving at eight apparently. He returned at nine, but spotted our men moving towards him from the opposite side of the road. He shot into the house, but our chaps had the door open within less than a minute. When they got inside, they found an empty building. We had men watching the rear as well and nobody was seen coming out. We've searched the damn place from top to bottom, every cupboard, nook and cranny, the loft space, everywhere, but nothing. The man has literally disappeared into thin air. Frankly, I'm desperate - who on earth are we dealing with, Houdini? We keep getting so near, but always end up further away than ever. I need you to cast a fresh pair of eyes over the place. There's something we're missing I know and there's little that escapes your gaze."

"Is there a cellar?"

"Yes, we've checked down there. There's no sign of anybody."

Gus walked up and down the long, marble floored hallway, looking into the rooms that led off from it. He inspected the furniture in each, running his hands along the tops of cabinets, tables and chair arms. He then walked up to Mr. One and showed him his palms. He said,

"What do you see, Angus?"

"What? Dirt, dust."

"Yes. Lots and lots of dust, enough to suggest that this is a house that isn't actually lived in. Let's have a look at the food supply."

He strode quickly into the kitchen at the back of the house and threw open all of the cupboard doors. The shelves were completely empty. He said,

"Which was the house that identified our target?"

"The one on the right."

"What about the one on the left?"

"Our chaps couldn't get any answer. The people on the right said that they'd seen a thick set, middle-aged woman going in and out from time to time, but they didn't know much about her and said she always wore a headscarf, which made it difficult to see her face properly. She seemed to have some sort of disability, she always walked with a limp and her head down."

"Has she been seen going out of the house this morning, most particularly, during the time since the Kerryman came in here?"

Mr. One instructed one of his men to go and check with those still watching the rear and the watcher who had been left stationed outside the front of the house. When the man returned, he said,

"The chaps at the back noticed a middle-aged woman with a limp going out about half an hour ago. She was carrying a couple of shopping bags apparently. They didn't get much of a look at her because of the headscarf she was wearing."

Gus said,

"It's probably far too late now, but you need to send a car to see if they can spot this character and pick them up. I think you'll find that they're our man in the simplest of disguises. It looks like your people were asleep on the job, Angus. Let's take a closer look at the cellar."

He led a little party down into the musty undercroft. The dividing wall between it and the house next door appeared to be solid all along. Gus crouched down by a section of brickwork that was about ten feet from the front of the house. He ran his finger through a small but noticeable mound of brick and mortar dust on the stone flagged floor. It stretched for about three feet along the line of the wall. He said,

"It's just an informed guess, but I think this little lot has been the result of repeated heavy vibrations from above impacting on old brickwork and shaking off any loose flakes. I suspect that we're standing directly under the fireplace in the room above. If you look at it closely you may well find that it has a false back, behind which a hole has been knocked through from one house to the other. The builders have used such force that they've created this little mound of dust. If I'm right, then that's the very simple explanation for our target's mysterious disappearance. Does he actually own this house, Angus?"

"He rents it according to the landlord, using an alias of course. We've got him in the back of a car outside in case we need him."

"OK. I think our target has probably been renting the house next door also under another alias. He has a concealed means of moving between the two houses, which, as I've said, I think we'll find is the fireplace above. When he's dressed as himself, he goes in and out of this house. When he wants to move around in disguise, he goes in and out of the one next door. But whatever he's wearing, he only actually lives in the one next door for security reasons. Anybody seeing him going in here and attempting to follow him would have ended up as baffled as you were this morning. I suspect he also has some kind of a warning device in this house to let him know if there are intruders, to give him time to make good his escape from next door. If we had the time to look, we'd no doubt find it. Let's go and check the fireplace upstairs. If it contains the concealed exit that I think it does, we need to have a look next door to see if our man's left us any clues when making his hasty escape."

It took Gus less than ten minutes to find the mechanism which controlled the concealed door between the two houses. It was indeed at the back of the large Georgian fireplace in the room above. The device released a three-foot-by-three-foot square of brickwork, which slid backwards easily along guide rails in the floor of the house next door. Gus and Mr. One eased themselves through, followed by Mr. One's several helpers. Unlike the Kerryman's 'entrance house', this building was very obviously in constant use. A half empty cup of coffee from breakfast sat on a small side table, next to what was obviously the Kerryman's favourite armchair in the drawing room. His bed upstairs was only half made and a freshly damp towel was draped over the side of the bath. The kitchen cupboards and two American fridges were full of food and the wine cellar was heavily stocked with expensive labels and vintages. The previous day's Times newspaper rested on a cushion on the ornately decorated settee and a heavily gilded, hand-painted Royal Worcester bowl, full of fresh fruit, graced the centre of the coffee table in the lounge. His bedroom was most telling of all. The large wardrobes were stuffed with suits, jackets and shirts that collectively would have cost around five times Mr. One's annual salary. The large one in the middle was in some disarray. The escapee obviously had grabbed a variety of items from it, given several gaps on the racks. Those he had quickly thought about but then rejected lay strewn on the floor. Presumably the 'middle-aged lady' had been carrying the chosen items in the two shopping bags that she was seen with. The bird had most certainly flown in great haste and fooled everyone for long enough to make good 'her' escape.

Try as they might, neither Gus nor Mr. One could find anything of an incriminating nature in the house, which very obviously had been kept sterile in terms of evidence relating to the Kerryman's murderous business interests. They couldn't even find anything that definitely confirmed it was him that had been living there, or so they thought. Things changed somewhat when Gus opened the top drawer in the Chippendale dressing table. Staring up at him from a crumpled photograph were the eyes of two brothers. A hastily scribbled note was attached with a paperclip. When Gus read it, he gasped. Mr. One asked what was the matter. He said,

"Listen to this - 'Please return this to my brother Mr. Benedict. If you and your friends have located me here you will now know well enough what I look like.' He clearly knew that I was working with you and was after him. He's been keeping an eye on us all the time we were trying to find him - or rather, his alter ego, the middle-aged lady, has been observing us, without either of us even noticing her."

As he was speaking, the men who had been sent in pursuit of the heavily disguised escapee came through the door in the wall. When Mr. One asked them if they'd found him, the news, as expected, wasn't good. The more senior of the two men said,

"We looked for the bag lady everywhere and found nothing. We came across a couple of uniforms on foot patrol and, just on the off chance, asked them if they'd spotted anyone fitting her description. One of them was a bright spark with sharp eyes. He'd noticed someone he assumed to be a woman with two shopping bags and a pronounced limp getting into a Bentley that slowed down to pick her up. The only reason he noticed was because of the contrast between the shabbily dressed woman and the posh wheels. He didn't make a note of the numberplate unfortunately."

"We'll have that already," One said. "It will be the same car that dropped the target off at the house earlier this morning and one of the chaps made a note of the registration number then."

"Someone that smart will only have rented the car," Gus said. "It will already be dumped somewhere and he'll be in a much less noticeable vehicle by now, heading no doubt to a safe house that he will have kept for precisely such an emergency as this. You can and indeed must tell the police to watch out for the car, just in case, but I'm pretty certain that it will simply turn up abandoned in a car park, or some such."

"So, yet again we've failed," Mr. One said despairingly.

Gus said,

"Failed? It depends what you believe failure to mean. We've disrupted the network responsible for the killing of British and Russian intelligence officers from top to bottom, so much so that they've panicked and eliminated one of their own, the good, or rather exceedingly bad Mr. P. The Kerryman is ninety-five percent likely to have fled London and his gatekeeper is in your custody, so he's not going to be open for business again in this part of the world any time soon. We'll only have failed if we don't get to the bottom of who it is that's been driving all of this and that's where our gatekeeper friend could be really helpful. How's the interrogation going, Angus?"

"That I need to find out, urgently. Thank you for your words of comfort, Augustus, I'll try my best to believe you're right. I must get back to see whether our friend is being as cooperative as you hope he might be. My chaps have been offering him some rather compelling reasons as to why he should help us. The news that the man he's principally afraid of is most probably no longer in town may be that crucial little extra that persuades him to be talkative. I'll be in touch if I need you again today, so don't stray too far from your office. One of my men will run you back."

On the other side of London, a medium sized, everyday black Austin saloon was just about to leave the city boundary as it headed north, very far north in fact. In the back, the Kerryman had changed into some of the male clothing that he had spirited out of the house during his escape. He had acquired a false moustache, spectacles and a decidedly grey tint in place of his previously dark brown hair. His driver had changed from the chauffeur's attire he'd been wearing previously into cheap casual clothing. They were heading towards Scotland or, to be more precise, Loch Lomond. The Kerryman had a very impressive castellated stone house that looked down on the loch far below from the mountains. He liked buildings that resembled castles almost as much as he liked Georgian houses, although he had been careful never to tell his priestly brother of this fact. The grounds of his 'castle' were large enough for him to completely disappear from public view behind the high estate walls. Normally, he visited it about four or five times a year. It was now about to become his permanent residence, from which he could manage his very profitable secondary 'business interests' in Glasgow. Leaving London was inconvenient and he had been extremely fond of his Georgian town houses, even if he did only rent them. But he had made more than enough money there to be able to semi-retire if he so chose and Scotland was his second most favourite place in the world, so moving there quite appealed to him. His Glasgow operation was much less time consuming than his London one had been and he would have more time to pursue his various leisure interests. He rather fancied being a laird and unlike his London residences, he owned every stone and every sod of soil on the Scottish estate.

Among his many talents, he was an excellent mimic. He was

proud of his ability to speak very credibly with a Houston accent that he had picked up from an American client with whom he had conducted numerous telephone conversations. He used it every second of his time in Scotland, even when he was alone, in order to ensure that he remained in character as the rich American oil millionaire that everyone who knew of him around Loch Lomond and Glasgow presumed him to be. He always wore sunglasses outside of the house to further lessen the chance of being recognised and never let anyone see him without the walking stick that he needed as a result of the old war wound he'd never had. He was, as he well knew, in every way a consummate actor and enjoyed every minute of his performances. His skill had enabled him to spy freely on his brother, Gus and anyone he felt the need to observe closely in the interests of his own security. He felt particularly proud that someone like Gus, who his research told him was a particularly astute observer of almost anything, had never had the faintest idea when he was being followed or generally observed. It seemed almost a pity that their paths would never cross again, so great had been the satisfaction of putting one over on one of the finest intelligence operatives the British had ever had.

He felt extremely relaxed about his future prospects. Even if his pursuers ever did manage to discover where he'd escaped to, he had adequate preparations in place to enable him to evacuate himself and his now considerable wealth back to Ireland. He anticipated being long gone before they managed to navigate their way past the traps and obstacles that it had amused him to put in place along and under the lawns and the very long drive that led from the main gates to the house.

The police, meanwhile, had been highly efficient in tracking down the Bentley. It was found sitting in a north London car park. The officer who spotted it was not amused to find a hastily written note on the dashboard. It said,

"Dear Constabulary Friends, please return to Warren and Co Limousine Hire with my compliments and thank them on my behalf for their many years of supplying me with excellent cars. Don't forget to tip the gentleman who opens the door for you at their premises. Sorry I didn't have time to say hello, but may I instead use this opportunity to say a very sincere goodbye."

Several hours later, the Kerryman was still entertaining himself by imagining how infuriated the police would be when they found his little note. His attention switched to more mundane matters when the Austin suddenly pulled into the side of a steep mountain road. His driver had been instructed to look for somewhere to stop where they could relieve themselves. He had found a familiar spot that he remembered from their previous journeys to and from Loch Lomond. It was, he reflected, the perfect place for what needed to be done. It was now pitch dark and they were deep inside Scotland. The driver opened the rear door and said,

"Don't go beyond the fence at the side of the road. It's a sheer drop behind it."

His master nodded. He got out and walked to within about a foot of the fence, his thoughts now smugly focused on the ease with which he had managed his escape from the assembled forces of the British intelligence services. Looking out into the blackness, he could just make out the tiny lights of some dwellings far below. He was taken completely by surprise when his muscular driver, the man he had relied upon and trusted for the last ten years, grabbed him by his trouser belt and collar and in one swift, perfectly executed manoeuvre, lifted him above the fence and then hurled him into space. He'd always imagined that the great care he took with his personal security would allow him to live to a ripe old age. Before he died, he would think up some way to cover himself, just in case there was the God, judgment day and all the other stuff his brother believed in. He'd find some form of words to explain and excuse his actions – and of course, he'd never killed anyone himself. All he had ever done was give people choices - he might even argue that he was testing their mettle on behalf of the Almighty, principally by finding out if people like Malone had the moral strength to resist saving their own worthless lives by becoming hitmen and taking those of others. But in the fleeting seconds between his being hurled over the edge of the six hundred feet drop and his skull being smashed to pieces on the rocks below, he had no time for any such thoughts, or the pleas for forgiveness of his sins that his brother would have wished him to make - no shriving time, as Mr. Malone would have put it. The only thoughts that went through his head were a simple, terrified question, followed by his final denial of reality - "What the hell is happening? It can't be happening to me." But it was. When he hit the rocks, for the merest nano second his brain was filled with an almighty flash, followed by nothing, a long, permanent nothing. From being the cleverest of killers, the Kerryman had been transformed in an instant to a simple everyday corpse, awaiting discovery, burial and the slow, damp rot of the earth.

Six hundred feet above, the driver unlocked the car boot, opened one of the several bags within it, and shone a flashlight inside. There, staring back at him, were the three hundred thousand pounds of non-bankable cash that had been too much of a temptation to resist. It was non-bankable because the Kerryman had been certain that it had come from the proceeds of heists where the notes would be traceable by the police. Some of his clients could and would only pay him with this type of money. The driver wasn't aware of this fine detail. He had opened one of the bags in a moment of idle curiosity when loading the boot and all that he had seen was an incredible amount of wealth that could be his for the asking. This was a little bit of ignorance that would cause him considerable problems in the future when he tried to bank some of the money. For now, all was anticipation and delight. He smiled to himself and closed the bag. He got in the car and drove on until he found a place where he could safely reverse and turn round. Then he headed back towards England, back towards a large empty cottage that the Kerryman kept in Yorkshire as one of his several safe houses to be used in emergencies. It would be the perfect place to hide away until any hue and cry had subsided. The man he had worked for during the last ten years, and whom he had so successfully convinced of his undying loyalty, hardly crossed his psychopathic mind as his body lay, face down and broken on the rocks.

Like the Kerryman, the driver felt very relaxed about his future prospects.

CHAPTER EIGHTEEN

Jennifer Marquis slipped into the office so quietly that Alice didn't hear her. It was only when she turned round from the filing cabinet that she saw the familiar figure in black disappearing into Gus's office. Alice had a bad headache and was less than delighted to see someone who, privately, she had now come to regard as utterly and wholly bad for Gus. Initially, she had found Marquis's effect on him to be amusing, but the more she saw of her the more she appeared to be bad news. There was something about the woman that seemed to spell trouble with a capital 'T'. It was nearly half past four and Alice's prior thoughts had been entirely focussed on going home at five, taking an aspirin and retiring for a nap for an hour before dinner. This was very much an interruption that threatened her schedule. She said, sharply,

"He's not back yet. He said he'd be about five minutes. I don't wish to sound rude, Miss Marquis, but it might be just a little bit courteous if you'd knock and take a seat like everyone else instead of always assuming you own the place. That part of the office is supposed to be private."

The lady in black wandered casually over to her and smiled. She said,

"I'm not a client, honey, I'm an equal to your boss and superior in every way to you. I don't need to take a seat. I can do what the hell I like and if I could I'd get your sweet little ass fired."

That was the match that lit the fuse. Alice's throbbing headache was in charge and it did the talking. She said,

"Well, sadly for you, that's not possible and if I could I'd give your 'sweet little ass' a great big kick. Frankly my dear, far from being superior, you strike me as the nearest I've seen to the Whore of Babylon. Quite what Gus sees in you is impossible to fathom."

"My, how it misjudges its position in the world. You're just a jumped-up office girl, lady, so don't try muscle talking to someone who could snap you in two if she was so inclined. You want people to sit down, then you sit down - and shut that prissy little mouth of yours until the big boy arrives and he and I can have a grown-up conversation. You can play with your dollies on the floor if you like, or is that too advanced an activity for someone with your capabilities?"

They were eyeing each other like two lionesses about to strike. It was at that moment that Gus walked in. He pretended not to sense the atmosphere of menace and loathing, preferring a quiet life as a result of having had two whiskies too many while celebrating an old school friend's birthday at lunchtime. He said,

"Good afternoon ladies. How nice to see you, Jennifer - is this a business or a social visit?"

The lady in black switched in an instant from menace to charm. She said,

"Well, seeing you is always a pleasure, Gus, so there's a little bit of the social side of things, mixed in with a little bit of business. Can we talk privately?"

As she entered his office, she turned and smiled angelically at Alice, while shutting the door behind her. As Gus eased himself into his comforting leather desk chair he said,

"I've not heard from you since our last little rodeo - you remember, the one following your ritual humiliation of the man in the Savoy? Have things been busy in the American Conspiracy Theory Factory?"

"Well, someone's been busy, that's for sure. It seems that Mr. Polmonovski has ceased to be a man whose interview I could attend."

"Has he indeed?" Gus asked nonchalantly. "And who is to blame for that do you think?"

"I was wondering what you thought."

"Oh, I think very little nowadays. Too much whisky, too few rodeos, you know the kind of thing."

"Well, the social part of my visit just happens to be about rodeos as it happens. I was wondering if you'd care to join me for dinner at the Savoy tonight. Perhaps we could see if my little friend turns up again and then, after I've humiliated him even more than last time, we could slip-slide our way over to your place for a little bit of this and a little bit of that."

"I'm always in favour of this and that," Gus said, "although I'll have to moderate my intake of the hard stuff at dinner. My head is still recovering from a liquid lunch that had a little too much liquid."

"Oh, I'm sure I can cosset it back into rude health, or certainly the rude bit anyway."

"I'm sure you can my dear," Gus said, smiling sweetly.

One taxi ride, three hours and half a bottle of wine later, they had almost finished their dinner at the Savoy before the lady in black returned to the topic of Polmonovski. She said,

"If I could divert our little chat away from pleasure to business for just a minute or two, I was wondering if those super-acute pussycat ears of yours had overheard any gossip as to who might have been responsible for the murder of Mr. P and his cronies. I know you pleaded ignorance earlier, but you are not an ignorant man, Gussie baby."

Gus smiled enigmatically. He said,

"Well, I've heard the occasional whisper floating in the breeze. There appears to be a theory in some parts that the CIA might have had a hand in things, although, as I say, that's no more than a whisper."

"Really? You may be surprised to hear that it's a whisper we've heard as well, and like all such whispers that concern our good name, we've been taking it rather seriously."

"Does that mean that the whisper might be true?"

"I didn't say that. My own number one suspects are your friends in Brit intelligence. I still think they're trying desperately to cover up something that's really embarrassing - and my suspicion is that it's all about Russian moles in the hole again."

"But clearly there's now a number two suspect as well."

"Well, not so much a suspect as the need to eliminate possibilities."

"What kind of possibilities?"

"Oh, the kind that suggest we may have a freelance operator or two working under our roof with agendas that are rather more radical than ours. It's been my job to come up with a shortlist of possible candidates. I've found a couple that we need to run a check on, but I wondered if the whispers you'd heard contained any names or other possible identifying factors that might be of help. It would, of course, be very much in British interests if we could be told of these. While, as I say, your guys are still my primary suspects, if we were to find that we had bandits in the camp, then we could deal with them in a manner that would benefit Washington and London equally."

"Well, much as I'd like to help, the whispers I've heard haven't had any names attached," Gus lied. He decided that it would be best if she remained ignorant of the fact that Mr. One considered her as much of a suspect as anyone else.

"OK. I just thought I'd see what you'd heard. If we do come up with anything on our side of the bridge, I'll let Angus know, or would you prefer to tell him yourself?"

"Oh, Angus and I only talk about chess nowadays. We're both in the same chess club, or didn't you know that?"

"And there was me thinking it was tiddledywinks you spent all your time chatting about. Your friends seem to have upped their game, by the way, I still haven't worked out which of the people in here tonight are the ones keeping an eye on me - or am I staring him straight in the face?"

"Perhaps if they've decided you're on the side of the good guys they aren't watching you at all."

"Perhaps. Are you looking forward to our little rodeo tonight?"

"I've got my cowboy boots sitting ready by the side of the bed."

"Well, that'll be a first, I've never ridden a steer with boots on before."

At that interesting point in the conversation a waiter approached with a sealed note on a tray, which he promptly gave to her and retreated. Her face clouded over as she read it. She said,

"Drat. It looks like things have developed a little faster than I thought they might. I'm afraid I have to fly honey pie. You stay here and finish your meal, it's on me. I'll ride that steer with the boots on another night soon, I promise."

She gave him a peck on the cheek before she left and then

hurried out. Gus felt very much like a man who'd been offered a glimpse of the northern lights in all their luminescent glory, only to find that he'd been left staring disbelievingly at faintly glowing Manchester street lamps, in the rain.

He was still reflecting on paradise lost the following morning, when Mr. One's driver burst into the office with an urgent request for his presence at an upmarket pub in the West End, the Unicorn and the Dragon. When he arrived, Gus was ushered through to a private room at the back, where his host sat drinking alone, while reading an exceedingly fat file. Mr. One looked up and said,

"Ah, Gus, take a seat. This file is non-existent by the way, a figment of your imagination - as you will be aware, nothing of a highly sensitive nature ever leaves the office."

Gus smiled wryly and nodded. Mr. One said,

"What's your poison - whisky as usual?"

"No, thanks anyway, Angus, it's a bit early for me."

"Whatever. I'm sorry for the radio silence over the last week or so. I've had three deeply serious problems coming to a head at once, I'm afraid, so I haven't been in a position to keep you as updated as I would have liked. There have been some interesting developments which you need to know about."

Mr. One took a sip of his port and leaned forwards in his most confidential mode. He said,

"It appears the Kerryman is no longer a problem. We got the police to put out his description nationwide, including the possibility that he may be disguised as a woman, and got a quite unexpected result four days ago. A body had been found in the Scottish mountains, not far from Loch Lomond. At first it was thought that it was just some careless winter tourist who'd fallen while out walking, but during the post mortem the deceased, a middle-aged man, was found to be wearing a false moustache. There were also traces of lipstick around his mouth, which alerted the bright young investigating officer to the possibility that the victim might be our man from the wanted list. The body was in such a broken state as a result of the fall that it was difficult to identify the face, so we sent someone to ask the Kerryman's brother if he had any distinguishing marks that might help us identify him. It turned out he had a highly distinctive birthmark on his left thigh and a stub instead of a thumb on his left hand as a result of a farming accident as a boy. The body in Scotland was an exact match. Once we told our friend from the Fox and Squirrel that the man whom he so obviously feared had taken an unexpected trip to the afterlife, he relaxed a little. In return for us promising to keep him out of it, he told us that on the day before Polmonovski was killed he had been given a message to send to the Kerryman about an urgently needed gangland hit. He'd been given a sizeable wedge of cash to cover his own fee in the matter and he believes that the sealed note to the Kerryman promised a huge payment in exchange for the killing, as long as it was done asap. That was what his client implied during their conversation. He wasn't told who the target would be, that was in the sealed note and the penalty for opening a sealed note to the Kerryman was so unpleasant that he never dared dream of having a look inside. But it was clear that the target was a very big name in the criminal underworld."

"Has he given you the identity of the client, the person who gave him the message?"

"He has, but only on the basis of us telling that person that he was seen talking to our gatekeeper friend by one of our men and not that it was the gatekeeper himself who grassed on him. I'm perfectly happy to honour such a promise. Our man is a Welshman, Owen Grazeborn."

"Have you pulled him in?"

"That's where things have got a little bit messy again. My men have asked around and he hasn't been seen since his conversation with the gatekeeper. It seems he's involved in all kinds of rackets and he's rumoured to have used the Kerryman's services to erase a couple of problem individuals in the past. If the CIA wanted to approach the Kerryman via someone who already had his trust, then Mr. Grazeborn was their man. Nobody has a clue where he now is. You are a man with underworld contacts that we don't have. I'm thinking particularly of Mr. Tasty, or whatever his name is. We've tried talking to him but got nowhere. One of my men is still nursing a black eye and a severely sprained wrist after arousing Mr. Tasty's wrath and I'm rather short of chaps at the moment with all the things that are going on. I suspect your friend might be rather more cooperative if you talk to him. He's famously the man who knows pretty well everything that's going on under the radar, or so I'm told, so he may know where we can find our Welsh chap."

"Tasty can be a very helpful man if he so chooses. I'll have a word and see what he says."

"Please do - and as soon as possible. I don't want another trail going cold before we've had time to catch the wildlife. If we can find this Welsh chap, we're only one step away from the people behind all these killings. I think this man can give us the final piece to complete the jigsaw, Augustus."

"Well, jigsaws certainly beat tiddledywinks," Gus replied.

Mr. One looked baffled and said,

"What on earth are you on about, Augustus?"

"Oh, it just reminded me of a bit of banter with Jennifer Marquis."

"Really? Speaking of Miss Marquis, how did your little tete-a-tete with her go last night?"

"Did your man not tell you?"

"Now, now, Augustus, we don't pry to that extent, not when a trusted 'one of our own' is involved at least. We were more interested in seeing where your lady friend went when she left the Savoy."

"And where was that?"

"The American embassy. There was something big underway - she was picked up in a car with the bureau chief, his right-hand man and a gentleman who we believe conducts all of their most significant interrogations. It's unusual to see that combination of individuals going into the embassy together at such a late hour. All of those people are still in the building. I think there is someone inside who they hope might gift them some extremely useful information, if given a little bit of encouragement, shall we say."

"Have you any idea what the information might be about?"

"That's where you might be able to help, Augustus. Did Miss Marquis give any hints as to what was going on? She does like to play games with me, through you, as you well know, so it's possible she might have said something that gives us a clue, if she thought there was some mutual advantage in our being alerted to whatever was underway."

Gus said,

"Yes, she had a message - I was going to mention it anyway.

She very obviously wanted you to know that she was looking into suspicions that there may be a rogue operator on the American side, somebody who needed Polmonovski dead if his cover wasn't to be blown. She made it clear that her main suspects for his murder were still your people, but I think she's giving you the message that the CIA is taking the trouble to look under its own floorboards as well as ours. She said something about things developing more quickly than she'd expected when she left, so maybe they'd found a trail that led all the way back to a specific suspect."

"Interesting. Did she say anything more?"

"She offered an olive branch - she said if your people had any leads on possible suspects among her people, she'd be appreciative if you could let her know."

"Even more interesting. Did you tell her that she's on my list of suspects?"

"I thought it would be best to plead ignorance on that point."

"Indeed. Whatever you do, don't give her any idea that we're looking for our Welsh friend. If word of that gets through to the same person or persons who ordered the killing of Polmonovski, I wouldn't fancy his chances of surviving until the end of the week."

"Well, if it is a rogue element within the CIA, they won't be able to use the Kerryman as their cover to go after the Welshman."

"Indeed. Well, don't let me detain you, Augustus, the sooner you have a word with Mr. Tasty and get back to me the better."

It was fortunate that Thursdays were the one day of the week when Gus always knew where he could find Tasty at lunchtime. He had some kind of a money collection round during Thursday mornings, probably a protection racket, that always ended in Nellie Nolan's Pie and Chips Restaurant, at around midday. Gus was already seated at what he knew to be Tasty's favourite table when the big man rolled in, right on cue. Tasty laughed and said,

"You're a cheeky chancer, Gus, me old china, nobody dares sit at that table without an invite. You're just about the only one I'd let get away with it."

"So, can I be reasonably sure that my fork isn't going to be inserted into my nostrils?" Gus enquired with a smile.

As Tasty took his hat and coat off and sat down opposite, he said,

"Depends why you're here Mr. Augustus Benedict. I do like that name of yours, very grand, fit for a bishop. Here, Stella, I'll have what he's having, cod and chips and a cuppa."

The young waitress smiled and nodded, then disappeared into the kitchen to place his order. He pinched one of the chips off Gus's plate and bit it in two, savouring the taste. He said,

"As the bill is on you, me old mate, you won't mind if I have a little starter off your plate - that's what they call it in all the posh restaurants isn't it, a starter? I was a minder for a while when I first began my illustrious career and I used to have to watch while my boss sat there scoffing posh nosh. I was lucky if I ended up with much more than a cup of tea and a sandwich. He was a mean old bastard, so mean I looked the other way when he eventually bought it. Now then, to what do I owe the pleasure of your company, Gus, me old mate?"

"My 'hush hush' friends, as you call them, are in urgent need of your help Tasty. They just need to know where someone is so that they can ask him for some information that might stop a few more of their people being killed. They won't hand him to the police or anything like that, in fact they've no interest in his criminal activities whatsoever, but he does have some vital information that they need."

"Oh, I get it, it's all to do with that geezer that tried to muscle me yesterday about Taffy Grazeborn isn't it? Just like a toff, thought he could throw a posh accent at me and I'd doff me hat and give him whatever he wanted. When that failed, he tried the heavy stuff. Now that was a mistake. He was a big man but not big enough - I gave him a shiner and a sharp pain in his arm, then shoved him head first into a dustbin round the back of the Bull and China. It was ever such an entertaining sight to watch his dainty legs thrashing about in the air. You see, they just don't understand how to ask for things politely some of these geezers. That's why they've sent you isn't it? You know how to ask properly."

Gus smiled and said,

"You know me Tasty, I'm extremely polite. Besides, the dustbins here are all full and you'd never get me in."

Tasty laughed and said,

"You are a one, Gus, me old china. If you want me to let you know where Taffy is it's on condition that you tell a little porky pie to your 'hush hush' friends in return. You tell them that you couldn't get a civil word out of me and that I told you to sling your hook, but say that you got lucky from another source. That way I don't get the hassle of Taffy turning up on me doorstep wanting to know why I've been saying what he thinks I shouldn't and I also don't get your lot bothering me again. I wouldn't want them to think that I'd turned friendly. Is that a deal?"

"Absolutely," Gus said.

"I don't need to tell you that deals are break-a-leg things with me - as in you double cross me and I break your leg. But then you're an honourable man, so I mention that little warning more as a courtesy than a threat. As you know, Gus, me old mate, I'm a very courteous man."

Tasty laughed at his own dark humour. He said,

"Right then. Taffy has a business partner in Cardiff who looks after their interests in Tiger Bay, while Taffy looks after the London end of things. You'll understand if I don't go into the nature of their business. Taffy's mate is called Blind Bill on account of his having glasses lenses that look like they've been cut from the bottom of a beer bottle. Every now and then Taffy goes over to Wales to stay with him when there's a spot of bother that needs his attention. If Taffy's not around at the moment that's where you'll find him."

"And where do we find Blind Bill?" Gus asked.

"Bill's a dedicated lunchtime boozer, so you'll find him in one of the docklands pubs. He always wears blue suits a size too small for him for some reason. So look for a fierce looking gent with bottle glasses and a suit that's too short in the sleeves and you'll most likely find it's him. All you need do is follow him and he'll lead you to Taffy."

"Great, that's really helpful Tasty."

"You know me, always a helpful gent, I'd even help a copper to cross the road if there was a bus with no brakes hurtling towards him. Oh, just one thing, your friends had better think carefully about how they're going to get Taffy's undivided attention and stay in one piece. He's not partial to strangers and the razor he carries isn't just for giving him a shave that'll make the gals swoon."

"I'll pass that on. Thanks."

"While we're on the topic of geezers of an elusive nature, I hear the Kerryman's go-between has vanished. He's not been seen in the Fox and Squirrel for days."

"Well, as we're in the business of information exchanges, I've heard from very reliable sources that the Kerryman is pushing up daisies."

"What? Him? Never! Where did you hear that?"

"Oh, a man in the know. It'll be in the papers soon, no doubt. But until then, you haven't heard it from me."

"No, gotcha. How did he end up brown bread?"

"A mountaineering misadventure in Scotland."

"With or without a helping hand?"

"Who knows? The hand didn't stick around to tell anyone."

"Well, well, would you Adam and Eve it? The geezer that's the most careful in the world ends up falling off a slab of the old rock solid. It makes you think, Gus, me old china. Eat your chips and be merry, for tomorrow we may all be dead."

When Gus got back to the Mayfair office there was a client waiting. He looked very much like the archetypal husband of the 1950s' advertising world, impeccably groomed, handsome and dressed in a dark business suit that had senior manager stamped all over it. He was leaning forwards on his chair, his hands clenched and his brows deeply furrowed, as if he were at the dentist's, waiting for a tooth to be pulled out. Alice, who was sipping a coffee, put her cup down and said,

"This is Mr. Mallory, he'd like to talk to you about a case he hopes you'll take on. I wondered if you'd be able to see him this afternoon. He says it's quite urgent."

The man started, as if suddenly woken from a dream, and jumped up. He said,

"You're Augustus Benedict?"

"Yes, that's right. I can spare a few minutes for an initial discussion if you like. Would you care to come into my office?"

"You did the snooping that cost me my marriage and left me virtually penniless. I've got creditors on my trail, nowhere to live and my Jag's just been repossessed. You've left me feeling so down that I might as well be dead. But then I thought, 'Why should it be me that's the dead man, why shouldn't it be the bastard that's caused me all this grief?' So I've dressed for the occasion of your funeral, Mr. Grandly Named Augustus Benedict. I've come to give you a ticket to the afterlife."

While they came out in a surprisingly coherent fashion, his words were slurred and it was obvious that a large amount of alcohol was doing the talking. Alice had noticed the tell-tale traces on his breath when he'd arrived, but he'd been so good at selling her a bogus sob story that she'd taken pity on him and let him wait. She was now bitterly regretting her decision. That regret turned to alarm when suddenly he pulled out a gun from his jacket pocket and took aim at Gus. Without a second's hesitation, she grabbed her half full cup of hot coffee and hurled it at his face, hitting him full on the nose and causing him to yell in pain. The gun went off simultaneously, but her action had made him lose his already delicate balance and the bullet tore into the ceiling. Gus had him pinned face down to the floor within seconds, ripping off his tie to bind his hands behind his back. Placing the gun safely on Alice's desk, he picked up the phone and rang for the police. When he'd finished giving them the details he said,

"Your name didn't ring a bell at first, Mr. Mallory, we've had so many cases during the past few months, but now I remember it perfectly. You married an older woman for her wealth and then spent more time in other women's bedrooms than you did in hers, living the life of Riley, using her money. The fact that she hired me to collect the evidence needed for her to be able to jettison a gold-digging, two-timing little rat like you was entirely your own fault, so don't come in here trying to pin the blame on someone else. All you've done is turned what was already a bad situation into one that's even worse. You'll be going to jail for attempted murder. But there is a silver lining to your cloud. They'll give you a roof over your head for free, so you'll no longer be looking for a bed for the night and your creditors won't be able to come knocking on your cell door."

His angry homily was greeted with muffled curses from the floor.

As the police were leading the exceedingly disgruntled and coffee-soaked Mr. Mallory away, fifteen minutes later, Gus turned to Alice and said,

"You'd have made a first-class fast bowler, Alice Harding. I know old George plays cricket, but I didn't know you did too. That was dead square on the wicket, which is just as well, because I'd have been dead as the proverbial doornail if you'd missed."

"Oh, I practise on George all the time. I've had to get really fast because he's so quick when it comes to ducking. I got him with the teapot as well last Sunday when he made a smarty pants remark about my burning a cake."

"I hope it was an everyday pot and not a Spode."

"Oh I save the Spodes for his birthday and Christmas. I always like to throw something special at him when there's a reason to celebrate."

Detective Chief Inspector Hawthorn, a pedantic man with a sense of humour that only came out of hiding once every leap year, stood in bafflement at their banter. His one and only thought was that if Alice hadn't been on hand the bullet that was now wedged in the ceiling would have been exhibit A in a murder investigation. In that respect, at least, he was in tune with their conversation.

Gus said,

"Amazing, isn't it? I survived every kind of danger you could imagine in the war and yet nearly came to grief today over something as mundane as a vengeful philanderer with a drink problem. Perhaps the Kerryman and I had more in common than we knew. I very much suspect that his end came from an equally farcical direction."

CHAPTER NINETEEN

"Feared London crime boss killed in Scotland!"

The dramatic headline in the London Evening News was the direct result of Mr. One prompting the police to release a full statement about the Kerryman's demise. He then gave copies of the newspaper to the four-man team he despatched to Cardiff to find and talk to Owen Grazeborn. He calculated that if the Welshman could be shown evidence that the fearsome Mr. K was no more, he would be much more likely to divulge who had used him as the go-between to arrange the murder of Polmonovski. His men had been instructed to assure Grazeborn that there was no need to incriminate himself, they weren't looking for any evidence that could be used against him in court as an accessory to murder. All they wanted was for him to reveal who had paid him to put 'a proposal' to the Kerryman's gatekeeper on the day before Polmonovski's murder. To further encourage his cooperation he had equipped the search party with a generous number of used five-pound notes that were to be offered in return for solid and genuine information. Given the Welshman's fearsome reputation, he had selected four of his most combat-capable operatives and equipped them all with pistols, just to be on the safe side. He then sat back and waited for a phone call.

A week later, at eleven am, at the precise moment when Gus had removed his trousers while changing for a trip to the East End, Mr. One burst into his office with his customary lack of warning. It was difficult to know which of the two men was the most startled.

"Ah, Angus. I was just in the process of changing into my East End clothes - I have a spot of surveillance to do at lunchtime where I need to try and blend in a bit."

"Oh, yes, I see. Well, you'd better put your Mayfair trousers back on, Augustus, I think you'll want to look your best for what I have in mind."

"Would that involve a trip to your club by any chance?"

"No, I'm afraid not. Somewhere much less grand I'm sorry to say. I've got a car waiting outside - if you'd care to come down and join me when you're ready there's somewhere I need to take you, something I need you to see. It's only fifteen minutes away."

Mr. One looked and sounded uncomfortable and Gus was sure it was nothing to do with the trousers situation. He smiled - a distinctly unusual, indeed almost unprecedented gesture, and then nodded, in a rather odd manner, before exiting.

When he got in the car Gus asked straight away about the progress that had or hadn't been made in the search for Taffy Grazeborn. He'd heard nothing since passing on Tasty's tip as to how best to find the elusive Welshman. Mr. One seemed oddly hesitant on the matter, as though he were wrestling with the question of how much he could say. After a brief, contemplative silence, he said,

"I think I can safely say that, thanks to the information that Mr. Grazeborn eventually gave to my men, the matter of the murdered British and Russian intelligence officers is now closed. This is strictly between you and me and is to go no further, as I'm sure you'll understand. It turned out that the Americans did have an unauthorised freelance operation going on under their roof. I'm not permitted to divulge the name of the individual at its centre, the key player who ordered the Polmonovski killing through Grazeborn. I'll refer to them simply as Person X. Our wily Welsh friend arranged for one of his associates to follow that individual after their first meeting so that he knew a little bit more about whom exactly it was that he was dealing with. The tail was able to note the full details of where Person X lived and the name that the said individual goes under in the United Kingdom - a name that is on our list of known American intelligence officers. That rogue CIA operative had clearly decided to have Polmonovski killed after hearing your neatly planted ruse about us being near to locating him. The only reason that operative could have wanted him dead was the fear that he would reveal who had been paying him to organise the killing of the various British and Russian intelligence officers. That would have exposed the rogue operation and those behind it for all to see. I met with my chief contact in the CIA and put our evidence to him. To my surprise, he said it merely confirmed what he'd already known for several days. The individual concerned had been dealt with, severely apparently, and the relevant operation had been terminated. He had already met unofficially his KGB counterpart for the simple reason that, like us, the Russians had worked out that the problem was an American one. They have pronounced themselves satisfied with the resolution to the matter and have said they consider it closed. I don't think anybody is particularly keen about the idea of a shooting war on London's streets - it would get completely in the way of good honest spying."

A faint smile flickered momentarily at the corner of his lips, which again struck Gus as unusual. He continued,

"The Americans said they had been intending to tell us as well, but I suspect that they were really rather hoping to try and brush the matter under the carpet, if at all possible. It is, after all, a little embarrassing for them, given all of the time they've spent complaining about the Russian moles they imagine to be hiding under our roof and our incompetence in spotting them. It seems they've been rather incompetent in spotting a rogue intelligence officer in their own midst. The information from Mr. Grazeborn was the key that unlocked American tongues and removed the need for us to search any further for the mystery assassins. Ah, we're here."

Gus was surprised to see that they'd arrived at St. Thomas' Hospital. Once they were out of the car, Mr. One started looking distinctly grey around the gills, almost as if he were in urgent need of treatment himself. He ushered Gus inside and strode past reception in a determined manner, heading onwards at a rate of knots. Puzzled, Gus said,

"Might I enquire what we're doing here?"

Mr. One seemed almost to be trying to avoid crossing that particular bridge. There was another short, awkward pause and then he said,

"While the Americans were pursuing their rogue operative, there was a casualty on an apparently unrelated operation unfortunately."

Gus noticed that they were now following the signs to the hospital mortuary. Mr. One continued, unusually softly for a man who preferred normally to speak in the manner of a senior officer, used to giving orders,

"I think this is someone that you will want to see, Augustus."

They were now in the mortuary itself. There was an attendant ready and waiting, who nodded at Mr. One as they entered. By now Gus had a deep, sinking feeling in his stomach. The attendant took them to one of the drawers, which he pulled open. He waited for instructions from Mr. One, who said,

"As soon as I heard that the body had been identified I thought I should let you know, given that you were both, shall we say, close in a number of ways, so that you were able to pay your last respects: in private of course."

He nodded to the attendant, who then pulled back the cover from the head of the corpse. It was, as Gus had feared, Jennifer Marquis. She had a bullet wound, very precisely placed, right between her eyes. He lifted the cover as far as her navel and found what he expected, a second wound, directly over the heart, with a third, in the stomach. He looked at Mr. One and said, sharply,

"This was an execution. What happened?"

Mr. One asked the attendant to leave them and then said,

"From what I understand, Miss Marquis unwisely confronted a highly dangerous target without back-up. What we are looking at is the consequence. The Americans have told me that it was nothing to do with the KGB."

Gus nodded, but Mr. One was not convinced that his words had been believed. He said,

"I'll leave you to pay your respects in private. I'll be just outside."

When they were driving back to Mayfair twenty minutes later, Gus said,

"The rogue operative that Grazeborn named, who was he, or she?"

"I'm afraid I'm not at liberty to say. The Americans promised us one or two things of high value and in return I promised them that the name of the operative would remain confidential. There is some potential embarrassment to them should that name and the full nature of what has been going on become known - domestic embarrassment I should say, particularly in Congress."

"And you're telling me that Jennifer Marquis was most definitely not executed by the KGB?"

"That's what I've been told, but you'll understand that I can't say any more. I believe also that Miss Marquis will be awarded the Intelligence Star for her bravery. I think it's the CIA's equivalent to our Victoria Cross, or as near as dammit."

Gus nodded and they sat in silence for some minutes. Then, just as he was getting out of the car outside his Mayfair office he said,

"It's strange, you have to admit. If I'd have been examining that body without any information as to what had happened, I'd have said it had more the look of a KGB execution than anything else. The two precisely placed wounds in her chest and stomach are the trademark of their veteran hitman, Oleg Karmininovski. The extent of the outer flesh damage is characteristic of the type of hand-finished bullet that he uses. They're a statement of ownership of the killing, a traditional message. Why wouldn't the CIA want that to be known?"

He raised his eyebrows quizzically and then shut the car door behind him.

When he walked into the outer office his face was grim. Alice said,

"You look as though you've had bad news."

"Bad news?" he said distractedly. "Yes, indeed. Angel eyes has gone to meet the angels, or, who knows, the devil. If anybody rings or calls this afternoon, I'm out."

He disappeared into his inner office and slammed the door behind him. He was a man who rarely slammed doors and Alice knew him well enough to ask no further questions on the matter.

Mr. One, meanwhile, was not easy in his mind. There was one thing he had omitted to tell Gus in any explicit sense. The truth. What was worse was that he knew full well that Gus had probably worked most of it out for himself, as his parting remarks had indicated. But the deal he had made with his CIA counterpart meant that he couldn't say anything more than he had done. He'd chosen what he felt to be the lesser of two evils. If he had not shown Gus the body and had let him simply discover for himself that his former lover was dead, he would have been put in an impossible position. Gus would have demanded to know what had happened and all that he would have been able to tell him were the lies that he had just offered him. Mr. One was fundamentally a decent man and one of several aspects of his job that he disliked was the requirement frequently to lie. In particular, he loathed lying to people for whom he had the highest professional regard. However, in showing Gus the body, he knew that his experienced eye would note various details, most particularly the nature of the wounds, that would lead him to suspect that Jennifer Marquis had been executed by the KGB. Equally, the fact that the Americans were not up in arms about the killing - and were trying to pass it off as something that had nothing to do with the KGB - would lead him to deduce that they had a reason to turn a blind eye. That reason could only be that Marquis had been the rogue operative and that a tacit deal had been done whereby the Russians could eliminate her without retaliation. Karmininovski would be precisely the man they would use for the operation. That would prevent any further unauthorised killings of intelligence officers being organised by her, provide the KGB with a means of retaliating for the killing of their own people without provoking a shooting war and solve an otherwise embarrassing problem for the Americans. Mr. One had given Gus the information that they wanted to bury the whole matter of the rogue intelligence officer's operation to avoid the domestic scandal and unwanted scrutiny that would follow. That was a large enough piece of the jigsaw for him to be able to fill in much of the rest. So, in effect, Mr. One had given Gus the truth of the matter implicitly, without giving it away explicitly and in so doing had got as near as he could to both honouring his promise to the CIA and letting Gus know what had really been going on. Gus's parting remark made it clear that he had pretty well filled in most of the dots. Mr. One just hoped that he would come to appreciate the subtle nature of what had been going on during the mortuary visit and realise the difficult situation that he had been in.

The full details of what had been going on within Marquis's rogue operation had startled Mr. One, as much as they had no doubt startled her CIA bosses when they had discovered them. His moment of enlightenment had come two days earlier, a few hours before Marquis's body was fished out of the Thames. It had been spotted, bizarrely, by somebody who had been considering throwing himself into the same dark, murky waters and had changed his mind when seeing just what the merciless, cold river could do to frail human dignity. Mr. One had agreed to meet his chief CIA contact on a deserted part of the Thames river bank, at three o'clock on a dull and windy afternoon. Hamish - they were on reasonably convivial first name terms - was an erudite, conservatively suited Bostonian, with owlish spectacles and the physique of an American football player, despite having a lifelong loathing of the sport. He wore the kind of high-collared coat that would keep out the bitter cold of the worst of the winters of new and old England. They shook hands with an awkward formality when meeting and then the CIA man pulled a pipe out of his pocket and began to load it with tobacco. He said,

"You're looking well, Angus. I always wonder how you cope with this miserable British weather, having spent so much of your army career out in India and the Far East."

"Oh, one adjusts," Angus said. "I go where my country needs me and India is now back in the hands of its people."

"You don't regret the decline of empire?"

"The empire means different things to different people, Hamish. For some it was all about economics, strategic positioning, or the desire for grandeur, for me it has always been about a civilising, benign mission. I'm happy enough that we succeeded in passing on the torch of democracy to India and Pakistan, although considerably less happy about the tragic loss of life that followed partition."

"You're a man we can do business with, Angus. We talk the same language you and I when it comes to the role of the West. Not all of our fellow countrymen would agree with our view of the world."

"Indeed. It's one of your fellow countrymen with a rather different view of the world that I want to speak to you about, Hamish. Or, to be absolutely precise, I should say countrywomen."

"I'm intrigued."

"You're aware, obviously, of the series of killings of British and KGB intelligence officers recently."

Hamish nodded, while lighting his pipe.

"We have finally established who has been behind them, although we don't as yet know why. I believe that you, like us, have suspected that the person organising the killings has been operating under the cover of the CIA and the American embassy."

"Really?"

"We have the name of that person and the necessary evidence to establish her guilt. If I give it to you, it is my anticipation that you will put a stop to her little operation, find out why it has been conducted and be so kind as to let us know the result of your enquiries. In the spirit of the good relations that one would expect between two such close Western allies, of course. I would hope that you would then have the said person arrested and find a diplomatic way of informing the Soviets that the matter has been dealt with, so that they know that what has been going on has been authorised neither by your people, nor by us. That way, we should be able to avoid any further unnecessary casualties on British soil."

Hamish took a long puff on his pipe and said,

"So, if you think something has been going on from our side of the bridge, who would you presume to have been behind it?"

"I don't presume, Hamish, I know. Our evidence is rock solid, based on lengthy and detailed enquiries and reliable witness statements. The name of the operative is Jennifer Marquis. In particular, we have a first-hand witness account that it was she who set up the Polmonovski killing, using a third party to make the arrangements with the Kerryman's gatekeeper in the Fox and Squirrel public house. Previously, she had arranged the various killings of intelligence officers using Polmonovski as her go-between with the Kerryman, but when she found out that we were on to him, she arranged to have him eliminated via another middleman. He was killed so that there was no danger of him spilling the beans about her."

In reality, Mr. One knew that he only had rock solid evidence with regard to the murder of Polmonovski, thanks to Taffy Grazeborn. Everything pointed to Marquis having organised the other killings, but given that both the Kerryman and Polmonovski were now dead, it would be much harder to make an unchallengeable case for her being behind them. He had a reputation as a man who didn't bluff, so he was relying on that being enough to swing the American in the direction that he wanted him to go.

Hamish took the pipe out of his mouth, knocked the tobacco out of it on the railing on which they were leaning and gazed into the mist that sat like a shroud on the river. He said,

"My, you people have been busy. We were going to tell you of course, as soon as we'd tied up all of the loose ends. As for the Soviets, you needn't worry. They worked it out three days before you - we've already smoothed things out with them and the prospect of any shooting war has gone away. Jennifer's little operation is now purely a matter of unfortunate history and she has been dealt with in an appropriate manner, as you would expect."

Mr. One tried to digest the fact that the Americans had discussed the matter with the Russians before even thinking about talking to London. His eyes searched his counterpart's face for any sign of guilt or regret in the matter, but could see none. Hamish continued,

"As you'll appreciate, all of this has been a considerable embarrassment to us and to me personally. Should the details get out there would be one hell of a stink back home and it would probably be the end of my career. That in itself may mean little or nothing to you, but it could well lead to my replacement by someone who is a lot less pro-British than me and a lot harder to deal with. The politics of things back home at the moment might well make things go that way. The walls of the White House and the Capitol Building are still echoing from the poisonous legacy of the McCarthyite witch hunts and the problems you guys have had with communist infiltration in the past have not made you popular in some quarters. Some feel that your past penetration by Russian spies - and what they see as British complacency about the possibility that there may be more still at work - helped fuel the McCarthy paranoia back in the States. If the Russians could dig their way into the British state, then they must be doing the same thing in Washington and all that stuff that some of mad eyed Joe's chums came out with. They really resent you guys for that. I'd like to think that we've always had a smooth relationship, you and I, helping each other out from time to time, although I appreciate that our late confirmation of the Marquis business has not been ideal. So, I'd appreciate it if you could keep this under your hat. If we put our heads together, we should be able to come up with a way of presenting all of this to our respective masters that masks the finer details of what has been going on. I've already constructed a picture of things that gives the Soviets enough knowledge to satisfy them, without letting the whole of the cat out of the bag."

"You want us to lie?" Mr. One said.

"Not so much lie, as construct an amended version of reality," Hamish replied, "one that keeps the wheels of Western politics and diplomacy grinding along without the unnecessary major hiccup that this scandal would cause, should it break. I would, of course, be prepared to offer something in return."

"May I enquire what?"

"Well, our level of cooperation has been somewhat circumscribed by the continuing fallout from past discoveries of Russian spies within the British end of things and I regret that. I would be prepared to help the two of us circumvent that a little, so that we can get closer to what we would both wish that cooperation to be like."

"I see."

Mr. One contemplated the matter in silence for a couple of minutes. Information was the lifeblood of the espionage business and the past scandals at 'the British end of things' had damaged the information flow between Washington and London. He took the point that if Hamish were replaced his successor might be someone who would be much less amenable. Anything that might improve the current information flow had to be seriously considered. If he agreed to his counterpart's proposal and helped cover up what had really happened, he would obviously need a get-out-of-jail-free card if his subterfuge was discovered. The ability to demonstrate that his deception had improved the quality of intelligence available to the British might well do the job, although he would still be unpopular in Westminster. His very knowledge of what had been going on in the American camp would be a powerful asset. It should be enough of a lever to extract the promised improvement in the information flow if Hamish subsequently tried to go back on his word. He said,

"The offer is welcome, but a little vague, Hamish. I'd really like it to be more detailed and to benefit both Five and my colleagues in Six, with everything going through me of course. Shall we agree to see how things work out in practice? Until then I'll keep what I can under my hat and find a way of presenting our findings that filters and fillets the real picture of what has happened in a way that should prevent any major ructions arising. From a practical, day-to-day point of view, I don't see any benefit in bringing about a major flare up in British-American relations at a time when our Soviet adversary is busy equipping itself with the most powerful nuclear weapons. However, if I don't find that the promised levels of increased cooperation materialise, things may start to escape from our files. Does that seem reasonable?"

Hamish looked distinctly uncomfortable with Mr. One's threat, but nodded his agreement. Mr. One continued,

"And just to make doubly sure that our little deal is honoured, I'd appreciate it if you could give me the full picture of what happened with Miss Marquis. I'd like to know precisely why she did what she did, if she was acting on behalf of any third parties - pretty well everything that I would expect to have come out of her interrogation. We've both done enough interrogations in our time, Hamish, so I'm sure you'll appreciate that I'll spot instantly if things are being left out, or don't seem quite to fit. Should I see any such evidence of bad faith, our conversation will be over and my files may well pass from my desk upwards, if you understand what I mean."

Hamish looked somewhat taken aback. He said,

"That sounds pretty much like an interrogation of me, Angus. I thought we were supposed to be friends and allies. You're asking a hell of a price - and not in a very brotherly fashion."

"Friends don't discuss things with the people who are supposed to be the common enemy and then avoid disclosing them to their major ally until they are literally forced to do so, Hamish. You'll forgive my directness, but the great virtue of frankness in such matters is that it removes the danger of misunderstandings and very serious fallings out further down the line."

"OK. You're a hard taskmaster, Angus, but you do have me over a barrel on this one. I'll tell you what you want on the strict understanding that it remains exclusively between you and me."

"I'll require the right to share it with one other person. He is absolutely leak proof, but needs to know for reasons that needn't concern you."

"That's not an idea that sits easily with me, Angus."

"No, I appreciate that, but without your agreement our conversation is at an end."

"Really? That would be a lost opportunity for you of considerable proportions, just as much as it would be unfortunate for me. OK, let me tell you just how far I can go in allowing things to be shared. These are my red lines, beyond which I cannot move. First, providing that this person is one hundred per cent rock solid, you can share the fact that we have been unknowingly hosting a rogue operation under our roof, that we have found out who was behind it and that we have closed it down. What must remain between us only is the name of the rogue operative, why she did what she did and who was behind her. I consider these things to be so high risk that I'm prepared to trust them only to you. Should Jennifer Marquis be found dead, then you must tell your trusted colleague that she was killed on a mission unrelated to the rogue operative issue, in the line of duty and not, not in any circumstances, by the Soviets. You must specifically tell that colleague that the KGB had nothing to do with it. I can't afford to have anybody outside of our little magic circle putting two and two together. We may be in a business that uses lies and deception as its currency, Angus, but we both know that at our level, and in the context of our alliance, if one of us breaks his word to the other, then the damage that results can last for years. On the core matters of this affair, I trust only you."

Mr. One considered the matter for a few moments and then said,

"What you require makes life more difficult for me than I would ideally wish, Hamish, but on reflection I can just about work with it. You have my word, but that is my first and last concession on the matter."

"OK, I'll go with that. What I've got to tell you isn't a pretty story, Angus and it threatens to reopen deep wounds in America if it gets out, so I really am trusting you to keep a lid on things. Frankly, we told the Soviets a pack of lies to make them happy and keep our side of things as much under the blanket as possible. I won't insult you by trying the same routine because, as you say, you'll see straight through it. So here goes with the real story. To cut to the chase, Senator Joe McCarthy and his poisonous allegations that respected, key American citizens are card carrying communist subversives, came to a swift and bitter end politically last year, as you know. However, not all of his fellow travellers got the memo. Senator Hunter Wastbrane has been continuing to peddle evidence-free communist conspiracy theories under the radar and he has a particular fixation about communist plots and influence within our NATO allies. You may ask what's that got to do with the price of chicken shit, but Wastbrane was godfather to Jennifer Marquis. Her family and his go way back and she was very much brought up in a family culture that believed every communist was the personal representative of the devil and that they were in the business of infiltrating all levels of Western society. Joe McCarthy caused us no end of trouble because of his bone-headed belief that the CIA was full of communists and Wastbrane swallowed his nonsense hook, line and sinker. So his little protégé, Jennifer, was deliberately encouraged to join the CIA after doing spectacularly well at Harvard - Bachelor's, Master's, PhD, you name it. She seemed to be just the kind of person we needed - sharp, pretty damn fearless and thorough in everything she did. What we didn't know was that she was effectively Wastbrane's plant in the organisation. She was feeding all kinds of classified stuff back to him, much of which it seems he completely misunderstood, or took wildly out of context in his attempts to prove communist infiltration, either within our ranks or those of our allies. As far as recent events in Britain are concerned, things came to a head when Leonid Kryslowski, a low-ranking KGB intelligence officer, defected to us, supposedly with a whole bag of goodies to give us in terms of information. Among his offerings was the claim that two British intelligence officers were working for the KGB, the two guys recently killed. He also named several Russians as being the masterminds that handled them and whose job exclusively was to blackmail and turn British intelligence officers. I checked all of this out and found it to be complete horse shit. The guy was desperate to earn himself a new identity and a safe house in the US because he'd found a way of accessing Soviet state funds without being spotted. This had worked quite well for about a year, but he'd then got a little over-confident and made an error that had given him away. He was simply in the business of telling us any old rubbish in an effort to earn our protection and save his hide. He'd named the KGB operatives who were after him as the supposed handlers, together with a couple of random, completely innocent British intelligence officers whose names he knew, and hoped we'd swallow what he told us. After a long interrogation, I dismissed him as a completely unreliable source and we threw him back onto the streets. I've no idea whether the KGB caught up with him, or whether he's eking out some kind of a squalid existence in the shadows. What I didn't realise was that Marquis had fed his nonsensical story back to Wastbrane. Wastbrane then told her that he had irrefutable evidence that it was in fact true and that I was a communist sympathiser who had rejected it and thrown it out to protect the supposed Brit double agents and their KGB handlers. He didn't tell her what the supposed evidence was. I think he was most probably making things up as he went along, in the ideologically blinded belief that the KGB man's lies were so close to what he imagined to be the case in Britain that they must be true. He then made a dangerous transition from conspiracy theorist to fantasy policeman, judge and jury. He instructed her that it was her patriotic duty to take out all of these individuals if the CIA proper wasn't prepared to do its job. That way, he could cut out the communist heart from the intelligence operation of our major European ally and thereby protect the interests of both the United States and NATO. He set up a secret account for Marquis to access in London that allowed her to fund all of the killings. She was the most detailed master planner you could imagine. She researched the London criminal underworld and selected the Kerryman as the best guy to handle what needed to be done. He had a reputation for being untraceable and that made him a very attractive proposition for an operation whose director needed to be invisible. And by using a local crime organisation, she hoped to completely disguise the fact that the assassinations were American organised. She specified that the killer the Kerryman used should have army training, but not be a professional hitman, hoping that the lack of the professional touch in some of the killings would create convenient confusion amongst the Brit and KGB guys trying to work out what the hell was going on. She created further distance between herself and the killings by hiring the sons of exiled Russians to act as the middlemen. Should you guys or the KGB discover that it was them arranging the hits through the Kerryman, she hoped that you'd all set off on a wild goose chase centred on the idea that what was happening was some kind of a Russian dissident operation designed to create a shooting war between Russian and British intelligence. As soon as you rumbled Polmonovski, she had plans to take him off the streets and, if necessary, kill him, in order to protect herself from being exposed as the real prime mover. Those plans as, we know, she activated. It was purely by good fortune that a couple of our guys intercepted one of her coded communications to Wastbrane and became suspicious. She was using code that was hellishly difficult to crack, but we managed it eventually and that alerted us to the fact that she and he were up to no good. She was so good at picking up on stuff that it was difficult to conceal from her completely that we were on her trail, so I fed her a line about my suspecting that we had a rogue operator freelancing under our roof and that this rogue operative might be behind the killings of British and Russian intelligence operatives here. I wanted to see her reaction, but her training kicked in and there was none. So I put her in charge of the investigation, as she thought, feeding her just enough information to panic her into trying to cover up her tracks. We were following her every move by that stage, building a case that would nail her ass to the wall. We got one step behind, unfortunately, which is how Polmonovski ended up dead before we fully realised what was going on. Given the powerful backing she had from Wastbrane and the junk he was peddling about me, I waited until our evidence against her was absolutely watertight and then pulled her in for interrogation. We had her on multiple charges, starting with the theft of classified information and ending with the murder of British intelligence officers, among others. Because her killings were unauthorised and resulted from claims and evidence that we had previously shown to have no basis in fact - and included the murder of two innocent allied personnel - we put it to her that she was likely to face a capital punishment. That might be within the British or US judicial systems, depending on legal and diplomatic considerations, or it could be that we simply failed to protect her against the KGB retaliatory hit that she could expect if we didn't arrange for her formal arrest. They would find out about her sooner or later and, indeed, as I mentioned earlier, they did, very recently. What you may not know is that she has a son back in America - the father died fighting in Korea several years ago, four months before they were due to be married. That was why she disappeared back home for a time after her first posting here. Her parents are now bringing up the child so that she can continue her career. We asked her if she would want her son to learn that his mother had gone rogue and died as pretty much a traitor, or whether he might prefer to be told that she had been heroically killed on a mission defending American interests. If she preferred the second option, then I would even be prepared to arrange for her to be nominated for the posthumous award of the Intelligence Star. I had only one condition and that was that she told us everything. She thought about it and went for the second option, which is why I am now able to give you the full picture of what has been going on. I tell you this because some time soon, maybe even today, her body will be pulled out of this very river. We brought her down here recently, a little further down, half a mile or so perhaps, and then walked away, leaving her fate in the lap of the gods, as it were. Through a back channel we'd let the Soviets know she'd be here. Once we'd left her alone a KGB sniper took her out and it was all over. Officially, she was on a mission and was killed in the line of duty. In a way, that's true enough. She had agreed to go on a final mission that would prevent an unnecessary shooting war between intelligence agencies, one which she knew would be impossible for her to survive. All of that's hardly in line with normal protocols, but it resolved the situation with the Russians and solved a problem for us. It also made things better for her son. Instead of his mother dying as a rogue or a traitor, or at best getting life imprisonment in the US, she is a hero in line for a medal. So when you hear about the medal, don't be surprised, that's what's really going on."

"Good God. What a mess, Hamish. What a God-awful mess. What's going to happen to this lunatic Wastbrane fellow, how do we know that he's not going to do even more damage?"

"I'm told that Senator Wastbrane had a coronary last night and that he passed away before the ambulance arrived, so the answer to your question is that I can assure you that he will cause neither you nor us any further problems Angus."

"Was that a genuine coronary, or one that was, shall we say, induced?"

"I believe that expert medical opinion is confident that it was

216

genuine."

"I suppose it is a question of whose experts we're talking about?"

"And there might be those who say that those who live by the sword die by the sword. Life is full of doubts and uncertainties, Angus, but the passing of Hunter Wastbrane is not a matter that I intend considering for any longer than it takes me to say his name."

Angus stared into the fog that sat on the dark, dank river water like a veil between life and the afterlife. He said again,

"What a God-awful mess."

"I don't deny it, but it's a mess whose details must largely stay between us. You mustn't tell your mystery colleague anything beyond what we agreed, Angus. You've always stuck rigidly by your code of honour as an officer and a gentleman in that good old English way you have and I've respected you for it - and respected your word. If I'm to deliver on my promise, to improve the information exchanges between us, then I need you to stay firm to your commitment."

"You already have my word. Deliver your side of things and nothing will leak."

"Good, that's agreed then."

The two men shook hands as stiffly as they did on arrival and then departed, each going in the opposite direction to the other.

The fog that had been sitting on the river gradually swirled landwards as they walked. It embraced each of them with the same cold, damp arms that cradled the body of Jennifer Marquis. At the beginning of its process of slow decay, it nestled under the edge of a wharf that Mr. One passed by without even seeing, so deep was the vaporous gloom.

CHAPTER TWENTY

For the two weeks or so following his traumatic experience in the hospital mortuary, Gus left the Mayfair office ticking over in the capable hands of Alice, while he buried himself in the accumulating caseload of his one-man East End operation. It seemed the perfect way to try and take his mind off the latest in a long line of deaths, tragedies and betrayals that had been his experience ever since his time within the British intelligence services during the Second World War.

It was on a Thursday afternoon that he found himself reuniting a young West Indian woman with the money that her thieving landlord had stolen from her room while she was out at work. The police had shown no interest and the scale of the loss threatened to make the woman destitute. She had been advised to seek Gus's assistance by a client he had previously helped. He had quickly and deftly established the landlord's likely guilt, but his attempts to persuade him to return the woman's money had come to nought. He'd resolved the deadlock after he'd managed to interest Tasty in her case, a feat that required no small amount of skill, given the big man's busy schedule. He'd spotted previously that his outwardly ungentle friend paradoxically had an almost gentle side hidden away and that part of him had zero tolerance for the mistreatment of women. He'd once confided in Gus that his childhood had been marred by a violent drunkard of a father, who amused himself by beating up the big man's mother from time to time. He'd been unable to do anything to protect her until he was sixteen, when he was finally strong enough to best his father in a fight and succeeded in throwing him out of their rooms. He never allowed the tyrant back and began his criminal career as a way of providing the income necessary to support his mother and his two sisters.

Tasty dealt with the light-fingered landlord with the same imaginative approach that he had adopted when visited by Mr. One's inquisitive underling. Having inserted the unrepentant thief, upside down, into one of his own dustbins, he then proceeded to bed him in like a potted plant, using the richly smelling contents of the adjoining bins as compost. Following this persuasive intervention, the landlord had a sudden flash of inspiration as to how to make amends for stealing from his tenant's room. It came just as Tasty was about to block up the last narrow airway down to the thief's inverted head with some foul-smelling rotten meat and a very deceased cabbage. Rosie, the young woman in question, was startled to find that she not only got her money back when she turned up for her appointment with Gus, but that her rent was considerably reduced from the extortionate levels of the previous six months. Ever the pragmatist, Gus turned a blind eye to the fact that Tasty had also added the landlord's properties to the list of businesses that he 'protected', preferring to focus on the positive outcome for the young woman, given that she also was being protected by her unlikely and very large new guardian angel, but without any fee, charge or other expectation.

As Rosie was stepping out into the street at the conclusion of their business, she turned round and said,

"Thank you, thank you again. For everything you've done. I don't understand why you won't charge me for your services, but I'm more grateful than you'll ever know."

Standing behind her, waiting to enter the office, was a man in a docker's jacket and trousers. The clothes were so ill-fitting that they looked like they'd absconded from a theatrical costumes shop. The noise in the street outside from truanting children playing and shouting was such that Gus didn't hear him enter. He was engrossed in reading a background file on his next appointment, due in half an hour. His visitor coughed and Gus looked up from his desk. He gasped in amazement.

"Angus! You look as though you've just walked off the set of Oliver Twist."

"How flattering. I thought I'd try and blend in with the locale. My men found me these items from our props store, but I see now that they were having a little joke at my expense. May I sit down?"

"Please do. What brings you to these humble parts?"

"Well, as you seem to have vanished from your Mayfair office, I thought I'd better try and find you in this curious little subsidiary operation that you run - for free, I gather, from what that young lady just said. What an amazing chap you are, Augustus."

"I'm just clearing up a backlog of cases. I should be holding the reins in Mayfair again within a week or two."

"I wondered if you might be trying to take your mind off recent events."

"That too I suspect."

"I wanted to find out if we were still friends, if we could still work together. You seemed to be rather angry with me when I dropped you off on the way back from St. Thomas'."

"Angry? I think I'm probably most angry with myself for not realising how much I was being both used and deceived."

"By me?"

"No, Jennifer. I joined all the dots together for myself when I got back to the office on that rather miserable day. I realised what you were trying to do, that you were communicating by other means what you weren't allowed to say in words. I know now that she was behind the killing of Tony Gregory and the other intelligence officers - and that the KGB took her out. It was all there, when I put together what I saw in the mortuary with what you told me - once I separated the truth from the no doubt 'necessary' lies of course. I presumed that you had an agreement with the Americans to speak from the same script."

"On that I couldn't possibly comment, as you'll understand, as, equally, I'm unable to say anything more about Miss Marquis than I did then. But I'm glad that you're content with the way things were presented."

"I'm mortified that, in my blissful ignorance, I happily went to bed with a woman who'd arranged the killing of a former colleague, Tony Gregory. What I can't understand is why she did it. What bizarre plan was behind it all?"

"All I can say is that I am certain that the killings have now stopped. We will not lose any more Tony Gregorys, thank God."

"With Marquis, Polmonovski and the Kerryman all dead they could hardly continue. It would be like trying to put on a performance of Hamlet with only the ghost available to appear on stage."

"The one person who would seem to be unaccounted for is the hitman who carried out the actual killings. With the Kerryman's impenetrable organisation it's unlikely that we'll ever find out who it was, unless he has a sudden fit of conscience and hands himself in."

"Indeed. What's really on your mind, Angus? You didn't come this far out of your normal habitat just to see if I was still speaking to you."

"Surprisingly, I did, Augustus. Our long association has been one of the things that has persuaded me that, despite all of the pressures and politicking of governments, the intelligence business can be made to work on some kind of ethical basis. You have those rare things called principles that some of my colleagues and the politicians to whom we answer at best see in a rather elastic way. That's why you're no longer in the service of course. But if we can keep up our collaborations, where you feel comfortable with what is involved, I'll feel like I'm still anchored on some kind of rock. That within the miasma of all the 'cover stories' and deceptions of our work, I'll have the privilege of working with someone who never loses sight of the core values which should drive everything we do. You are a most valued colleague, Augustus, even if you only keep one foot in our waters nowadays. Several of your many talents exceed in quality those of anyone currently working for me and your various contributions to this most recent case have been game-changers. I'd like to hold on to all of that and to think that we could continue to work together in the future."

Gus looked pensive initially, but then smiled, in a restrained kind of way. He said,

"Give me a week or two to blow this thing out of my hair, then look me up again when you think there's something on the table that might be right for the agency, and that includes Mrs. Harding, as you call her, as well as me. As you'll have noticed, I hired her for her most excellent research skills, among other things."

"Indeed," Mr. One replied, while rising suddenly and unexpectedly, in his customary fashion. He pulled a small bottle of the most expensive of brandies out of a deep pocket in his jacket and put it on the desk. Gus said,

"You're determined to turn me into an alcoholic."

"Not at all old man. I just wanted to leave you something fitting with which to drink to the memory of Tony Gregory. I'm sure the bottle will last for some time beyond that, given your moderation in all things, apart from women of course."

Gus laughed, the first time that he'd done so since their visit to the mortuary. Mr. One was a man much relieved to part this time on the best of terms.

It was past five o'clock before Gus finally said goodbye to his last appointment for the day. Looking out into the evening gloom, as he donned his hat and coat, he decided that he would walk all the way back to his apartment. It would be a useful opportunity to stretch his legs, after an afternoon stuck largely at his desk, and a good, long walk always gave him the chance to reflect on things that he would otherwise be distracted from by the hurly-burly of the London Underground, or the chatter of a cab driver. The edginess of the area in which his office sat was also useful in helping keep his streetwise survival skills finely honed. As he strolled on through the early evening, weaving in and out of little groups of people in various stages of intoxication, some with ill intent towards those of an unwary nature and some so far gone they had no intent at all, he chewed over and over again in his mind the complex puzzle that had been Jennifer Marquis. Without Mr. One's privileged knowledge of her role as the ideological twin of the now deceased Hunter Wastbrane, he couldn't understand why she should have wanted to kill a man so far beyond reproach as Tony Gregory, never mind the other British intelligence officer that she'd sent to an early grave. The KGB men at least were 'the enemy', but he had heard no explanation as to why she would want to kill the specific Russian operatives that she did. Clearly, her CIA superiors did not agree with what she had done, otherwise they would have been up in arms about what any expert eye could confirm had been her execution by the KGB. As he had intimated to Mr. One, the thing that most concerned him was how she had so readily shared his bed and many intimate moments, while simultaneously being the killer of key people within an organisation that, she well knew, he was still closely involved with. This conundrum sent his mind back to the interrogations of key Nazis that he had either conducted, or sat in on, following the end of the Second World War. He had been struck time and again by how comfortably they had fitted together apparently normal family lives with the brutal killings that they had ordered, or themselves committed, in the name of the Nazi state. Frequently, he had concluded that they had given themselves licence to do their murderous Fuhrer's bidding by simply dehumanising their victims. He wondered if that was what Jennifer Marquis had done, whether she also existed on two levels within her mind, one that treated those whom she regarded as human according to one set of principles, and one that treated those whom she didn't according to another. He might have supposed that she was far too intelligent to think in those deluded binary terms, but he had met many highly intelligent Nazis whose intellect was no guardian against absurd ways of thinking.

As he walked on, a thick fog descended and he doubled his concentration on the faces that appeared suddenly and without warning out of the miasma in front of him, checking for any signs of hostile intent. It was the perfect weather for street criminals. Simultaneously, he listened carefully for the soft, rapid footsteps behind him that might suggest the approach of a hopeful felon with robbery in mind. He was startled suddenly by the face of a man that appeared under a street lamp in front of him. The eyes were hollow, bloodshot and desperate. The man was not old, but he looked as though he had seen things that had given him the burdens of someone three times his age. It was a face almost without hope, that seemed to be searching for something which it couldn't define and which it had little expectation of finding. Most of all, it was the face of a man who hadn't eaten properly for some time. Gus being Gus, he couldn't simply pass by on the other side. He couldn't see any way in which the forlorn and deflated figure could be a threat, so he walked quickly over and pressed twenty pounds into the palm of his hand, saying:

"Get yourself a good meal. There are people who will help you, listen to you. Use them. There's always hope old chap, even when the sky seems to have fallen in."

The money was enclosed in a flyer advertising the address of a soup kitchen that promised a warm and friendly ear for those in need. Gus walked on through the fog, back towards the bright lights of Mayfair, without thinking any more of his characteristic act of spontaneous generosity. The man leaning on the streetlamp looked down at the money in a puzzled sort of way. He might be scruffily dressed and unkempt, but he wasn't short of the stuff. He had a considerable stash of well-thumbed five-pound notes back home. What he was short of was a means of clawing his way back to a normal life, one where he felt free of the crippling guilt that wrecked his attempts to sleep at night and left him frequently wandering the streets as a means of keeping his mind off the horrors of the past. He separated the flyer from the money and read it distractedly. Specifically, it was inviting him to use the social services provided by the parish run by the Kerryman's brother, the canon. At first, he didn't know what to think, but he hadn't known what to think for some time. But then, something his past tormentor once said came back to mind, that while a confession in a court of law would lead him to the hangman, a confession to a priest would have to be kept forever a secret, to go no further than the confessional box. There was someone he could unburden himself to with no risk of a trip to the gallows as a result. He could ask the parish priest, whoever he may be, to hear his confession and grant him absolution. He had no idea whether such an exercise would banish or at least reduce his crippling burden of guilt, but anything that might seemed worth a try. He changed his mind about throwing the flyer away. He stuffed it and the money into his pocket and then shuffled away, to see if he could find the location of the church in the flyer - he, Mr. Malone, unknowingly walking towards the Kerryman's sibling, while Gus, equally unknowingly, walked away from the man who had shot Tony Gregory. The canon, at least, would be a man enlightened as a result of the combined actions of each.

He would finally learn just what his brother had done.

Other mysteries by P.J. Anderson available from Nine Lives Original Books

'The Spy with an Angel's Eyes' is the first in a series to be written around the character of Augustus Benedict. The next book should appear around the middle of 2022.

Nine Lives Original Books has published two other of P.J. Anderson's mysteries. 'A Man Twice Dead: an almost perfect crime' at first appears to be very much in the vein of traditional whodunnits. But as the story unwinds, it becomes apparent that something a little different is going on ... 'The Ghost Fabler' is a hidden gem which contains several compelling ghost stories, themselves woven within another ghost story, which in turn merges into a chilling tale of the macabre ...

A Man Twice Dead: an almost perfect crime.

For A.B., a former book editor, 'A Man Twice Dead', "... fizzes with inventiveness and ingenuity." For Delwyn Swingewood, it is, "... a country house murder mystery with a difference."

Country house murder mysteries are, of course, a fiction, unless a vengeful and brilliant mind decides to create a real one to right a wrong – and kill those who he, or she, presumes to be killers. What better way of playing with them, gradually rooting them out and then imposing the ultimate penalty? The assassin makes his victims the centre of a real-life plot, inspired by the whodunnit novels of the past, one which is perfectly executed, until ... In real life, of course, not everything goes to plan. It seems that, in the end, only the unexpected is to be expected ...

The Ghost Fabler: supernatural tales told within a chilling tale of the macabre

Who is the icily charming 'Mr. Green' and what is the real nature of his influence over powerful American business mogul Sebastian Engel? Why is he so determined to force traditional Irish storyteller Christine O'Donnell to work for him and why does he threaten the children she tutors? Can she turn detective and discover what his real purposes are and save both herself and the children? This is a unique and genuinely chilling book, a web of traditional ghost stories woven within a Faustian tale of evil at its most deadly and ambiguous. "Well, what can I say – what a creation …. It's like walking across Morecambe Bay without a guide: put a foot wrong and you don't know what you'll step into. Evil is to the side, at the front, behind, below, above … I do not remember breathing as I read the final chapter." A.B., a former book editor and previously of the Financial Times.

Made in the USA
Middletown, DE
25 April 2022

64747467R00139